Ro

Black CHESS

A Novel

URAEUS
PRESS

URAEUS PRESS, LLC

8309 Laurel Canyon Blvd. #328
Sun Valley, CA 91352
www.UraeusPress.com

Copyright © 2020 by *Roberta Roberts*
All Rights Reserved.

This book, or parts thereof, may not be reproduced in any form without written permission from the publishing company.

Black CHESS

Library of Congress Control Number: 2020940153

ISBN: 978-1-7351408-2-7

This is a work of fiction. All characters are fictitious and not intended to represent specific persons. Any resemblance to actual persons, living or dead, is entirely coincidental. The events, locales and business establishments described are products of the author's imagination or are used fictitiously.

Kamari Smith **– Cover Design; Graphics**

Printed in the United States of America
First Printing

Dedication

This book is dedicated to my cherished father and maternal grandmother.

Thanks for your unconditional love, encouragement and support. R.I.P.

Survive, Strive & Thrive!

Robbie

Prologue

Chess is the Game of Kings.

Royalty used the game of chess to teach war strategies to their children and military. Now used as mental training for children, chess debatably gives them psychological advantages over others.

The game of chess originated in India between the 3rd and 6th century when the game became known as *Chaturanga*, referring to four divisions of military – infantry (pawns), cavalry (knights), elephants (bishops) and chariotry (rooks).

In the 7th century after the Arabs (an ethnic group widespread in North Africa and the Middle East) conquered Persia (now known as Iran), the game became popular among Muslims.

The first reference to chess, called *Xiang Qi*, in China occurred around 800AD.

Only after the Moors conquered Spain did the game of chess spread to Europe around 800AD. Moors were Muslims from North Africa who inhabited the area now known as Spain and Portugal, and had a powerful impact on the culture of those countries.

A famous Arab chess player authored the oldest known chess manual, written in Arabic between 840-850AD.

The game did not reach Northern Europe or Russia until the 9th century and did not become widespread until the 10th century.

Black CHESS

A Novel

PAWNS

The PAWN, the chess piece of least value, can only move forward along the file on which it stands, one square at a time. However, on its first move, each pawn has the option of advancing two squares. En passant (French for 'in passing') is a unique circumstance where a pawn has just made the initial double move. The opponent can use a pawn to capture it as though it had only moved one square. An en passant capture occurs only between two opposing pawns and must be made on the next move, or the opportunity is lost. The pawn captures forward diagonally, one square to the left or right. If a pawn avoids capture and reaches the opposite end of the board, it must be promoted to any piece of the player's choice, except a king. A pawn is usually promoted to the most powerful piece, the queen.

PAWNS

Robert bolted into his mother's bedroom giggling, with his black Labrador Retriever puppy chasing behind him, and dived onto her disheveled queen-size bed. Celeste smiled as she watched her little prince through the reflection in her vanity mirror, hoping he would continue to live a carefree and happy childhood and find that same happiness as an adult. Her eyes scanned the room, as she added hair-extensions to her chestnut-colored beach-waves. The state of her room echoed the state of her life. She regretted painting her room white. It seemed like a brilliant idea at the time. The perfect backdrop to display some black-and-white photographs from her collection of thousands. Now unbalanced collages covered every dingy wall. The only color photo in the room, a gold-framed picture of Robert, was sitting on her vanity. She needed some color in her life and order in her world.

"Robert, isn't it time for your nap?" Mr. Alexander asked, appearing in her doorway.

"I'm not taking no nap!" Robert protested, launching himself from the bed into his grandfather's arms.

"Getting dolled up, Princess?" Mr. Alexander inquired, throwing Robert back onto the bed. "You have a date?"

Celeste took an exasperated breath and began grooming her eyebrows with an old pink toothbrush. "No, Daddy. Just going to brunch with Bianca and Kennedy, so they can finally meet."

"When are you going on a date?" he asked, moving a pile of unfolded clean clothes so that he could sit on the edge of her bed.

"I don't know," she responded, fanning her hand in the air. "I'm focused on my career, not men."

"Life is multidimensional. You need to make time for your social life."

"I go out."

"I don't remember the last time you went out with someone other than your girlfriends."

"It's not like I'm turning down offers."

"I bet if you decide to give your heart another chance, you'll find love."

"I think love is something that just happens. It's not something you search for."

"How will you ever find a husband, if you don't date?"

"What makes you think I want a husband?" Celeste asked, staring at her father through the mirror.

"You need a husband."

"For what?" she asked, turning to face her father with a furrowed brow.

"To create a safe and stable home for you and Robert."

"We have a safe and stable home," Celeste stated, standing up and walking to her jewelry armoire. "Sounds like you're trying to get rid of us."

"That's absurd! All I have is the two of you. This will always be your home."

"I'm never leaving!" Robert chanted.

"Right now, my only concern is getting my career started so that I can be self-sufficient and *finally* independent."

"How's work going?"

"Ugh, horrible!"

"What's wrong?"

"I'm sick of shooting models!"

"What's your plan for change?"

"I don't know," Celeste said, putting on teal-blue tassel earrings to match her t-shirt.

"You need to get a plan. Are you still interested in photojournalism?"

"Yes."

"What's your major obstacle?"

"Experience."

"How did your classmates get jobs as photojournalists?"

"Probably personal contacts or financing their own projects to build their portfolios."

"What about volunteering?"

"I can't afford to work for free!"

"Why not? You have no expenses here."

"I can't build financial independence volunteering," she answered, grabbing a handful of hangers from her closet.

"You can get experience to put on your resume while pursuing your goals."

"I'm not willing to sacrifice the next six months to a year with limited or no income."

"Seems like a small investment of time, for the career of your dreams and financial stability."

"Isn't that what I did when I spent four years of my life earning my degree in photojournalism? After doing a year-long internship, along with most of my classmates, I was one of the few who didn't get hired at the place I interned."

"Princess, I want you to be happy."

"I'm content," she specified, picking t-shirts out of the pile of clothes on her bed.

"Do you want to live or simply exist?"

"Right now, I'm just dealing with basic survival for Robert and me."

"What are your long-term goals?"

"I just wanna prevent Robert from ever experiencing the pains and disappointments of life I've experienced, by making sure he's well equipped to succeed. I want him to survive, strive and thrive."

"That's what you want for Robert. You can't dedicate the rest of your life to mothering, nor can you make up for his father's absence by sacrificing *your* life."

"I'm not sacrificing my life. I just wanna be a good mother. It's not easy figuring out what to do. It's not like I got a baby manual, and I never had a real mother. I'm just doing the best I can."

"You need to stop putting the burden on Robert of providing your happiness. What do you want for *yourself*?"

"I've found my purpose in life. My contribution to the universe is my son. I enjoy being his mother, and I don't look for him to provide my happiness," Celeste declared, hanging up her t-shirts.

"Name something you do that brings you joy, not involving Robert."

Celeste thought for a while but did not provide an answer.

"Has life dealt you such a bad hand that you don't even want to play anymore?"

"I haven't given up, Daddy. I wanna be successful."

"What does that mean?"

"Having all my needs, many of my wants, and some achievable dreams."

"Is marriage a part of that?" Mr. Alexander asked, extending his arm to prevent Robert, who was jumping on the bed, from falling.

"No."

"You don't want to get married?"

"I'm not against it. I'm just not concerned about that."

"A fulfilling life includes romantic love."

"So you think I need a man to fulfill me?"

"Life and achievements are much more fulfilling when you have a committed partner."

"So why didn't you remarry?"

"I don't know. Guess I was too busy raising you."

"That feels great," she replied sarcastically. "I kept you from romance."

"You didn't keep me from romance. I wasn't interested because I couldn't get over your mother. I don't want you to walk this life alone."

"Well, I wanna walk alone. I wanna be independent. I need to know I'm capable of taking care of myself and Robert."

"You don't need to be single to be independent. Many married women have successful careers."

"Well, you and Robert are all I need. Nothing like unconditional love," Celeste said, putting on brown snakeskin gladiator sandals. "I can't count on emotional security from any man but you."

"The world is a tough place for a single mother. You need a life partner, and Robert needs a father."

"Robert has a grandfather."

"I'm Mommy's partner! I don't want her to have nobody but me!" Robert shouted.

"That's right, Sweetheart," she responded, winking at her son.

"Robert deserves a complete and healthy family unit."

"You seemed to make it work, as a single parent."

"A woman can't raise a man. You don't know what it takes to be a man."

"You're probably right, but I'm not worried about that cause we've got you."

"I won't always be around."

"Where you going, Grandpa?"

Celeste and her father's eyes froze momentarily on each other. "I might be at work or on vacation."

"Well," Robert paused, sensing his mother and grandfather's discomfort, "we'll wait 'til you get home."

Celeste smiled at her son. "That's right."

Mr. Alexander picked Robert up, tickled him, and dropped him back on the bed. "Go walk your dog, so we can finish our chess game."

Robert grabbed a black towel and held it around his neck, impersonating Superman. "Can I be white next time?"

"If you win, you can be white."

Robert jumped off the bed and took off running, with Zeus following, through the door.

"You don't have confidence in me," Celeste complained.

"I'm just concerned about your future."

"I'm gonna be an entrepreneur, just like you."

"You need a steady job with benefits. That's the only way to guarantee independence."

"You were able to establish your own company. Just because I'm female doesn't mean I can't do the same thing."

"I do have faith in you and your abilities."

"I hope so, Daddy," she said, putting on her jean jacket. "Well, I'm running late, as usual. Thanks for babysitting."

"I'm not babysitting! Don't try to use Robert and me as your excuse for not getting out. If I'm here, he can be here. If I need to go out, there's nowhere I go that he can't go. I'm not doing you a favor!"

"Alright, Daddy! Thanks for being the best Grandpa." Celeste headed down the stairs, escorted by her father. "Robert, I'm getting ready to go."

Robert and Zeus came running from the backyard to meet Celeste in the foyer. "Bye, Mommy!" Robert screamed, jumping into his mother's arms.

"Bye, Sweetheart. Be good and have a great day!" She leaned Robert back like a baby and struggled with him to plant three kisses on his neck. "I don't understand why you continue to try to stop me. You can't!" she said, handing Robert to his grandfather.

"Do you have money?"

"A little bit."

Mr. Alexander sat his grandson down and handed his daughter a hundred dollar bill from his pants pocket. "Bye, Princess. Have a good day. Be safe."

"Thanks, Daddy. Love you," Celeste said, kissing her father on the cheek.

"Love you too."

Zeus began whining and jumping on her legs. "What's wrong with you?" she asked, scooping Zeus up with one hand. "You're not going with me," she added, rubbing her nose back and forth across his. Celeste handed Zeus to Robert, picked up her black camera case and navy-blue leather Coach Hobo purse, and slung one over each shoulder.

Robert studied the sparkling palm tree on his mother's tee, which read *Life's A Beach*. "Are we going to the beach tomorrow?" he asked.

"Of course, Sweetheart." Celeste headed down the walkway and got into her 2011 light-blue Honda CR-V, her 21st birthday and graduation present from her father. She looked through the passenger side window at Robert holding Mr. Alexander's hand in the doorway. Smiling to herself, Celeste waved and pulled off thinking how fortunate she was to have her father and son.

Celeste drove into a middle-class area of single-family homes that was once a status location. The loss of neighborhood pride was evident in the lack of curb appeal. Trash, clutter, peeling paint, uninviting porches, neglected lawns, and numerous properties resembling auto repair shops highlighted the deterioration. She stopped in front of a single-story home where an old Chevy sitting on bricks and two new vehicles lined the driveway. Sitting shirtless, on the dilapidated porch, was a man with bulging muscles gleaming in the sunlight. Two toddlers playing in an inflatable pool scrambled out, one running towards the house, the other towards the front gate.

"Hi, Auntie Celeste!"

"Hello, China," Celeste said through the open passenger side window.

"How did you know it was me?"

"Your smile." Celeste got out of her SUV and walked towards the gate. "You and your sister can't trick me."

"Where's Robert?"

"At home with his grandfather," she said, entering the front yard.

"I wanna go to your house."

Celeste leaned over to give China a kiss on the cheek. "Well, I can't take you today because your Mommy and I are going out."

"Where you going?"

"China, stop asking Celeste a million questions. Get back in the water," the man on the porch insisted.

"Auntie, watch me swim," China said, skipping back to the inflatable pool.

"Hey, Pierce."

"What's up?"

Celeste climbed the worn stairs, wary of splinters and uneven footing. "Nothing much. How you doing?"

"Tired as hell. Kennedy is about to kill me."

"What's she doing?"

"Got me out here in the hot sun, cutting grass. Now all of a sudden, she doesn't wanna waste money paying kids in the neighborhood to do it, so I have to."

"Why don't *you* pay some kids?"

"I already suggested that. Kennedy wants *me* to do it. Says their work is mediocre."

The raggedy screen door flew open, banging against one of many mismatched chairs scattered across the porch. "Hi, Auntie."

"Hi, India," Celeste said, squatting to receive a tight hug around her neck.

India carefully descended the porch stairs and ran to join her sister in the pool.

"The grass has been overgrown for more than a month!" Kennedy shouted from inside. An exotic beauty with porcelain skin and short bone-straight black spiked hair emerged onto the porch. "Are you gonna finish this tiny yard today?"

"I'm taking a break."

"A break from what?" Kennedy asked baffled, standing over him wearing a taupe shorts suit. "You haven't done any real work!"

"I finished half the yard, and set up the pool for the twins," Pierce replied, admiring her beautiful legs in shorts and heels.

"It wouldn't be so hard if you maintained it more frequently. You're just lazy."

"It'll be done by the time you get back. When you coming home?" he asked, still gazing at her legs.

"Don't clock me! I rarely go out."

"You're never home!" he responded in disbelief.

"Somebody has to work to keep a roof over our heads."

"Don't worry 'bout this house. It's my responsibility."

"So you inherited this house from your grandmother, and now you plan to sit on the porch for the rest of your life?"

"You plan on doing makeup the rest of yours?"

"At least I'm a functioning member of society."

Pierce looked at Kennedy with aggravation. "Please leave your car keys, or move your car so I can get out."

"Where are you going?"

"I don't have plans, other than watching the game and drinking a few beers. But I wanna be able to leave if I get bored."

"Okay," Kennedy said, leaning over to kiss Pierce on the lips. "Bye, Honey."

"Bye, Sugar. Have a good time," he said, patting her on the butt.

Kennedy and Celeste headed for their vehicles. "Bye, little sharks. Be good," Kennedy said, waving to her daughters.

"Bye, Mommy. Bye, Auntie Celeste," the twins said in unison.

"Goodbye. Please come visit Robert and me soon."

Kennedy got into her jet-black 2014 BMW Z4, backed out of the driveway, parked behind Celeste, and got into Celeste's SUV. "I'm so glad to be out of there!" Kennedy sighed.

"Why are you harassing Pierce?" Celeste asked, pulling off.

"He's driving me crazy! He has no motivation! We are going nowhere fast!"

"You should have thought about that before you had the twins."

"When we started dating he had dreams. He has given up. He's weak and a quitter!"

"Why don't you and Pierce take a short weekend getaway just to talk and reconnect?"

"No way! He'll bore me to death, and I'll have to pay for everything!"

"Why don't you start doing different activities with him, instead of doing different men?"

"It's exciting meeting different guys and having new experiences."

"So what are you gonna do about your Baby Daddy?"

"Nothing, but I'm gonna keep passion in my life."

"Don't you think your relationship is worth trying to improve for the twins?"

"Nope. The twins need productive parents, and I need to be happy."

"Do you love him?"

"I love him, but I'm not in love with him."

"Were you ever in love?"

"I don't think either of us was in love, more like in lust."

"If you don't want Pierce, why don't you leave him?"

Kennedy ignored Celeste and began searching social media for potential dates.

"Well, it's bad karma to be cheating on a man committed to you."

"If he was committed to me, he'd be working. He knows I want a better life."

"Alright, I'll leave it alone."

"You need to quit this celibacy madness and find a man," Kennedy stated. "I see some great guys for you right here."

"Does it look like I have time for a man or trolling social media?"

"Yes. You're just gun shy."

"My Dad just finished hassling me about getting married. What's going on?"

"I don't know about you, but I'm gonna find me a rich husband."

"You're only attracting one-night stands."

"I have to kiss a lot of frogs to find my prince," Kennedy said, continuing to swipe left on her phone.

"You have to become that which you seek."

"Don't start that Agape talk again."

"It's *Law of Attraction*, not Agape."

"Whatever."

"Why should a rich man choose to marry a broke woman with bad credit? Why should a man who takes pride in his health and fitness marry a woman who doesn't care about her own health and fitness?"

"I don't have bad credit," Kennedy replied, before answering an incoming call.

Celeste merged onto Interstate 405 North, closed the windows and turned on air conditioning, while Kennedy held a 30-minute conversation with a mystery man. Cruising onto Pacific Coast Highway, the stress in Celeste's body began to subside. "This day is gorgeous. I'm gonna make a quick stop to t–"

"I know. You need to take some pictures."

"I won't be long. It's just rare for me to be in Malibu on such a perfect day."

"What time are we supposed to be at Gladstones?"

"One o'clock."

"We've got fifteen minutes," Kennedy said, looking at her phone.

"Have you gotten any more stylist assignments?" Celeste asked.

"Not yet, but I'm hoping to make some connections for music video shoots."

"Has the agency been keeping you busy?"

"The last few weeks have been busy. What about you?"

"My schedule is still inconsistent, but photographing models is getting frustrating."

"Doing makeup is getting really boring."

"I wanna do something meaningful."

"At least we're both working the beach shoot next Wednesday and Thursday," Kennedy said, freshening her lipstick.

"Maybe we can meet Bianca for *happy hour* on Thursday."

"Great. Then *maybe* we can find you a rich man to date."

"Do you wanna be in love or just have a rich husband?"

"I'm only interested in certainty," Kennedy said, taking a selfie.

"Certainty about what?"

"Being able to take care of me and my kids. I'm looking for security and luxury, not love."

Celeste drove to a scenic parking spot overlooking the rocky cliffs and ocean. "Come on. Walk with me down to the beach."

"What's wrong with this dramatic view?"

"Isn't the beach rejuvenating?" Celeste asked, removing her shoes and rolling up her jeans.

"Not really. I don't like getting sandy."

"Just come on. Let me show you my secret meditation spot."

"Yeah, I'd better go before you lose track of time," Kennedy replied, removing her jacket and shoes.

Kennedy followed Celeste down the steps descending onto the beach. Celeste hiked towards a cliff, where a rolling stream of large rocks terminated at the water's edge. "Maybe you lack confidence in your ability to love."

"I'm not the problem. Men are incapable of love. They're only interested in sex. For them, sex *is* love."

"Do you think not knowing your father causes you to lack confidence in men?" Celeste inquired, continually snapping photographs of the coastline.

"Do you think growing up without a mother handicaps your femininity?" Kennedy asked irritably, already knowing the answer.

"Probably," Celeste answered, ignoring the jab. "But I think it's possible, subconsciously you feel rejected by your father and don't believe you deserve to be loved."

"Plenty of men are after me."

"Are you trying to prove to yourself or others that men love you?"

"I'm not trying to prove anything to anybody. And I don't appreciate you judging me."

"I'm not judging you. Your need for variety is inconsistent with your desire for a monogamous relationship . . . marriage."

"It is nice to be loved by a man. You should try it sometime."

"Lust and love are two very different experiences."

"How would you know? I think you're insecure about your feminity."

"No, I'm not."

"You wouldn't be such a tomboy if your mother had been around."

"Maybe, but I adore the tomboy in me."

"Where are you going?"

"The other side of those rocks."

"I'm not getting wet."

"We can easily climb over the rocks." Her effortless feline movements were in sharp contrast to Kennedy's awkward and guarded climb. "Isn't this great!" Celeste said, jumping onto the sand and throwing her arms in the air.

"Yeah, this is nice. Great place for a secluded date. Ever been here with a man?"

"Of course," Celeste said, photographing Kennedy on the rocks. "This is my favorite beach in California."

"Don't you already have plenty pictures of this place?"

"Yeah. I usually take black-and-whites. On overcast days, I like to capture the eerie shadows appearing in the fog," Celeste said, wading in the water, taking a meditative stance and several deep breaths of salt air, before whispering to the ocean.

"That's spooky! You're giving me the chills."

"I've decided to redecorate my room, so I need some color photos."

"Redecorate? You need to move. How you gonna get a man living with your father?"

Bianca was seated at a patio table facing the beach when Celeste and Kennedy arrived. Her long light-brown soft curls danced in the ocean breeze, while she dangled a powder-blue leather sling-back three-inch sandal from her foot, clearly bored with her phone conversation. She quickly terminated the call and let out a sigh of relief. "Hi, Sweetie," Bianca said, sharing double kisses on the cheeks with Celeste.

"Hey," Celeste replied. "Bianca, this is Kennedy. Kennedy, this is Bianca."

"Nice to finally meet you," Kennedy replied, selecting the seat facing Bianca, with her back to the beach.

"Nice meeting you," Bianca said, with a nod.

"How's Wade?" Celeste asked, standing between them taking photos of the ocean.

"He's fine. How was my nephew's Easter?"

"Great. Robert was in the children's program at Agape, and then went to an Easter egg hunt at his friend's house."

"Are you going to sit down anytime soon?" Bianca asked.

"Sorry we're late," Celeste said, joining them at the table.

"Guess who had to make a stop to take photos," Kennedy revealed, putting her designer purse on the left side of her plate and her phone on the right side face up.

"Whenever Celeste is in Malibu she always needs to stop for photos. Did you tell Mama *hi* for me?" Bianca asked while Kennedy looked confused.

"Of course. Did you get blonde highlights?"

"Yes," Bianca said, with a mischievous grin. "Thought I'd try something new for spring. I might go blonde for summer."

"Looks gorgeous."

"Thanks. Want a taste?" Bianca asked, offering Celeste her mimosa.

"No, thanks. I'll wait. The waitress is coming."

"Good afternoon, ladies. May I get you something to drink and some appetizers?"

"I'd like a mimosa," Celeste requested with a smile, putting her purse and camera bag on the ground.

"Give me a Coke or Pepsi, whichever you have," Kennedy answered, never looking up from the menu.

"I'll have another mimosa. I don't need appetizers this early in the day. I'm ready to order."

"So am I," Celeste agreed.

"Okay," Kennedy said, continuing to study the menu.

"I'll take the seafood ceviche," Bianca replied.

"I'll have lobster bisque and a Caesar salad with shrimp."

"Give me a hamburger," Kennedy demanded.

"We have Angus burgers," the waitress informed Kennedy.

"That's fine."

"And I'll also have a glass of champagne with my meal," Bianca requested.

"Me too," Celeste added.

"I'll be right back with your drinks."

"Kennedy, you're the designated driver," Celeste announced.

"As usual," Kennedy responded.

"Can I ride home with you?" Bianca asked. "Wade can pick me up later."

"Sure," Celeste replied. "Where's your Prius?"

"Wade has it. His car is in the shop. I rode to Santa Monica this morning with Mom."

"Farmers Market?"

"Yep. Is Robert home?"

"He should be."

"Great. I'll have time to visit with my nephew," Bianca said, with a big smile. "And Wade has another Lego set to bring Robert."

"How are you getting home?" Celeste asked Kennedy.

"I'm not going home. I have a date later. I'll take an Uber from your house."

Celeste cut her eyes at Kennedy and glared.

"Love your old-school charm bracelet," Kennedy said, ignoring Celeste's glare.

"Thanks," Bianca said, gazing at her gold bracelet.

"Is it vintage?"

"No. My thirteenth birthday gift from Celeste. One charm every year, age thirteen to twenty-one."

"Nine charms, blessing different aspects or phases of her life," Celeste added. "Nine is the power number."

"Why is nine so special?" Kennedy asked.

"The sum of all multiples is nine," Celeste explained. "18, 27, 36, 45, 54, 63, 72, 81, 90, 99, 108."

"How long have you two known each other?"

"Since kindergarten," Celeste and Bianca said in unison.

"You two sound like my twins!" Kennedy laughed.

"I love your pixie haircut," Bianca said to Kennedy.

"Thanks," Kennedy replied, glancing at her phone.

"Not many women can pull off short hair."

"Kennedy is known on social media for her sexy short hairstyles and dramatic makeup."

"Celeste says you're an Instagram Celebrity."

"I have a large following. Several hundred thousand."

"Is your Instagram business or personal?"

"Business," Kennedy said, swiping left several times on her phone.

"What's your business?"

"I'm a make-up artist and wannabe stylist."

"What type of stylist?"

"Video shoots."

"So how do you use Instagram to promote your business?"

"I post photos of my hairstyles and makeup, MUA bookings, and all video shoots."

"How does that help your business?"

"It's my online portfolio."

"Are you a hairstylist?"

"No."

"Then why photos of your hairstyles?"

"Branding. Short sexy hair is my brand."

"How did you get so many followers?"

"Beautiful women, great makeup, great photos, and mastering hashtags."

"I've heard timing is important," Celeste added.

"I post whenever. Hashtags ensure my photos reach my target audience. Do you have an Instagram account?"

"No," Bianca answered, finishing her mimosa.

"Why not?"

"I'm a private person and not hyped about social media, but I do have a Facebook work page, which I neglect."

"Social media is a necessity for every person in business. What's your business?"

"I'm the Assistant Fashion Editor for a local magazine."

"So what's happening at work?" Celeste interrupted.

"I didn't get a fashion week assignment for Milan or Paris."

"That's horrible!" Celeste cried.

"My work is not being acknowledged. It's like I don't exist."

"Who got fashion week assignments?"

"My former summer intern got an assignment in Milan."

"How insulting! A couture show?"

"Yep. He has no experience. I don't understand."

"The guy from FIDM?"

"Yes!" Bianca quietly confirmed, drumming her gel manicured fingernails on her face-down phone.

"He obviously has connections," Celeste said, shaking her head.

"Sexism is real."

"Why do you think sexism is the problem?" Kennedy asked, looking perplexed.

"The magazine is owned by a man. Men appear to be getting most of the promotions and opportunities, and they're getting paid better than women."

"I thought women had the advantage in the fashion industry," Kennedy said, swiping right on her phone.

"It's so hard for women to advance their careers in any field," Bianca complained. "Female superiors often are the worst because they see other women as competition rather than comrades."

"Is your boss female?" Kennedy asked.

"Yes, and I'm sure she's threatened by me."

"Just getting in the door is difficult," Celeste added. "We struggle to get real jobs with benefits. Careers seem out of reach."

"Graduating from a fashion institute is apparently more valuable than a degree in journalism."

"So you wanna use social media to get recognition at work?" Kennedy asked.

"Not necessarily for this job, but for my career."

"Are you trying to market yourself or what you do?"

"Myself," Bianca replied, handing her empty glass to the waitress.

"What's your brand?"

"*L.A. Lifestyle Expert.*"

"Fashion, entertainment, real estate?"

"Fashion, beauty, health and fitness. What type of photos or articles should I post?"

"I'm not a social media expert. My focus is Instagram, where you tell your story with photos."

"Then, what type of photos would you suggest?"

"You'll need to attend *every* fashion show in Los Angeles, and some FIDM events, making a fashion statement yourself. Feature trending beauty services and products in L.A. or California."

"She can also feature spas and fitness clubs, and alternative health modalities," Celeste added.

"You're gonna need a theme. Not just random photos."

"What do you mean by theme?" Bianca asked.

"Vibe, focus, location, angle, filter, selfies, color," Kennedy answered. "And I strongly suggest the use of blue."

"Why blue?"

"Blue photos get more likes. People are drawn to soothing blue," Celeste stated.

"Some people use a soft blue filter on black-and-white photos or frame photos in blue."

"How do you use blue?" Bianca asked Kennedy.

"I don't use blue as often as I should, but when I do, it's usually a blue frame."

"Have you thought of possible names for your Instagram page?" Celeste asked.

"I was thinking of something with *L.A.* and *style* in the title. Any suggestions?"

"All of my social media is Kennedy Vance MUA. If you're branding yourself, use your name."

"Would you use Sullivan or Michaels?" Celeste asked.

"I don't know, probably Sullivan."

"Wade might be offended," Celeste warned.

"You can decide that later. You definitely need to decide on a theme first."

"You can research Instagram themes on YouTube," Celeste suggested.

"Use sex appeal as part of the vibe."

"Why?" Bianca inquired bewildered.

"Sex sells and drives the world," Kennedy responded.

"I'm not playing into sexism."

"Then, you probably won't get many followers."

"Maybe you can do a stylish young professional look," Celeste proposed.

"Women endure sexualization while being sexually oppressed," Kennedy acknowledged. "We might as well benefit financially."

"This society is too concerned with genitals and what people do with them."

"Sexism and homophobia are negatively impacting society," Bianca said. "The basic human rights to pursue your dreams and love who you please are being threatened."

"Some people just don't want alternative lifestyles flaunted in their neighborhoods."

"I'm not homophobic, but I'm not on board with the *Transgender Agenda*," Celeste added. "Some of us are concerned with the images our children see."

"What *agenda*?!" Bianca interrupted. "I can't believe you'd impose your gender biases and sexual beliefs on others!"

"I'm not trying to influence anyone's sexuality or gender identification. I just don't want alternative lifestyles paraded around my family," Celeste stated.

"So they should hideout?" Bianca protested. "Ain't nobody trying to push anything on you or your people!"

"Everyone should have the right as a human being to live their lives out loud. I also have the right as a parent to censor the world my child experiences," Celeste responded.

"People need to learn tolerance for others," Bianca declared. "How are you going to teach Robert tolerance if he is not exposed to different types of people?"

"He's learning religious tolerance at Agape," Celeste revealed.

"Religious fanatics are morons," Bianca replied. "The hypocrisy of religion…sexism and hidden homosexuality."

"People in power attempt to stay in power by controlling religious beliefs."

"I think most of the intolerance is for nontraditional religions and/or religious extremists," Kennedy added.

"No one has the right to force their religion on others."

"Who determines what's traditional and who's a radical?" Celeste asked.

The waitress arrived with their meals, and all conversation stopped. "Is there anything else you ladies need?"

"No, thanks. This lobster bisque smells delicious."

"Some ketchup, for my burger."

"Nothing for me."

The ladies began enjoying their meals. "What's going on with you?" Bianca asked Celeste, breaking the awkward silence.

"Not much. Same shit, different day."

"She needs to find a man," Kennedy proclaimed.

"Daddy wants me to get married."

"He's probably ready for you to get out of his house," Kennedy added.

"He doesn't want you or Robert out of his sight," Bianca snickered.

"I'm not paying attention to Daddy."

"She doesn't need a man. Celeste needs a career with growth potential. She can get a man whenever."

"There's certainly no growth potential in model shoots arranged by talent agencies. It's just a racket to sell portfolios to people who will never work as models or actors."

"I'm sure it's mind-numbing," Bianca said sympathetically. "You've got the skills and talent to get a job as a photojournalist."

"I'm ready to get back to building my photojournalism portfolio."

"It's time for us to get serious about our careers and stop accepting any job for income," Bianca said. "You know we always reach our goals."

"Kennedy and I work together a couple days this week in Santa Monica. We could meet you on Thursday in Westwood for *happy hour*."

"We can talk more about your Instagram page then," Kennedy suggested.

"That works for me."

"Let's toast to reaching our goals," Celeste said, tapping glasses with her friends.

Champagne splashed on Bianca's white lace tank top. "I'm running to the ladies room to get this stain out," she announced, grabbing her blue Valentino purse hanging on a jeweled table hook. All eyes were on Bianca as she weaved between the patio tables and disappeared into the restaurant. Her perfectly proportioned hour-glass figure, girl-next-door beauty, classic style, and confident stride were impossible to ignore.

OPENINGS

The primary goal in chess is to checkmate your opponent's king. The secondary goal is to reduce your opponent's manpower by capturing material, making it easier to force mate. Both of these goals are achieved through tactical play; however, most moves in a game of chess are strategic. Strategic play positions you to execute tactical play. There are three elements to a chess game. The first element, the men, determines who leads in force. The board, the second element, represents your strength in space. Whoever controls most of the chessboard is most likely to win. The third element is the moves. The player with the most moves commands the power of time.

In both strategic and tactical play, there are numerous familiar circumstances, which you can quickly learn to manage correctly. A game of chess always begins from the same position, called the initial position, in which white always moves first. The OPENINGS are the plays of both sides, at the beginning of a game, where the players are repeating moves that have been played for eons. It is critical that you know what you are trying to do in the opening, and how to do it, instead of repeating moves that have been taught to you, which you do not fully comprehend. Defeat can come quickly in the opening if you sin against principles. Two of the most important focuses are to (1) get your pieces onto good squares, and (2) strike at the center. Do not become so fascinated with your own plans that you fail to analyze your opponent's moves! Stay focused and controlled, ignoring the lures of your opponent into reckless play.

OPENINGS

Celeste entered the trendy Westwood bar wearing black raw silk trousers and a white tailored blouse, with her hair pulled back into a fishtail braid, utilizing her three-inch black-and-white herringbone pumps to scan the *happy hour* crowd. Squeezing between clusters of people oblivious to her presence, despite being six feet tall and excusing herself, Celeste felt invisible. The conversations she overheard, passing diverse individuals, all echoed shock and horror at the brutal arrest of Freddie Gray in Baltimore, Maryland being broadcast on the bar televisions. A familiar laugh prompted her to turn right finding Bianca dressed in a pink floral wrap dress, at a nearby table surrounded by men. Celeste apprehensively moved towards them fearing male scrutiny. "Hey, Girlfriend," she said, leaning over to double kiss Bianca.

"Hi, Sweetie!" Bianca beamed at the men and announced, "This is my BFF, Celeste!"

"Hello," Celeste responded, to the nods of the men.

"This is Bryce," Bianca said, introducing the white guy sitting on her right.

"Please, have a seat," Bryce offered, standing up. "We were just keeping Bianca company until you arrived. May I get you a drink?"

"Yes, thank you. I'd like a strawberry daiquiri," Celeste requested, taking a seat.

"Anyone else want anything?" Bryce asked.

"I'd like another martini," Bianca replied, with a smile. Everyone else shook their heads, indicating *no*. "This is Hunter," she continued, introducing the Black guy on her left. "And this is Dez," she said, introducing the Latino guy sitting across from her. "Where's Kennedy?"

"Outside on the phone. She's coming."

"How was your day?" Bianca inquired, offering Celeste her cocktail.

"Ridiculously superficial," Celeste replied, declining a sip. "How was yours?"

"Frustrating as usual," Bianca answered, crossing her legs exposing her soft pink suede pumps matching the soft pink suede purse on her lap.

"Have you been following what's happening in Baltimore?" Celeste asked Bianca.

"I've seen it. How can I miss the trending topic of the day?" Bianca asked, clearly indifferent sitting with her back to the televisions.

"I can't believe they dragged that man in pain and threw him into a police wagon like a bag of trash, after detaining him for no reason!" Celeste criticized.

"They had a reason. The police knew him and his record," Bianca rebutted.

"The police said they detained him because he was walking around early in the morning looking suspicious. They found nothing. I don't understand how that leads to being arrested," Celeste questioned, furrowing her brow.

"Hey," Kennedy said, arriving in a sexy animal print dress.

"Guys, this is Kennedy," Bianca presented, finishing her martini.

"Have a seat," Hunter offered, quickly standing up.

"Thanks," Kennedy replied, sitting down.

"Your hair is so sexy," he stated, admiring her wavy black pixie.

"Thanks," she responded, with a flirtatious smile.

"I'm Hunter," he said, extending his hand. "Would you like a drink?"

"I don't drink alcohol, but I'll take a Coke," Kennedy answered, shaking his hand.

"You working this weekend?" Bianca asked Celeste.

"No."

"Feel like beach yoga?"

"Definitely need it. Haven't been to that class in at least six months."

"Do you do yoga?" Bianca asked Kennedy.

"Nope."

"You workout?"

"Nope. Just dance."

"What type?"

"Hip-hop, modern, ballet."

"You ladies are beautiful," Dez interjected. "Whatever you're doing, keep doing it."

"Thanks," Kennedy responded, looking him over.

"I'm Dez," he said, shaking Kennedy's hand.

"Do you guys work together?" Kennedy asked.

"Yes. We're interns at a law firm."

"From UCLA?" Celeste probed.

"Yeah."

"When are you taking the bar exam?" Bianca inquired.

"This summer," Dez sighed. "The preparation is brutal."

"What kind of law do you practice?" Celeste asked.

"We research and discuss civil rights legislation," Dez replied.

"Why is police brutality growing?" Celeste queried, dipping a tortilla chip in the bowl of guacamole on the table.

"I doubt it's growing," Dez responded. "It's just that cell phone cameras, body cams, and the Internet are now exposing abuse by law enforcement."

"Feels like we're living in the Stone Ages," Bianca uttered.

"Law enforcement is supposed to represent safety, but now illicit fear and flight responses," Celeste complained.

"Menacing for Black folks," Kennedy specified.

"And Latinos," Dez appended.

"Everybody is scared of everybody else," Bianca said, eating chips and guacamole. "And too many people appear to be unhinged."

"What happened to *Protect and Serve?*" Celeste asked perplexed.

"The L.A. Police Department came up with that motto in 1955," Dez stated, stuck on Kennedy's cleavage.

"Other law enforcement agencies nationwide adopted that same motto," Bianca added.

"It has never been about serving or protecting people of color," Kennedy scoffed. "In the ghetto, the police are just another gang who bully, hurt and kill people."

"There's no one in ghettos to protect people, and no attorneys, judges or politicians with power," Dez explained, then dropped his eyes back on Kennedy's cleavage.

"The police are becoming more blatantly racist, and promoting the spread of racism," Kennedy grumbled, crossing her legs away from Dez.

"Law enforcement no longer has the respect it once had for having skilled, physically fit, and mentally stable officers with some basic knowledge of psychology and sociology to deal with troubled people," Bianca said, watching the interaction between Kennedy and Dez.

"Police officers don't use psychology or sociology to diffuse situations in ghettos. They use physical force and violence," Celeste stated.

"White criminals are troubled people. Black criminals are rabid animals," Hunter said, returning with sweet potato fries and Kennedy's Coke.

"Why is *blue blood* above the law?" Kennedy asked.

"Because they are the law," Celeste replied.

"No organization can be trusted to self-regulate with integrity," Bryce said, returning with a martini and daiquiri. "Courts are supposed to be our safeguard."

Kennedy burst into laughter, "The judicial system is even worse for people of color!"

"You *cannot* defend yourself in U.S. courts, although every citizen is supposed to be able to do so," Hunter stated. "No money, no proper representation, and you lose."

"It is not about right or wrong. It is about color and wealth," Dez revealed.

"Wealth can get you out of damn near anything," Celeste scoffed, tasting her daiquiri.

"They're trying to lock up all Black men," Kennedy said, sipping her Coke.

"The goal is to *kill* or lock up as many African American men as possible," Celeste amended. "Or at the very least profit by incapacitating them through addictions to drugs, alcohol, sex, consumerism."

"Exactly. Decrease our manpower," Hunter added.

"To accomplish what?" Bianca asked bewildered. "They pose no real threat to society."

"How about population control?" Celeste proposed. "Limit the number of African American men producing offspring."

"And institutionalized slavery through the prison system," Hunter said, standing behind Kennedy.

"One of the main strategies of white supremacists is to keep minorities out of positions of power so they can get away with our annihilation," Dez asserted.

"Black men are treated like Pit Bulls," Kennedy sighed. "They need to act more like Pit Bulls, defending themselves, their families and their territory."

"Well, going ballistic only justifies the actions of law enforcement," Bianca warned, enjoying her fresh martini. "Most officers have integrity and won't tolerate sick people tarnishing the shield."

"Too many police officers are unfit mentally. Some of them were bullied or abused as children, are bigots, or suffer from Napoleon complex," Hunter said, eating sweet potato fries.

"Police officers have been allowing their colleagues to violate rules, regulations and protocols since their organizations were formed," Bryce enlightened. "It's not that the crazy people are in charge. It's that the bond of *blue blood* outweighs everything else, even race."

"Their lives are at risk daily," Bianca said, dipping a few sweet potato fries in the honey chipotle sauce. "They must be able to trust that their colleagues have their backs."

"That bond should represent brotherhood and honor, not a place to hide your crimes and psychological problems," Dez said, joining Bianca eating sweet potato fries.

"Well these days, nobody sane would choose a career in law enforcement," Bianca decided. "It is irrational to expose yourself to dangerous criminals, mentally ill people and morons for inadequate compensation."

"So they should get paid more to kill Black folks?" Kennedy asked in disbelief.

"If salaries and benefits were better, the quality of employees would improve significantly," Bryce stated.

"They might be able to hire some martial artists who don't need guns, and some psychologists and sociologists who can masterfully eliminate threats without violence," Bianca considered.

"We need more African American police officers in all jurisdictions," Hunter suggested.

"Black officers who have a stronger bond to their people than the *blue blood*," Kennedy added.

"Ladies, it has been nice talking with you," Bryce interrupted, looking at his watch. "We have to get back to the office. Enjoy your evening."

The guys took one last gulp of their drinks, sat their glasses on the table, and left.

"You ran those guys off discussing racism," Bianca complained. "I didn't even have a chance to introduce Bryce to Kennedy."

"What do you care? You weren't interested in them," Celeste responded.

"That was the perfect time for you to practice socializing with men," Kennedy said, continually swiping left on her phone.

"You weren't interested either," Celeste said, rolling her eyes. "Those were nice guys with real careers."

"Nerds are more your type."

"Why didn't you just engage in casual conversations?" Bianca inquired.

"Men don't wanna get into a debate the first time they meet you."

"My consciousness will not allow me to engage in small talk, while my people are being murdered by the very people who are supposed to be protecting us," Celeste declared. "I can't sit around posting pictures of my belongings, the fabulous places I go, and the beautiful people I know. People are dying."

"The earth won't stop spinning because of child prostitution, slavery, or ethnic cleansing," Bianca revealed.

"Well, it should. Serious life-threatening issues need to be addressed immediately," Celeste said, dipping a handful of fries in the sauce.

"That's never gonna happen," Kennedy pooh-poohed, eating a tortilla chip.

"We can't fix social issues if we can't discuss them in social settings with opposing views," Celeste explained.

"Those topics are avoided by families, friends and coworkers," Bianca clarified. "How are you going to have a meaningful conversation with strangers?"

"We have to decide what kind of world we wanna live in and create it," Celeste insisted, drinking her daiquiri.

"What kind of world do you desire?" Bianca asked.

"Utopia."

"No such thing," Bianca replied.

"Of course there is. There's a word for it."

"It's a word for a concept, not a reality," Bianca refuted.

"Whatever the mind can conceive, man *or woman* can achieve."

"Sweetie, you've always been a dreamer."

"Why is that unrealistic? All realities are possible in this field of infinite possibilities."

"But that certainly isn't probable."

"We have to be definitive about our goals and desires, and brave enough to pursue them."

"Not many people ask themselves or the Universe the correct questions," Bianca said. "Most people just moan and groan about what's wrong, instead of focusing on change."

"When you respect your morals and values, your actions reflect that," Celeste said. "I'm gonna start living with more integrity."

"We have to respect ourselves enough to be a part of the change we seek," Bianca added.

"We need to become more involved," Celeste stated. "I'm joining *Black Lives Matter*."

"I'm with you," Kennedy agreed.

"Let's go to the Baltimore protest next weekend," Bianca suggested.

"I'd love to go, but I can't afford it," Celeste sighed.

"Sweetie, you know I've got you," Bianca said supportively.

"How much do you think it'll cost?" Kennedy asked.

"Around $500 each for airfare, and spending money. My husband will get a hotel room for us."

"I could probably do that. Might be fun," Kennedy smiled.

"Let me check the flight prices," Bianca said, taking her phone out of her purse.

"I've gotta make sure Daddy can babysit next weekend."

"You know babysitting is not a problem. Robert can spend the weekend with Mom if your father is busy."

"This will be the first time I travel without Robert."

"Both of you will be fine," Bianca reassured.

"I'm hungry. Don't they have any wings in here?" Kennedy asked.

"Probably," Bianca said, finishing the fries.

"I'll order wings or sliders when the waitress comes by," Kennedy offered.

"I've only seen a waitress once since I've been here," Bianca said. "Might be a while."

"I'll go order food," Celeste decided. "You two check the flights."

"Wow, Freddie Gray's arrest is blowing up social media!" Bianca said, scrolling through her phone. "This protest is gonna be huge!"

Bianca, dressed in black calf-length yoga pants and sports bra, and Celeste, wearing black ankle-length yoga pants and a pink *Hamsa* tee, stood in *mountain pose* on their matching fuchsia yoga mats facing the Pacific Ocean.

"This is simply the best way to start a Sunday," Bianca said, closing her eyes and leaning her head back to bathe her face in the bright sun rays.

"The meditation service, before Agape's worship service, is rejuvenating just like this," Celeste replied, bringing her hands together in the prayer mudra and taking slow rhythmic breaths of the fresh morning air.

"Listening to the surf is so relaxing," Bianca sighed, moving into *tree pose*.

"The ocean is calling me," Celeste murmured, joining her with the mirror image.

"What time do you need to be back home?"

"Whenever. Daddy and Robert don't have any plans today."

"Let's have lunch at the Venice Beach Whole Foods after class."

"I'm already starving," Celeste complained, switching her *tree pose*. "Hopefully, I can survive until then."

"You're just cranky because you're not surfing," Bianca said, changing to her left foot.

"I went yesterday morning."

"Damn!" Bianca grumbled, annoyed by the continual beeping of her Apple watch. "Freddie Gray's death has been the breaking news all morning!"

"Terrifying!" Celeste said, dropping her left leg. "Dying in police custody . . . incredible!"

"Police officers accuse him of causing his own death," Bianca said, turning off her notifications.

"Something was wrong with him when the police were dragging him to the wagon."

"The police claim he threw himself around on the ride to the station."

"His hands were handcuffed behind his back, and he was thrown inside on his stomach!" Celeste exclaimed. "Wow! Racial profiling is still leading to deaths in the 21st century!"

"Looks like the police have already raised reasonable doubt about their guilt, and will not be held responsible for the death of another African American man in their custody," Bianca said, returning to *mountain pose*.

"Black folks want justice," Celeste declared, facing Bianca in *mountain pose*.

"In spite of debates and scrutiny in all forms of media, police brutality is not declining," Bianca said, moving into *triangle pose*.

"Law enforcement officers don't give a damn what we know about their brutal acts," Celeste stated, turning to her left in *warrior one pose*. "Who's gonna stop them or hold them accountable?"

"Cell phone cameras and social media will hold them accountable," Bianca assured.

"White people close their eyes to the racism, abuse and injustice they know minorities experience."

"People are silent because most civilized human beings are stunned and appalled," Bianca said, moving into a left-side *triangle pose.*

"It's okay for people to hide in their comfortable lives, while people are being killed?" Celeste questioned, moving to a right-side *warrior one pose.*

"No one knows how to resolve this crisis."

"Anyone remaining silent is supporting racism. Either you're with us or against us."

"African Americans need to do more and stop looking for white people to save them."

"African Americans, who could make a difference, also hide in their comfy white sponsored lives. Those who experience discrimination daily are getting involved."

"Exposing racism through protests will bring about justice," Bianca affirmed, returning to *mountain pose.*

"There will never be justice for African Americans experiencing racism and abuse by law enforcement until other groups of people stand with us," Celeste stated, joining Bianca in *mountain pose.*

"Other people are standing with us."

"Other minority groups, but not enough white people in positions of power."

"Why should other people put themselves in potential danger to save us?"

"It's everyone's duty as a human being to defend the rights of others . . . Black, Latino, Native American, Asian, female, LGBTQ, poor, uneducated, young, old, religious, spiritual, atheist, disabled, sick," Celeste said, taking a *warrior two pose.*

"We'd be protesting all the time! You've got to focus on you and yours first."

"It's a shame we live in a world with so many inequalities. Ignoring discrimination of others leaves us vulnerable to those same abuses."

"Too many human beings choose to live in hate, confusion and war," Bianca said, leaning forward into *downward facing dog*.

"There are far more people who wanna live in a peaceful, loving world," Celeste countered, switching *warrior two* to her right side.

"Including me. We came here to relax. I came here to destress," Bianca complained, collapsing into *child's pose*.

"What's your problem?"

"Wade," Bianca answered, never lifting her head.

"What's wrong?"

"Your brother-in-law is ready to be a father," she revealed, rolling over into *corpse pose*.

"Oh my God!" Celeste whispered, sitting down on her mat and submerging her feet in the warm sand. "So . . . how do you feel about that?"

"I want to be Editor-in-Chief of my own magazine."

"Alright, Oprah. But what about your marriage?"

"You know I don't want a baby now. I don't need a baby."

"You've been married three years. When do you think you might be ready for children?"

"Maybe never. I've got my nephew. I'm good."

"When we were young girls, we dreamed of being mothers. You wanted a daughter, who you were gonna name Dominique. What happened?"

"I don't want to end up like Mom."

"I don't think Mom's life is so bad."

"She's a miserable, prescription drug-addicted housewife, with no personal identity."

"Wow! Why are you being so mean? Did you and Mom get in an argument?"

"It's the truth. And no, we didn't have an argument."

"Why do I sense hostility in your voice?"

"I'm angry at her for not pursuing her dreams. She should have set a better example for us. Dad focused on and pushed Quentin."

"Your father tried to inspire all of us by exposing us to the world. Mom sacrificed so that we could have the best chance at life. She attended every one of our events. Threw the best parties for us. Kept us *best dressed* and well fed."

"No, she took the easy route . . . marry wealth."

"Obviously it wasn't that easy. Evening cocktails were necessary to ease the pain."

"We're all she had," Bianca said, gazing into the blue sky. "Now, all she has is Robert."

"She has your father. You or Quentin need to have some babies."

"Robert keeps us all busy enough. Quentin's not ready to settle down, but it's not on me."

"Robert needs cousins," Celeste said, dusting the sand off her feet and admiring her pink pedicure and gold toe rings.

"Talk to Quentin. I want to make a name for myself, not be known as Mrs. Michaels."

"Have you decided a name for your Instagram page?"

"My maiden name. I'll need you, as my personal photographer, more often."

"I've got you."

"Do you think Kennedy can help me get a good start on Instagram? She's sort of ghetto."

"Kennedy is willing to show you exactly what she did, and share what she's learned about Instagram."

"If she can do it, I can do it. It's not like she took classes."

"She's a bit ghetto fabulous, but she has a good heart."

"Did she go to college?" Bianca asked, doing a *seated forward bend*.

"No."

"Did she graduate high school?"

"Damn! Yes, she graduated, and yes, she can read!"

"The company you keep either lifts you up or brings you down."

"We have to stop being judgmental of our less fortunate sisters," Celeste said, moving into a *half spinal twist*. "Real queens fix each other's crowns."

"The three people, with whom you spend most of your time, determine the quality of your life. How does she enhance your life?"

"She's a coworker whose company I enjoy. We share the struggle of working mothers. She helps me keep my sanity."

"Has she exposed you to anything new and valuable? Or are you just helping her grow?" Bianca asked, crossing her legs into the *lotus pose*.

"You can learn something of value from absolutely everyone," Celeste declared, twisting to her right side.

"That doesn't mean you should be friends with everybody," Bianca said, placing her hands on her knees in the healing mudra.

"Guess you don't like Kennedy," Celeste smirked, assuming the *lotus pose* facing Bianca.

"I just met her. She's nice. I'm not sure we'll be good friends. We're not from the same world."

"Please . . . just give her a chance. Let's try to enjoy our Baltimore trip."

"After we have lunch, do you mind if I stop by the Third Street Promenade to pick up some jeans and sneakers for the march?"

"No problem."

"You need anything?"

"No, I'll buy a tee at the protest to wear and support the *Black Lives Matter* movement."

"For sure. And we should purchase a few tees as souvenirs for the family."

"I definitely wanna get one for Robert," Celeste said, lying back on her mat.

"I bet you'll get some moving photos in Baltimore."

"I'll photojournal the protest to add to my portfolio."

"Figure out some media outlets where you can upload captioned photos during the march," Bianca suggested.

"I could livestream some of the speakers to Facebook or Instagram. People need to see and hear the pain caused by the devaluing of our lives."

"Intelligent, educated, sane people, who are helping us evolve as a species, will never let these reptilian-brain functioning homo sapiens take us back in time."

"We are too docile."

"Who's we?" Bianca asked, defensively.

"American citizens. We live in a bubble that filters out the purple elephants in the room. We must stand together facing these demons and demand changes, by any means necessary."

"*By any means necessary* suggests violence is an option."

"It should be. Lives are at stake. White supremacists want us to suffer silently and not force the issue. Threaten white lives, and see how quickly and forcefully they defend their lives."

"So you're willing to go to war with white people?" Bianca asked puzzled.

"Hell no. We don't have the manpower or know-how. But the fact that we pose no physical threat makes our voices irrelevant."

"We can demand justice by the choices we make. We need to start boycotting."

"You couldn't stop shopping for one week!"

"Yes I could . . . for a cause," Bianca said, chuckling.

"People who actually believe a better world is possible take action to create it."

"Peace begins with each of us."

"We can't have peace without justice."

"We can't have justice without communication."

"We'll have justice when we start electing more mayors, governors, state representatives, and Presidents who care about the quality of our lives," Celeste declared, sitting up.

"We'll have justice when we start removing elected officials who do not address our concerns, and who just tell us what we want to hear to get elected."

"Fortunately our generation is starting to wake up and get involved."

The yoga instructor arrived and laid out her yoga mat at the shore in front of them. She plugged her tablet into a speaker and began playing Native American flute sound therapy music. "Justice is coming for the atrocious acts against African Americans, now that all Americans witness police brutality more frequently," Bianca whispered to Celeste.

"I have to believe that," Celeste sighed.

"Good morning class. Namaste," the instructor said, bowing to the class.

"Namaste," the class responded in unison, rising to face the instructor in *mountain pose.*

"Take deep breaths of this cleansing ocean air, in through your nose, and release through your mouth to the sound of *A-U-M*," the instructor directed.

The class began taking deep rhythmic breaths while chanting *Om* in unison until everyone had transported from their present paradigm into the stillness.

Kennedy assessed the men in the LAX bar, while Celeste and Bianca watched protesters chanting *black lives matter* on the television over the liquor display. "I'm so excited to be leaving Cali for the first time!" Kennedy announced, running her fingers through her new curly brunette pixie.

Bianca briefly cut her eyes at Kennedy astonished.

"You mean on a plane. Haven't you been to Vegas? Arizona?" Celeste asked, dressed in all black standing up to remove her leather jacket.

"No. I've never been outside California."

"Wow," Celeste said, revealing a hot-pink long-sleeve tee with black *Cali Girl* graphic.

"It's also my first time on a plane. I'm a little scared," Kennedy confessed, flashing a big smile, taking a selfie, and posting it to social media titled *First Flight!*

"Scared of what?" Bianca inquired.

"Crashing."

"That's illogical," Bianca scoffed. "How often do you hear about planes crashing? The probability is minuscule."

"Just relax. We'll be fine," Celeste assured, gathering the auburn Havana twists on top of her head into a ponytail.

"Have a drink," Bianca suggested, adjusting the gold tribal bands in Celeste's hair.

"No! First flight and first drink?! She might get sick."

"I'll go to that coffee kiosk right outside the bar and get some hot tea to relax."

"I bought you a book," Celeste said, handing Kennedy *The Secret*.

"Perfect. That'll keep my mind off the flight."

"I got one for you too," Celeste said, handing Bianca *The Alchemist*.

"Thanks. I've been planning to read this book for a while."

"Two of my favorite books that every person should read."

"Don't forget about *The Four Agreements* by Don Miguel Ruiz," Bianca added, watching Kennedy swiping right on her phone.

"Definitely, a must-read once every year. See anyone interesting here at the airport?" Celeste asked Kennedy.

"Not anybody to take seriously."

"Probably not many desirable and eligible men need an app to meet women," Bianca considered.

"Hopefully I meet a lot of interesting dudes from all over the country at the protest."

"They might be too nerdy for you! Conscious African American men who spend their money and time fighting for civil rights!"

"Who don't like a strong alpha male?!" Kennedy giggled with Celeste.

"Should we have Bloody Marys this morning?" Bianca asked Celeste. "Probably don't have a decent bottle of champagne here to make a mimosa."

"Might as well. Hope there's real breakfast on the plane, not just a bagel and banana."

"I'll go get my tea. Either of you want anything?"

"No, thanks," Celeste and Bianca said in unison.

"Celeste, a magazine to read?"

"One of my absolute favorite things to do is sleep on planes! I do not read!"

"Celeste falls asleep before take-off," Bianca scoffed.

"What I really love is the sound of the engines and roar of the plane as it accelerates for take-off. And I love to hear the wheels lift-off and touch-down!"

"Apparently, orgasmic for her. Celeste is boring on airplanes."

"I'm not feeling any of that. Not my idea of a good time. I'm gonna just pray!" Kennedy responded, heading out of the bar.

Bianca returned to watching news coverage of Freddie Gray's death. Celeste dug through her black leather backpack, found her phone and checked her email, before placing a call. "Hi, Mommy!" Robert replied, answering the phone.

"Hello, Sweetheart. I'm at the airport. We're getting ready to leave."

"Where's Auntie?"

"Right here," Celeste said, handing Bianca the phone.

"Hi, Cupcake!"

"Hi, Auntie!"

"Enjoy your weekend. I'll bring you something from Baltimore."

"Okay. Love you."

"Love you more!" Bianca said, handing Celeste the phone.

"Are you gonna be okay?" Celeste asked Robert.

"Yeah. Me and Grandpa are going to the movies."

"That should be fun. I miss you!"

"Miss you too! You'll have fun, Mommy. Don't worry."

"Let me speak to your Grandpa."

"Hi, Princess."

"Hi, Daddy. You and Robert gonna be okay?"

"Are you gonna be alright?" Mr. Alexander chuckled.

"You know this is my first time taking a trip without Robert."

"What could go wrong? We're both at home!"

"Alright, Daddy."

"You're only gonna be gone a couple days!"

"Okay, see you guys soon."

"Stay safe. Call me if you need anything."

"I love you!" Robert said, getting back on the phone.

"I love you too. See you Sunday night," Celeste said, ending the call.

"Looks like there's going to be an enormous turnout tomorrow," Bianca said, watching the television.

"Hopefully other groups of people will be there supporting us."

"Black lives only matter to Black folks," Kennedy stated, returning with her tea.

"That's not true," Bianca resisted. "Plenty other people support the *Black Lives Matter* movement."

"Black lives are of least value in this world," Kennedy insisted.

"We've got to value our own lives, not beg other people to validate and save us," Bianca responded, handing the bartender her American Express card to pay for the drinks.

"First we have to believe a peaceful and loving world is possible," Celeste said. "That belief will transform our behavior, inspire us to participate in change, and lead us to the world we desire."

"White supremacists don't want the *Black Lives Matter* message spreading," Kennedy said, sipping her tea.

"Not only in the African American community but also in white America," Bianca added, drinking her cocktail.

"We've gotta expect the world is evolving into a civilized place that allows all people to live in peace."

"Not until bigots learn to accept that we are all created equal," Kennedy sighed.

"Although some of us are genetically superior," Celeste smiled.

"All human beings are equal biologically, but not as citizens," Bianca revised.

"Most white folks *do not* see us as their equals," Kennedy said, never looking up from her phone. "Even the ones who think they aren't racists."

"The quality of our lives sure aren't equal," Celeste attested.

"Racism and classism handicap my life," Kennedy grumbled. "Racism from society, and classism from Black folks."

"Affluent African Americans also experience discrimination from their own people," Bianca countered, signing the bill.

"So Massa got y'all discriminating against each other! Affluent?!" Celeste chuckled. "None of us got real wealth or power!"

"Our people can be like crabs in a bucket," Bianca complained, putting her Louis Vuitton wallet back into her large saddle-colored Coach leather tote bag sitting on the bar.

"*Jack and Jill, Tots and Teens*, only for light-skinned affluent African Americans."

"You enjoyed the ski trips, especially to Europe," Bianca said sarcastically.

"I certainly did. Robert deserves to have enriching experiences and inspiring role models."

"He gets that. Robert and Mom enjoy going to *Jack and Jill* meetings and events."

"He's only a member because of your parents. All African American children need those experiences and role models."

"Those old requirements are dead," Bianca enlightened Celeste.

"*The Boys Club of America* is all we had," Kennedy scoffed. "Poverty was the only requirement."

"No-class ghetto morons accuse people of talking and acting white," Bianca declared. "I speak standard English so that I can communicate with other members of society to achieve *my* goals, not to impress anyone. Are wealth, education, health, dreaming, comfort, safety, and peace only for white people? Those coons are morons working for racists, against their own people."

"Envy and jealousy. They don't believe they can achieve lives worth living," Celeste diagnosed.

"They want to be free to chase their dreams," Kennedy added. "They're mad at Black folks who got out for not lending a hand to help them get out."

"A deeper problem is men not recognizing women as their equals," Bianca moaned.

"Even some of the progressive ones believe they aren't chauvinists," Celeste added.

"Sexism is obstructing my life far more than racism," Bianca continued.

"That's only because you live in Cali. Californians are the most tolerant people in this country," Celeste replied.

"Try living in the South."

"Try living in Orange County," Kennedy pooh-poohed.

"Sexism is prevalent in SoCal because of the entertainment industry," Bianca countered.

"Black women definitely experience more sexism than other women," Kennedy declared.

"We are targeted more because of our race and gender," Celeste complained.

"We're easy prey," Bianca said. "African American men don't protect their women. And most women don't have the resources to get legal help."

"We are the most oppressed people on the planet! African American women endure racism and sexism daily," Celeste grumbled.

"And rejection by Black men and hostility from Black women," Kennedy added.

"*Women's Lives Matter* should be a movement connected with *Black Lives Matter*," Bianca uttered.

"The idea that *All Lives Matter* needs to be promoted," Celeste added.

"Oh my God! Please don't say that while we're in Baltimore! That offends Black folks!"

"Saying *black lives matter* offends white people," Bianca countered.

"This bullshit is so stupid! Saying *black lives matter* doesn't mean other lives don't matter. And we don't have to clarify our statements to please white people!"

"Whenever Black folks try to have some sense of pride, their methods have to be scrutinized and approved by white folks," Kennedy said, rolling her eyes.

"Obviously all lives matter. The only lives in question are those of Black people."

"Being more inclusive might open up communications," Bianca suggested. "No African American should be offended by the idea that *Women's Lives Matter*."

"We might as well save this debate for the weekend," Celeste suggested.

"Only in our hotel room!" Kennedy insisted.

"Can you help me get my IG page started this weekend?" Bianca asked Kennedy.

"Sure. We'll need nine images to get a nice 3x3 grid to launch your page, and at least ten hashtags to reach your target audience."

"How long before our plane departs?" Celeste interrupted.

"We have twenty minutes to get to our gate," Bianca said, checking her Apple watch.

"Let me get some photos of you before your first flight," Celeste said, removing her camera from her backpack.

"Okay," Kennedy smiled, taking a celebratory pose with both arms in the air.

KNIGHTS

The KNIGHT, representing armored cavalry, is sometimes referred to as a "horse" or "jumper," reflecting its ability to move over chess pieces to its destination. It is the only chess piece that can jump over any other chess piece, of any color. The knight moves in the most unusual way among chess pieces. It moves in an "L" shape, two squares horizontally (or vertically) in either direction, and one square vertically (or horizontally) in either direction. The jumper moves from one color to the opposite color. Each knight begins the game between a bishop and a rook. The knight is the only chess piece that can move before one of its pawns is moved. A horse is most powerful near the center of the action; "A Knight on the Rim is Grim." The knight captures by taking over the square occupied by an enemy piece. A fork, simultaneously making two or more direct attacks, is best executed by a knight because of its "L" pattern.

KNIGHTS

Kennedy, Bianca and Celeste, dressed in matching *Black Lives Matter* tees, zigzagged their way through the protesters moving closer to the stage. It was clear to everyone that they were not from Baltimore. Bianca's long straight light-brown weave and skin-tight blue jeans were flawless. Kennedy shouted celebrity with her Hollywood glamour makeup, perfectly aligned brunette curls glistening in the sun, black leggings and military-style ankle boots. Celeste, the tallest of the trio, wore an updo of auburn faux locs and black Levi 501 jeans.

"Ugh!" Bianca sighed under her breath to Kennedy and Celeste, annoyed by the advances of men. "We're here to protest!"

"Girl, I love it! There are so many handsome Black dudes here!" Kennedy responded, taking a Coke out of her backpack.

"Wish they would stop trying to talk to me and all talk to you instead," Bianca said, drinking her bottled water.

"Apparently protests are where you find a large selection of intelligent, woke men," Celeste declared.

"Doesn't mean they're single or available," Bianca warned.

"Stand here so I can take some photos." Celeste backed up a few steps, taking photos of Kennedy pumping her fist in the air chanting *Black Lives Matter*, in the crowd of protesters. Bianca turned her back and stepped aside to avoid being photographed.

"Hello," a guy said, approaching Celeste.

Celeste briefly looked away from her camera, "Hello."

"I'm Khalil," he said, offering his hand. "What's your name?"

"Celeste," she said, letting her camera hang from her neck so she could shake his hand.

"Where you from?"

"Los Angeles."

"How tall are you?"

"Five-nine. How tall are you?" she asked mockingly.

"Six-seven."

"Looking for models? You a talent agent?"

"Didn't mean to sound weird. Your height drew my attention."

"No problem. I'm used to it."

"Sorry. I know how that feels. Everyone thinks I play basketball."

"Really, no problem."

"Did you come with a group?"

"No, just me and two girlfriends."

"Is this your first *Black Lives Matter* protest?"

"Yes."

"How long are you gonna be in Baltimore?"

"We leave tomorrow."

"Are you a professional photographer?"

"Trying to be. You with the FBI or Census Bureau?"

"No," Khalil laughed, turning his BLM baseball cap around backward. "Just trying to get to know you. I noticed you taking a lot of pictures with an expensive camera. Thought you might be here working. I'm one of the community organizers of this protest."

"I saw you on stage."

"Real nice cartouche," Khalil said, looking at her necklace.

"Thanks. It was a gift from my father. He had it made for me in Cairo."

"Around here, you should probably hide that inside your t-shirt. The gold and diamonds are glimmering in the sunlight."

"Thanks for the warning," Celeste said, tucking her cartouche under her tee.

"You married?" Khalil asked, looking at a wedding band and engagement ring on Celeste's right hand.

"No. These rings belonged to my mother."

"Doesn't seem to be discouraging too many men!" Khalil laughed.

"If that was my intention, I'd be wearing them on my left hand," Celeste chuckled.

"What news outlet do you work for?"

"I don't work for any media outlet."

"You should consider working freelance for this movement. We need more coverage. Here's my card. Let's talk next week."

"Alright, Mr. Sloane," Celeste said, reading his business card.

"May I take you and your friends to dinner this evening in the harbor? Are you free?"

"We're actually staying in the harbor. I'd like to go, but I'll have to ask my girls."

"Maryland is famous for Chesapeake blue crabs. Do you like seafood?"

"Yes. Shrimp and lobster are my favorites, but I'd like to try some Maryland crabs."

"You've got my number. You can confirm later. If your friends don't wanna go, I can come get you and we can hang out in the harbor."

"I'm not gonna leave them. We're here together."

"Well, I hope you can convince them to join us for dinner. I'd like to talk more about you working with the *Black Lives Matter* movement."

"I'll call you later," Celeste said. Khalil smiled and walked away.

"What's up with him?" Kennedy asked, approaching Celeste.

"He works with *Black Lives Matter*, and is interested in my photography."

"Sure," Bianca doubted. "I saw that big country Negro gawking at you!"

"It was just business. He invited us to dinner."

"He'll probably be wearing a dashiki!" Kennedy teased.

"We don't need him to take us to dinner," Bianca said, frowning. "Why do you want to go to dinner with him?"

"I don't necessarily wanna go to dinner *with him*. It might be an opportunity for me to learn more about the movement and where I might be able to contribute and build my portfolio."

"Where does he want to take us?" Bianca asked, flashing a fake smile at a guy speaking to her.

"A restaurant in the harbor. Somewhere close to our hotel."

"You told that stranger where we're staying?!" Bianca questioned.

"No. I just told him we're staying in the harbor."

"Alright. He's probably harmless."

"Another opportunity for you to practice socializing with a man," Kennedy suggested, taking a selfie.

"I'll be there for business."

"Have some light conversation. Don't be so intense all evening," Bianca instructed. "Did you bring a dress and heels?"

"I don't need to wear a dress. I don't wanna be misleading."

"You wouldn't want him to think you're a real girl!" Kennedy said sarcastically.

"Show your class. You're not dressing for him but for the position you want."

"Calm down. I brought a dress."

"I'm about ready to go back to the hotel and relax," Bianca sighed. "I wonder if we can get massages there?"

"Probably."

"I need a nap," Kennedy said. "The time zone change is messing with me."

The ladies returned to their hotel, rejuvenated and then prepared for dinner.

"Where are we supposed to meet him?" Kennedy asked, exiting the elevator.

"There he is sitting by the escalator," Celeste said, heading across the lobby.

"Oh my God!" Kennedy murmured. "Is that the same dude? Tall, dark and sexy!"

"He cleans up pretty good," Bianca whispered. "Glad you wore a dress."

"Be quiet!" Celeste whispered.

"Good evening. Thanks for allowing me to take you lovely ladies to dinner," Khalil said, wearing black pants and a gray dress shirt.

"Thank *you*," Celeste smiled. "These are my friends, Bianca and Kennedy. Bianca, Kennedy, this is Khalil."

"Hello," Bianca replied.

"Nice to meet you," Kennedy said, looking him over. "Nice haircut."

"Thanks. Got my hair cut in the hood earlier this week."

"Should we get an Uber?" Bianca asked.

"The restaurant is just a short walk along the harbor," Khalil replied, holding the door for the ladies to exit. "I think you'll enjoy the sites. Hope everyone likes seafood."

"I do," Bianca responded. "I might try some Baltimore crab cakes."

"Seafood's okay," Kennedy said, "but I might get something else."

"Do you ladies smoke weed?" Khalil inquired.

"Not me," Kennedy responded.

"Are you a drug dealer?" Bianca questioned.

"Why I gotta be a drug dealer?" Khalil answered, with a grin.

"Why we gotta be potheads from Cali?" Bianca retorted, with a blank expression.

"I'm the only one who smokes weed," Celeste confessed. Khalil nodded at Celeste approvingly. "Do you smoke weed?"

"Occasionally."

"Are you from Baltimore?" Kennedy asked.

"No, Chicago."

"Where you staying?" Kennedy probed.

"The Renaissance."

"That hotel looks amazing."

"The Four Seasons is pretty impressive."

"Our suite is incredible. What kinda work do you do?" Kennedy continued.

"I'm a community organizer."

"For *Black Lives Matter*?"

"Yes, but not exclusively."

"How long have you been here?"

"Five days."

"Do you travel a lot?"

"All the time. And it's hard living on the road."

"You have a family at home?"

"Are you interviewing me?" Khalil asked chuckling.

"No," Kennedy recoiled, rolling her eyes and acting disinterested.

"I'd like to know more about the *Black Lives Matter* movement," Bianca interrupted. "How did it get started?"

"In 2013, three young women, just like you ladies, Patrisse Cullors, Alicia Garza and Opal Tometi, originated the hashtag *#BlackLivesMatter* on social media, after Trayvon Martin's murderer was acquitted. And I think Los Angeles was the very first chapter."

"Interesting," Bianca said. "I'll have to research them."

"What kind of work do you ladies do?" Khalil inquired.

"I'm a music video stylist," Kennedy announced, handing him a business card from her phone case.

"Celeste and I have degrees in journalism from USC," Bianca revealed. "I'm an Assistant Fashion Editor for a magazine."

"I have a minor in photography but have yet to land a job as a photojournalist. I work for a talent agency photographing aspiring models and actors, and I hate it."

"What did you think of your first *Black Lives Matter* protest?" Khalil asked.

"I was impressed with the turnout," Celeste said. "Thankful to have participated."

"People were here from every state. Is that normally the case?" Bianca asked.

"More folks are traveling to protests. Usually, most of the protesters are locals."

"Makes me proud to be African American," Bianca admitted.

"There's power in numbers," Celeste said, taking photos of the harbor.

"We must unite and stay united," Kennedy stated, stopping to take a selfie.

"Support from Black people all over this country is needed," Khalil explained.

"We need support from all ethnicities and marginalized groups, not just African Americans," Bianca added.

"We don't have community until a tragedy occurs, and never have national unity," Khalil said in disgust.

"Most Black folks can't afford to travel to protests outside their state," Kennedy replied, swiping left on her phone.

"That's the bullshit that keeps us enslaved," Khalil responded. "We can find the money to anesthetize ourselves to our reality, and pretend to be enjoying our lives."

"African Americans don't invest in the future of our people," Bianca complained. "All they want to do is hide from reality."

"What are you gonna do with the photos you took today?" Khalil asked Celeste.

"I'm gonna submit them to news outlets, and put together something for my portfolio. I wanna work in mainstream media."

"You should become a BLM photojournalist. We need more journalists to spread our message," Khalil suggested.

"Would she get paid?" Bianca asked, watching Kennedy taking selfies.

"No, she would be volunteering her time and donating her talent."

"What makes you think she has any talent?" Bianca questioned.

"I don't know if she has talent. I'm waiting to see what she creates."

"Celeste could reach more people working for the Huffington Post," Bianca countered.

"She'd start off working freelance or blogging without compensation at HuffPost," Khalil said. "We need her talent."

"I just admire what Adrianna Huffington has accomplished with the HuffPost. A woman excelling in the news industry, focused on politics, is remarkable."

"The HuffPost is a liberal news and opinion website," Celeste disclosed.

"We need Black people to contribute their talents not just money," Khalil explained.

"I'm open to all suggestions."

"This harbor is beautiful," Kennedy interrupted. "Have you spent your free time here?"

"I haven't had any free time. I've been out in Black neighborhoods promoting the rally. Most of the time, room service has been my best meal of the day."

"It's disappointing to see dilapidated housing everywhere," Bianca said. "Is this harbor the only civilized place to live in Baltimore?"

"I'm sure there are some livable neighborhoods, but Black folks don't live there," he said. "Black folks live in row houses, urban crates for the disenfranchised. Just like in Philly."

"People are forced to live like caged animals. What a tragedy," Bianca sighed. "I can't imagine enduring that for even a month."

Khalil escorted the ladies shopping for souvenirs, before heading into the restaurant. "What would you ladies like to drink while we're waiting for our table?" he asked, standing behind the ladies seated at the bar.

"I'd like a glass of champagne," Celeste requested.

"Champagne for me," Bianca added.

"I don't drink," Kennedy said. "I'll take a Coke."

Khalil ordered two glasses of champagne and two Cokes.

"So, you don't drink?" Kennedy asked approvingly.

"I drink, but rarely. Trying to maintain my health and fitness."

"Are you a gym rat?" Kennedy probed.

"Nope. Don't have time. I workout in hotel gyms on the road, and go to a fitness club in Chicago."

"Have you ever considered a vegan or vegetarian diet?" Bianca asked.

"I don't know the difference. I'm a carnivore."

"Me too!" Kennedy concurred.

"Vegetarians do not eat meat products. Vegans are vegetarians who also don't eat dairy products," Celeste explained.

"Are you vegan or vegetarian?" Khalil asked, looking at Bianca and Celeste.

"I'm vegan . . . most of the time," Bianca responded.

"I just try to eat healthy balanced meals and most of the time that includes meat," Celeste answered. "But I try to keep dairy to a minimum."

"Do you workout?" Khalil asked Celeste.

"Celeste is a California surfer girl," Bianca revealed.

"You surf?" he asked in disbelief.

"I love the ocean," Celeste replied.

"I love smart, attractive, athletic women," he said, looking at her with penetrating eyes.

"Do you swim?" Celeste asked Khalil.

"Of course, I can swim."

"Not like Celeste. She was a lifeguard at the beach, from high school through college."

"A lifeguard?!" Khalil said in amazement. "How old were you when you started?"

"Sixteen," Celeste answered. *"Junior Lifeguard."*

"At the beach?"

"Yep."

"And she's a Pisces. She's practically a fish," Bianca continued. "When she wasn't in school, she was either on her surfboard or on the beach. She was tanned year-round."

"How long have you known each other?"

"Since we were five," Bianca and Celeste said in unison.

"They grew up together. They're pretty much sisters," Kennedy explained.

"Do you two surf?" he asked Kennedy and Bianca.

"I don't know how to swim and have no interest in the ocean," Kennedy declared.

"I don't surf and only swim in private pools. And I'm not a sun worshiper like Celeste."

"Do you go to the gym?" Khalil asked Celeste.

"No, we go to the spa!" Celeste chuckled, clinking her champagne glass against Bianca's.

"We love saunas, steam rooms and hot tubs, not exercise equipment," Bianca clarified.

"Oh, it's all about water for you Cali girls!" Khalil teased.

"I sometimes workout a few minutes before going to the spa area," Celeste smirked.

"Obviously surfing is keeping you in shape," Khalil stated. Celeste gave him brief eye contact and a shy smile.

"Where the hell is President Obama?" Kennedy interrupted, looking at news coverage of the protest on the bar television.

"He can't appear in every city where African Americans are being murdered by law enforcement," Bianca said, taking a sip of her champagne.

"He's not *King of All Blacks*, he's the President of the United States," Celeste announced. "He can't show bias or favoritism towards one group of people."

"But he should be making sure no groups of Americans are being denied their human rights or Constitutional Rights," Kennedy complained.

"Obama is requiring federal agencies to investigate Black deaths at the hands of law enforcement," Celeste stated.

"African Americans were foolish to vote for him expecting changes in their lives," Bianca said. "He can't make substantial changes to the quality of our lives by himself. Our people don't even understand how the United States government works. This is not a dictatorship."

"I absolutely love President Barack Obama! He's doing an excellent job considering the mess he inherited from the former administration, and the assholes he has to work with now. Such a brilliant, classy, disciplined, and handsome alpha male! Now as much as I love him, I am fanatic about FLOTUS Michelle Obama. My fantasy is to fly on Airforce One with the Obamas!" Celeste revealed.

"You know I support my homeboy," Khalil responded. "He's doing what he can from the White House, trying to work with a discriminatory Senate and House of Representatives. We've gotta stop unifying only around death or injustice, and start organizing around a vision for the future."

"What kinda vision for the future of Black folks?" Kennedy asked.

"Liberation," Khalil answered.

"How can we unite for meaningful change?" Bianca asked.

"Wake folks up," he suggested. "Invest in our people, politicians and neighborhoods."

"Well, we're a long way from true freedom," Kennedy said, drinking her Coke.

"Fortunately the *Black Lives Matter* movement is growing, the message is spreading, and people are uniting," Celeste declared.

"Unity does not automatically translate into power or change," Khalil divulged. "It's only a starting point. Murders by police officers and no accountability are still happening."

"Your table is ready," the hostess interrupted, leading them out of the bar.

"I need to sit in a hot tub and get a massage," Bianca declared, entering San Francisco's historic St. Francis Hotel.

"I'm hungry," Kennedy whined. "Hope this bar has something good to eat."

"I just need to sit down," Celeste sighed, following her friends into the Clock Bar.

"When are you meeting Khalil?" Kennedy asked.

"I just texted him. He's coming down now," Celeste replied.

"Have y'all been talking by phone or just on social media?" Kennedy probed.

"We've talked by phone a few times."

"Business?" Kennedy inquired.

"Yep."

"You think he's legit?" Bianca questioned.

"It's definitely not his decision whether any of my work is used by *Black Lives Matter*, but he can help me get it seen. None of the media companies gave me any response."

"Maybe your packets didn't reach the correct departments or people," Bianca considered.

"That's a real possibility," Celeste said, taking a seat at a table with her friends. "That's why Khalil could be helpful with *Black Lives Matter*."

"Well, if *Black Lives Matter* isn't interested, you know mainstream news will never be," Bianca replied, sinking into her chair.

"Why is your phone blowing up?" Celeste inquired, frowning at Bianca.

"Wade is tripping!" Bianca said, turning off her phone.

"What's the problem?" Celeste asked, removing her jacket.

"He's pissed because I attended another rally. Says protests are too dangerous."

"Pierce said the same thing," Kennedy responded, changing from sneakers into brown leather flip-flops.

"Daddy is starting to get concerned."

"We haven't been near any violence," Bianca replied. "When shit gets crazy, we know how to immediately leave. Wade thinks I've become obsessed with oppressed people."

"Participating in two protests means you're obsessed?" Celeste asked befuddled.

"The bottom line is Wade wants a stay-at-home wife. He wants me to quit my job and work from home *since I'm so unhappy at work*."

"And what does he want you to do?" Celeste inquired.

"Build my Instagram following, and start the HuffPost L.A. lifestyle blog I've been talking about."

"Doesn't sound like the worst idea," Kennedy contemplated, removing her phone from her backpack.

"How am I supposed to earn money?"

"A large IG or blog following could lead to a job or financial perks," Kennedy considered.

"Has Instagram brought you a single dollar?" Bianca doubted.

"It has led me to paid gigs."

"Is that how you earn most of your income?" Bianca questioned.

"Unfortunately, no. Not yet."

"Wade's being sexist thinking I'd be more useful and happy at home. Even the two of you think being a housewife is worth my consideration. Is it reasonable for me to expect Wade to be satisfied living his entire life at home? It's time to eradicate sexism and homophobia."

"Maybe we should stop combining sexism and homophobia, and deal with them separately," Kennedy suggested. "More people might support the fight against sexism."

"No way!" Bianca resisted. "It's fundamentally about the same thing . . . evaluating people sexually and penalizing them if they're not like you. Sexism, homophobia and transphobia must end."

"Relationships between men and women are how mankind survives," Kennedy stated.

"Maybe there are too many people and procreating needs to slow down," Bianca offered.

"Maybe our species doesn't need to continue! We're an infection on Mother Earth!" Celeste scoffed.

"Here he comes," Kennedy whispered.

"Hey," Celeste said, turning around as Khalil approached.

"Hello ladies," Khalil said, leaning over to give Celeste a hug, before taking a seat between her and Kennedy. "You're looking regal," he said, responding to the colorful African headwraps adorning their heads.

"Hello," Bianca replied, sitting across from Khalil.

"Hey," Kennedy responded, taking off her headwrap and picking through her short natural curls with her fingers.

"What's up?" Khalil asked, looking at Celeste.

"We're exhausted. The march killed us."

"What's on your shirt?" he asked, looking at Celeste's chest.

"The Om symbol, the I AM," Celeste explained, pulling her red tee down over the top of her blue Levi 501's to cover her exposed belly button.

"Celeste is a yogi," Bianca divulged, wearing a *Say Her Name* protest tee.

"Celeste is the t-shirt queen," Kennedy said disapprovingly, removing her BLM t-shirt covering her long-sleeve tee. "She should start a business."

"She could sell t-shirts with protest images," Khalil suggested. "Celeste has some great photos on Instagram."

"T-shirts are all Niggas are allowed to sell in this society," Bianca scoffed.

"You can make money selling anything that most people need or use," Khalil responded.

"Most people have used paper clips," Bianca frowned. "Making them would be meaningless work."

"Spreading a positive message that impacts the world would be meaningful," he replied as the waiter arrived to take their order.

"Your drinks and appetizers should be here shortly," the waiter said, leaving the table.

"How was the protest?" Khalil asked, taking off his jacket.

"I expected a much larger crowd of women denouncing the deaths of African American females by law enforcement," Celeste complained. "We must make our voices heard."

"I expected a larger crowd and more men supporting the nationwide protest," Kennedy said, swiping left on her phone.

"Females need to show up correctly in the universe," Bianca declared. "Stand up for women's rights! Have some courage!"

"*I am my sister's keeper*!" Celeste sang.

"African Americans need to be vocal about racism and injustice, but most are afraid to get involved in these volatile situations," Bianca explained.

"Our oppressors are not interested in hearing anything we have to say," Kennedy scoffed.

"First, we need to reach our own people," Khalil clarified.

"The police murders of Meagan Hockaday, Natasha McKenna and Alexia Christian, just to name a few, should have brought out every African American," Celeste declared.

"Don't forget about the police murders of Rekia Boyd and seven-year-old Aiyana Jones," Khalil added.

"Obviously the lives of Black females are not as important as the lives of Black males, even to Black people," Kennedy sighed.

"Most people only hear about, or believe it is only, Black men being murdered by law enforcement," Khalil explained.

"Black people are cowards," Bianca replied.

"Slavery tortured that into our DNA to spread to future generations. We also suffer from PTSD," Celeste defended.

"Not all Black men are cowards. Some of us are warriors for our people."

"Not all Black women are cowards," Kennedy rejected. "We are infamous for being strong physically and mentally."

"You don't look as inspired as you did when we first met you," Bianca said to Khalil.

"I enjoy my work, but sometimes it's aggravating when I can't see any changes. But warriors never quit. I'm gonna unwind for a few days and get a second wind."

"Are you going back to Chicago when you leave here?" Kennedy inquired.

"Yeah."

"Guess you appreciate your time at home?" Kennedy probed.

"It's usually a sleep marathon for a few days, and then I prepare to get back on the road."

"Your Reisling," the waiter smiled at Celeste, returning to their table.

"A martini for you," he said, sitting a glass in front of Bianca.

"A Coke," the waiter said, handing Kennedy her glass.

"And your Reisling," he said, sitting Khalil's glass and then the appetizers on the table.

"Thanks," Khalil replied, handing the waiter his credit card.

"We need to stop spending our money where we don't see African Americans and women being recognized and respected," Bianca continued.

"Black people can't effectively boycott because we are addicted to consumption," Khalil opposed. "There are 41 million African Americans . . . that's a country . . . worth a trillion dollars."

"We wouldn't know where to begin," Kennedy said, picking meat off a chicken wing with her long manicured nails.

"How about the liquor stores and convenience stores in the hood owned by non-Blacks?" Celeste offered. "Far too often, those people treat their customers, our people, like shit."

"Those store owners rarely live in the neighborhood," Bianca added. "They set up shoddy shops in ghettos, with shoddy products from questionable sources, without regard for health, safety or hygiene, and then return to white communities hoping to be accepted using our money."

"Try buying all of your products and services from Black people for six months," Khalil suggested. "If we all had the discipline to do that, we would be spreading our wealth amongst our people, enriching the Black family, cleaning up our neighborhoods, and kicking the white supremacists' corporate world in the ass."

"We'd be living like the Amish!" Bianca laughed. "We would not be getting the best products or services, putting us at an even bigger disadvantage."

"Why do Black folks always think products and services by Black folks are of lesser quality?" Kennedy asked, licking her fingers.

"Why do we always need to have the best?" Celeste complained, splitting the veggie wrap with Bianca.

"We need the best because we have low self-esteem. The things on us and around us determine our worth. We don't respect the work of our brothers and sisters because white supremacists have us believing anything we're doing is mediocre," Khalil rationalized.

"Products and services improve over time," Celeste said. "White people can start with poor quality products and services, and are allowed to grow. We have to start with perfection."

"Everything we use to make our products, and the technologies we use to provide our services come from white people," Bianca explained, dipping her veggie wrap in the sauce.

"If we support our own people, eventually they'll be the ones providing the materials and technologies," Celeste envisioned.

"Do you have your portfolio?" Khalil asked.

"It's in our suite. I can go get it now."

"No rush. I have time if you do."

"You look refreshed. Did you leave the protest early?"

"I've been back about two hours. You wanna relax first? Later, we can grab something quick to eat around Union Square and discuss your work."

"What did you two wanna do this evening?" Celeste asked her girlfriends.

"I have a date," Kennedy announced.

"A date?" Bianca asked perplexed.

"Yeah. Just got a dinner invitation," Kennedy said, displaying her phone.

"Uh, I don't know if that's safe," Celeste paused.

"I'm gonna meet him in the lobby and walk somewhere nearby to eat."

"Whatever. I'm going to get a massage, order room service, and call my crazed hubby."

"Okay, we can meet later," Celeste said to Khalil. "What time should I be ready?"

"What's good for you?" he asked.

"Eight o'clock?"

"Perfect. I'll meet you in the lobby."

Celeste exited the elevator and immediately saw Khalil standing across the hotel lobby. He smiled as she walked towards him, clearly aware he was making her nervous.

"You look relaxed. Did you get a nap?" Khalil asked.

"Yes, thank you. I needed that," she responded.

"Love your hair," he said, admiring her shoulder-length auburn Havana twists.

"Thanks."

"Let's walk around Union Square and see what we can find to eat. Would you like me to carry your portfolio for you?"

"No, thanks."

"How long have you been working as a photographer?"

"I've been working as a fashion photographer for the past three years. Prior to that, I interned as a photojournalist at a newspaper for a year."

"Are you drawn more to photography or journalism?"

"I wanna be a photojournalist. I have the education but not the experience. Obviously, I'm gonna have to pay for the experience. The Baltimore protest was my first portfolio project."

"Looking forward to seeing your work."

"I always try to visit Union Square when I'm in San Francisco," Celeste said, exiting the hotel. "It's so beautiful at night."

"I always stay at the St. Francis, when I come to San Francisco."

"Where do you like to eat when you're here?" Celeste asked.

"Fisherman's Wharf."

"Me too, but I also love Chinatown."

"I've never been," Khalil said, looking around Union Square. "Is it okay for us to have dinner in Chinatown wearing jeans?"

"There are some world famous five-star restaurants, but for most places, we're fine."

"Let's find a place to look at your portfolio, and afterward have dinner in Chinatown."

"Okay," Celeste smiled.

Khalil and Celeste strolled around Union Square enjoying the crisp night air until they found a private place to sit on an unoccupied plaza bench. She unzipped her portfolio and removed a large envelope before handing him the portfolio.

"Do you only work in black-and-white?" Khalil asked, looking through her portfolio.

"I prefer to work in black-and-white. I love the sharp contrast."

"You really captured the pain, rage, sadness and frustration."

Celeste sat nervously looking over Union Square while Khalil continued flipping back and forth through her portfolio.

"I love how the last photos were about courage," Khalil said. "Do you mind if I take a few photos of your portfolio on my phone?"

"Feel free, but here is my resume, some business cards, and an 8x10 folder of this project," she said, handing Khalil the envelope she had removed from her portfolio earlier.

"Wow, thanks. This is even better. I'll share this with *Black Lives Matter* organizers and African American news sources."

"Thanks for your help. I'm not expecting you to perform miracles. Any feedback would be appreciated."

"I'm sure someone in media would be interested in at least a few of these photos. The question is, can you get paid for them?"

"I don't need to get paid. I need to build my portfolio and resume."

"Oh, you don't need money?" Khalil questioned, with a smirk.

"Of course, I'd love money," Celeste clarified, with a smile. "More money to continue following and supporting the movement."

"I love the way your photos have a gathering of Black men looking like warriors, rather than an angry mob."

"African American men are being feminized, and I refuse to see them that way."

"Abuse and injustice are beginning to wake up our confused brothers. Black men are beginning to embrace their king status."

"Black women are beginning to embrace their queen status," Celeste added.

"Do you have a man?"

"No, but I do have a four-year-old son."

"What's his name?"

"Robert."

"Where is he now?"

"At home with my father."

"Do you have children?"

"Nope. I can't imagine having responsibility for a family in this hostile world. I've gotta help make some changes 'round here first."

"I feel you."

"Are you ready to go? You look a little cold."

"Yes. Thanks for taking the time to meet with me."

"We're still going to dinner, aren't we?" Khalil asked.

"Sure," Celeste smiled, relieved that he still wanted to spend time with her.

"Californians showed up politically!" Celeste declared, removing her bottled water from her backpack.

"There were almost eight hundred *Black Lives Matter* protesters today showing support of the California Senate bill increasing police oversight," Khalil said enthusiastically, removing his black leather jacket.

"This year, California has the highest number of deaths by law enforcement," Celeste said, sitting next to Khalil on the grass across from Bianca and Kennedy. "L.A. police officers have killed more people than any other law enforcement agency in the U.S."

"I recently read that unarmed African American men are seven times more likely to die from police gunfire than unarmed white men," Bianca added.

"It's not fair that we have to live under constant stress from the threat of death from not only racists but law enforcement," Celeste complained. "We're sitting on the lawn of the State Capitol where that bullshit happened with the Panthers."

"Oh yeah, that's right," Khalil recalled.

"What are y'all talking about?" Kennedy asked, swiping left on her phone before looking up.

"They're talking about back in the 1960s when the *Black Panther Party* took over our State Capitol with weapons," Bianca explained, taking a few gulps of bottled water.

"That's not what happened," Celeste objected. "They were here in peaceful protest, just like we were today."

"They were carrying weapons," Bianca replied.

"They all had licenses to carry their weapons," Celeste insisted. "When white supremacists protest toting rifles, it's no big deal. Their weapons are only for protection," she said sarcastically. "Who do they need protection from? Probably the people they abuse, destroy and try to kill."

"Black folks carrying weapons for their own protection has always been unacceptable in this country," Khalil added. "Life's not fair for us. We're always on defense, losing ground, and being told we're wrong to protect our lives and families."

"We must start protecting ourselves again," Celeste asserted.

"Should we demand fairness through activism or revolution?" Kennedy asked, sipping her Coke.

"Revolution," Khalil responded.

"Activism," Celeste contradicted.

"So you believe in the nonviolence philosophy of Martin Luther King, Jr.?" he asked.

"I'm more influenced by the teachings of Malcolm X."

"But Malcolm X and the Panthers advocated revolution," Khalil replied.

"I admire the philosophy of the *Black Panther Party*, but their revolution quickly died without the strength in numbers of our people. Most Negros were scared to revolt," Celeste said. "Time to try something new."

"Activism isn't new," Khalil countered. "And Niggas ain't scared."

"Well, I'm an activist. People need to be educated."

"I'm a militant."

"Militants don't change minds. Activists enlighten people. Enlightened people are more evolved, reasonable and fair."

"Celeste is a militant," Bianca interrupted. "This is an Angela Davis protégé."

"My idol is absolutely the brilliant, courageous and stunning Dr. Angela Yvonne Davis!"

"We need a revolution," Kennedy said, removing her BLM cap. "We aren't traumatized children of former slaves."

"Are *you* gonna actively participate in a revolt?" Celeste questioned.

"No, I'm not fighting with nobody, but Black men need to revolt," Kennedy said, running her long red fingernails through her wavy burgundy pixie.

"I don't see how getting physical can help solve the problem," Bianca said. "We would be dealing with our oppressors like Neanderthals. Use words, not clubs."

"Our generation will vote your ass out, and get bigots fired from their jobs everywhere!" Celeste avowed.

"Law enforcement needs to be held accountable for their actions," Bianca said, tossing her medium-length weave of copper-blonde soft curls.

"How?" Celeste asked. "I don't believe that will ever happen."

"Black folks should be recording videos of everything," Kennedy replied, taking a selfie.

"Nobody, who can make a difference, cares about our videos," Celeste informed them. "African Americans are being denied their human rights."

"Did you get some good photos today?" Khalil asked.

"I hope so."

"You know you did," Bianca said. "Celeste is artistic."

"I know she is," Khalil replied. "Obviously, she's not just snapping random photos."

"I need to go back to the hotel and change," Kennedy interrupted. "I have a date."

"Who?" Celeste asked, concerned.

"A guy I met at the airport."

"What does he do?" Bianca asked.

"Says he's in the import business."

"Probably a drug trafficker!" Khalil teased.

"No," Kennedy scoffed. "He's a real businessman."

"I'm ready to leave," Celeste said, finishing her water.

"Ready when you are," Khalil said to Celeste. "You'll have time to relax before our eight o'clock dinner reservations."

"I have to post to Instagram, and want to write an article about today's rally for my portfolio," Bianca said. "I have no problem ordering room service."

"You're writing about the movement?" Khalil questioned, helping the ladies get up.

"I've got an inner urging to do something more to fight bigotry and injustice," Bianca replied. "I'm not sure how I'll use it or when, but I want to get this experience on paper while it is fresh in my mind."

"Wow," Khalil replied, strolling back to the hotel with the ladies.

"I think Khalil is here," Bianca shouted, looking up from her laptop.

Celeste opened the door to find Khalil standing there in a black suit and tie. "Hey," she said, inviting him inside. "I'm ready. Just need to get my purse."

"You don't need a purse," Khalil replied, quickly running his eyes over her black cocktail dress. "What's up," he nodded at Bianca.

"Hey," she responded, getting up to neaten Celeste's updo of individual auburn braids.

Kennedy emerged from the bathroom wearing a robe. "Nice suit," she said, assessing him.

"Thanks."

"Okay, I'm ready," Celeste announced, throwing her red Pashmina wrap around her shoulders and grabbing a small black evening bag. "Bye."

"Have fun!" Bianca replied with a warm smile.

Celeste and Khalil stood outside the hotel, waiting for an Uber. Khalil had been trying to covertly look her over since they left her room. "You are gorgeous!" he said, looking at her with seductive eyes. "I just realized I've never seen your legs. I can definitely tell you're an athlete."

"Thanks."

"Sexy dress and shoes," he continued, clearly looking at her butt.

"These shoes were a gift from Bianca," she said, turning her right foot sideways exposing the red bottom of her Christian Louboutin sling-back.

Khalil just smiled. "Here's our Uber," he said, helping her get in first. "Mmm," he sighed, sniffing the back of her neck, "you smell delicious!" Celeste giggled as she got in.

"The Firehouse restaurant?" the driver confirmed.

"Yes," Khalil answered. "They have one of your favorites," he said to Celeste.

"What?"

"Maine lobster bisque."

"Aah, I'm excited!"

"Your girl, Kennedy, is adventurous. She'd better be careful hooking up with strangers in strange towns."

"She hasn't traveled much and relishes every trip."

Khalil and Celeste sat silently until they arrived at their destination. "We're early. Let's walk around a few minutes," he suggested. "This is the Old Sacramento Historic District."

"Alright," she replied.

"How do you spend your free time?"

"Awakening my son."

"How?"

"Different experiences, places, concepts. We enjoy watching science programs together. I try to show him as much of the world as possible."

"You live with your parents?"

"We live with my father. My mother died during childbirth."

"Sorry to hear that."

"Thanks."

"You have sharp facial features. Are you part Native American?"

"No. My mother was Mulatto . . . from New Orleans."

"Do you have siblings?"

"Just Bianca and her older brother, Quentin. None by blood. Do you have siblings?"

"Three older brothers, and a younger brother and sister."

"Wow. You've got a big family. Do you wanna have a big family?"

"No," Khalil scoffed. "Too many people all the time."

"Do you have any hobbies?"

"I like to fish but rarely get a chance to go. I mostly watch sports."

"Which sports?"

"Every sport. I'll watch spitball fights."

"So, you're a sports fanatic."

"I'm actually a Bay Area fan. Raiders and Warriors. Do you watch sports?"

"Sometimes, with my dad. I'm a Cali fan . . . Dodgers, Athletics, Angels, Lakers, Warriors, Clippers, 49ers, Raiders, Chargers, Galaxy, LA Kings, and the Sparks. I don't really get turnt up until playoffs. And we're always in the playoffs!"

"What are your father's favorite sports?"

"Boxing first and then football. What are your favorites?"

"Football, basketball, MMA, boxing, in that order. Does your son like sports?"

"He loves sports. He plays on a soccer team."

"Does your family go to his games?"

"Bianca's brother, Quentin, takes Robert to all practices and games. When he has to work, my dad fills in. Quentin is an OB/GYN."

"What does your son enjoy doing?"

"Hanging out with his Grandpa, and playing with his dog. My dad is teaching him to play chess. He also loves cars and Legos. Obviously, he and I spend a lot of time at the beach."

"I play chess often, especially on my phone while waiting in airports. Do you play?"

"Yes."

"You're an interesting woman!"

"Are you being sexist? What's interesting about a female playing chess?"

Khalil laughed, "I'm attracted to brains and beauty, and don't meet many female chess players. I need intellectually stimulating conversation to keep my attention. It's also a turn on that you're athletic. Can you cook?"

"Nope. Bianca's mother prepared most of my meals when I was growing up. My father does a lot of barbequing now."

"It wouldn't be fair for you to have everything going for you!" Khalil teased.

"Do you cook?"

"Yep, and I am the grill master."

"My father thinks he is too."

"What does your father do for a living?"

"He owns a small real estate company."

"My goal is to become a real estate developer in Black neighborhoods."

"We've gotta start creating Black Wall Streets again."

"We're on the same page," Khalil sighed. "Have you been surfing lately?"

"I go a couple times every week. Usually early mornings, before work."

"Do you surf year-round?"

"Yep. And I wear a wetsuit year-round. The Pacific Ocean is too cold."

"You think the Atlantic Ocean is warmer?"

"Definitely. It's not as deep."
"Where do you like to vacation?"
"The beach. It's not a vacation without a beach."
Khalil chuckled.
"Where do you like to go?"
"Anywhere outside this country. Sometimes I just need a break from all this stupidity."
"When my father goes to Vegas boxing matches, Bianca and I usually tag along but don't go to the fights. Neither of us like all that blood and violence."
"You still single?"
"Yes. You have a significant other?"
"No. Hard to have a stable relationship living on the road. Why don't you have a man?"
"Focused on my career."
"What's happening with your job search?"
"I've wasted my time and a lot of other people's money. Mainstream media doesn't appear to be interested in African American perspectives on *Black Lives Matter* or any other social issues affecting minorities."
"Maybe it's a blessing that you didn't find work in mainstream media that might force you to censor your message. I believe you can make freelance photojournalism your career."
"I've gotta start making consistent money and stop fighting social causes. I need financial stability to contribute. I'm gonna try to use local college and professional sporting events to get into mainstream media. We've got so many good teams in SoCal."
"I might be able to help you get press passes for some games."
"That would be great and save me a lot of money."
"And field or floor position for photographing games."

"Right!" Celeste realized.

"You should keep your *Black Lives Matter* IG page alive. Add local protests of any civil rights or human rights issues. Your work does make a difference, and you are helping to build a better world."

"Good idea. L.A. always has something going on politically. I just can't do it as often. I'm gonna focus on sports photography, and start shooting color instead of black-and-white."

"Can't imagine what you'll capture in color," Khalil said, gently caressing her hand entering the restaurant.

BISHOPS

The BISHOP moves in a straight-line diagonally to any empty square, without jumping over another chess piece. The bishop is the messenger or runner, and sometimes the jester. Bishops can only move to squares of the same color, known as "Light-Squared Bishops" or "Dark-Squared Bishops." Each bishop controls half the board. The king's bishop starts between the king and the king's knight. The queen's bishop begins between the queen and the queen's knight. The bishop captures by taking over the square occupied by an enemy piece.

BISHOPS

Kennedy, Bianca and Celeste wandered through downtown San Francisco's Super Bowl City wearing protest tees and drinking frappuccinos. "I should buy one of these," Celeste said, holding up a *Super Bowl 50* football jersey. "Wish just Carolina was on it. I'll order a *Panthers Super Bowl Champions* sweatshirt online after the game."

"I should probably get one for Robert," Bianca said, looking through the choices.

"What time are you meeting Khalil?" Kennedy asked.

"He'll call me when he gets back to the hotel," Celeste said, purchasing a jersey.

"You excited about seeing him?" Kennedy pried.

"More like *uneasy*. I hope we have the same chemistry in person."

"You've only kissed once," Kennedy said. "What kinda chemistry could you have?"

"Mmm," Celeste recalled, closing her eyes. "He's a great kisser."

"Oh, you're just horny!" Kennedy teased.

"But seriously, really getting to know each other through long conversations has brought us closer. Our connection is mental, not physical. I'm concerned about the physical."

"Does he know you're celibate?" Bianca asked, purchasing a sweatshirt for Robert.

"Yes."

"What does he think of that?" Kennedy probed.

"Not much," Celeste responded, bursting into laughter with Kennedy and Bianca.

"I don't know how y'all gonna work that out," Kennedy said, swiping left on her phone.

"He respects and understands my choice. He's not trying to change my mind."

"Yeah, over the phone," Kennedy teased.

"Probably wasn't an issue for him," Bianca considered.

"You know females all over this country are after him," Kennedy added.

"Great. He doesn't need to bother me about sex."

"Well, finally there's a man in your life," Kennedy said, swiping right on her phone.

"He's not the best, but he'll suffice for practice," Bianca conceded.

"What's wrong with Khalil?" Kennedy inquired.

"I don't trust him," Bianca answered. "And she deserves someone better."

"Damn! He hasn't done anything wrong besides being Black. We're really friends."

"Men are *never* friends with women," Kennedy explained. "He wants your body."

"I don't think he's worth sacrificing your beliefs," Bianca warned.

"Khalil's a nice guy, and he respects me."

"What are you gonna wear?" Kennedy asked.

"One of the three dresses I brought. I wanna look nice but not too sexy."

"Why not?" Kennedy questioned disapprovingly.

"I don't wanna look like I need attention."

"I'm doing your makeup."

"I'm getting dressed in his room and will have to do my own makeup."

"What?" Kennedy grumbled.

"No way!" Bianca objected, furrowing her eyebrows. "He'll definitely try something."

"Don't worry. He's not like that."

"We should've done something with your hair," Kennedy complained, studying Celeste's head full of kinky weave.

"It's good enough for him," Bianca said, tossing her shoulder-length curly weave.

"If he's looking for an L.A. fashionista, that's not me."

The ladies continued strolling through Super Bowl City shopping and enjoying the opening day festivities. Khalil unexpectedly walked up behind Celeste gently taking her hand. "Hey!" Celeste said, throwing her arms around his neck.

"Hey, Gorgeous!" he said, hugging her tightly. "What's up, Bianca, Kennedy?"

"Hello," Bianca replied, attempting to be pleasant.

"Hey, Khalil," Kennedy responded, with a sincere smile.

"Blonde hair?" Khalil asked.

"Platinium blonde. Old school," Kennedy specified, running her fingers through her short wavy shag.

"This is why she's an Instagram Celebrity," Celeste explained.

"What are you wearing?" Khalil asked, looking at Celeste's tee.

"*Mario Woods, December 2, 2015.* I want these San Francisco police officers, enjoying their work in Super Bowl City, to remember why protesters are here!"

"Do you think this protest was successful?" Khalil asked.

"MLK, Jr. wouldn't be impressed with the number of Americans in attendance," Celeste responded.

"I expected to see more professional athletes here, and as speakers, since so many guys are in town for the Super Bowl," Kennedy said, swiping left on her phone.

"Apparently, people care more about the Super Bowl than people being murdered by law enforcement," Bianca complained, throwing her hands in the air and looking in every direction.

"As you can see, pro football is big business," Khalil replied.

"NFL teams are plantations featuring physically dominate Black guys," Bianca declared. "Their opinions, beliefs and concerns don't matter. They're slaves following orders."

"That's fucked up!" Khalil responded.

"Black athletes are simply equipment," Celeste added. "Like office photocopiers."

"Damn!" Khalil laughed.

"They're just mules employed for their bodies, not their intellect," Bianca scoffed.

"Wow!" Khalil chuckled.

"Athletes are celebrated until they get injured or in trouble," Celeste continued. "Then they're abandoned, forgotten, and often left with incapacitating damage to the body and brain."

"Name one African American athlete known for being intelligent," Bianca challenged.

Everyone thought momentarily, but no one responded.

"See what I mean. There are obviously plenty of highly intelligent male and female African American athletes, but you've really got to think about it."

"White supremacists fight images of Black men dominating physically and mentally," Khalil said. "They need us to look like tamed beasts, so they exploit our physical dominance."

"Black alpha males being exploited," Bianca mocked. "They can't keep scrawny white men from forcing them into dedicating their lives to chasing around a ball."

"Like circus elephants tied by one leg to chains they can easily break, thinking they are trapped," Celeste added.

"And they think they're getting paid," Bianca scoffed. "The owners are financially raping them."

"Just some field Niggas, occasionally healthy enough to be auctioned off to another plantation," Celeste said facetiously, laughing with Khalil.

"Black people are still being oppressed everywhere," Kennedy complained.

"And who or what do you think is oppressing us?" Bianca questioned.

"White supremacists," Kennedy responded.

"White supremacy being tolerated in our society as a whole," Celeste amended.

"White supremacy is dying because white people are becoming extinct," Khalil stated. "That's why they want to make abortion illegal. They don't want to lose any white babies. They'll find a way to get rid of us."

"African Americans don't understand basic genetics," Celeste declared. "They don't realize Black is the dominant gene. Everything else comes from Black. And you can't get rid of Black no matter how much white you mix in."

"Ignorance has too many of our people feeling inferior," Bianca sighed.

"The media creates, and spreads worldwide, the negative images of African Americans," Celeste added.

"Black folks need to put out more positive and realistic images of our people, and social media is a great place to get started," Khalil suggested.

"Black people were *Bred to be Led*," Bianca quoted. "Checkout *Brainwashed*, by Tom Burrell."

"The United States government is responsible for the oppression of African Americans by not enacting and enforcing laws to protect us," Celeste stated.

"African Americans are oppressing themselves," Bianca scoffed.

"How are we oppressing ourselves?" Celeste asked bewildered.

"Not getting an education, not valuing marriage and family, not participating in the political process, and not taking care of our bodies and minds," Bianca explained.

"We value education," Celeste scoffed. "The problem is we get a shitty education in urban schools, low scores on the SAT, and don't get admitted to the best universities where the best professors teach."

"We unified politically to elect President Obama," Khalil declared.

"Only because Obama is African American," Bianca replied. "If our people cared about financial freedom, they'd be voting Republican."

"What did you just say?" Khalil asked befuddled.

"She's a Black Republican," Celeste interrupted, throwing her hand up indicating stop. "Please . . . don't get her started."

"Poor people are destroying our country. They represent the largest percentage of the criminal element and strain our economy with their social services needs. It's not fair that successful, hard-working people have to be burdened with lazy, unproductive members of our society," Bianca complained.

"Wow, a real live Black Republican!" Khalil said in disbelief.

"Politics is theater acted out on government stages. None of it is real," Kennedy stated. "The drugs, alcohol and tobacco flooding Black neighborhoods are designed to destroy us."

"No one is forcing Black people to abuse their bodies," Bianca scoffed.

"Our coping mechanisms are drugs, alcohol and tobacco," Khalil explained.

"Learn to face and deal with reality," Bianca continued. "Stop being so weak."

"When there's no way to fix your situation, you have to find ways to tolerate it," Kennedy said, taking a selfie in the crowd of football fans.

"Chemically an organism must counter negative hormones with something or die," Celeste stated. "Nothing weak or ignorant about trying to survive. White supremacists wanna stress us into medicating ourselves with drugs they provide to our neighborhoods and profit from, and then make it criminal for us to use them. All of this is some bullshit!"

"The main drive for all life is survival of self. Any organism that does not defend itself, when being poked to death, is disabled mentally or physically," Bianca countered. "A dog will attack a bear to defend its puppies, expecting to be killed. Corner a rat, and it will attack you."

"Well, I feel the stress of being African American every single day," Celeste declared. "We are born into a lifetime of stress. Unending stress will kill anybody."

"There are so many forces opposing us it's difficult to identify all the ways," Kennedy complained. "I'm tired of walking. Let's find somewhere to sit down."

"Can I borrow Celeste for five minutes?" Khalil requested.

"We'll be sitting over there," Bianca responded.

Khalil led Celeste by the hand out of Bianca and Kennedy's sight, where he pulled her close to him and kissed her. "I couldn't wait to see you."

"I've been pretty anxious too," Celeste whispered.

"You ready to go to my room?"

"I've gotta go back to my room, shower, and get my portfolio."

"Oh, hell no! You can shower in my room, and I have two queen-size beds. We'll get what you need and bring everything to my room."

"Okay, but let's just hang out with Bianca and Kennedy a little longer."

"I can't take much more of your girls. We've waited five months to be together."

"We FaceTime almost every night," Celeste said, silenced by his lips on hers again.

"I don't care, Baby. I'm ready to chill with you. Let's be out of here in fifteen minutes."

"Alright, Boo," Celeste said, leading him by the hand back to Bianca and Kennedy.

"I got Robert a Denver Broncos t-shirt and hoodie," Khalil announced, handing Celeste an orange bag out of his backpack.

"You out here shopping while we're protesting?" Kennedy teased, striking a pose with her hands on her hips, featuring her *Black Lives Matter* tee.

"Denver Broncos?" Celeste asked perplexed. "You know we're Carolina Panthers fans."

"I know you're a Panthers fan. I don't know about Robert. He probably wants to wear winner colors."

"Man, please. Carolina will definitely win!"

"Why are you a Panthers fan?"

"I love Cam Newton! I'm all about Black quarterbacks. There was a time when football organizations didn't believe Black men were intelligent enough to be quarterbacks or head coaches!"

"Oh, you *love* Cam?" Khalil teased, squeezing Celeste's waist. "Cam and his long-time girlfriend just had a baby."

"I love him as an athlete. I'm not trying to marry him!" Celeste replied, elbowing Khalil in the side. "You aren't a Broncos fan."

"I'm a diehard Raiders fan. I've gotta root for my conference."

"Quit playing! The NFC is the best! Panthers, Eagles, Redskins, Cowboys, 49ers, Packers, Saints, Seahawks!" Celeste declared.

"You don't like Atlanta?" Khalil asked.

"Nope. We parted ways when the Falcons abandoned Michael Vick right before he was released from prison."

"I thought you'd probably be a Bears or Lions fan," Kennedy interjected. Celeste looked confused.

"Oh, you know about football too?" Khalil asked.

"A little."

"I'm a Raiders and a Golden State Warriors fan. People often think I'm from Oakland."

"You know any of the professional athletes in town?" Kennedy asked.

"A few guys."

"Going to the game or any parties?" Kennedy probed.

"Hopefully, I'm gonna watch the game with Celeste and Robert."

"When are you coming to L.A.?" Celeste inquired.

"I'm not going to L.A. You and Robert are flying here for the Super Bowl."

"Huh?" Celeste murmured.

"There's no way I can get you a press pass for the Super Bowl."

"I didn't expect you to do that."

"But I was able to get three Super Bowl tickets!"

"Oh my God!" Celeste squealed. "How?!"

"One of my teammates from Howard, who plays pro football, hooked me up. They're not the best seats, but they're decent."

"I've got a zoom lens!"

"Robert is going to be thrilled!" Bianca declared. "That'll make a great first impression."

"I've booked a two bedroom suite at the St. Francis for Saturday and Sunday. We'll take Robert to the NFL Experience at the Moscone Center on Saturday."

"Sounds amazing! I'm not gonna tell Robert until after I give him your gifts."

"Hopefully you'll get some great shots for your portfolio," Khalil said, receiving a kiss on the cheek from Celeste.

"I'm gonna take full advantage of this opportunity," Celeste said excitedly.

"This evening, we can go through all your sports photos and choose the ones that best relive the competitions. Tomorrow, we can work on your portfolio and resume."

"The last photos in my portfolio will be of the Super Bowl."

"Your portfolio is going to be impressive!" Bianca stated.

"I'll be ready to approach media outlets the week after the Super Bowl! Thanks, Boo!" Celeste said, giving Khalil a long tight hug around the neck.

"You know I've got you, Baby," Khalil said, holding Celeste in his arms.

"Now y'all have nicknames for each other?" Kennedy asked.

"This is definitely *my girl*!" Khalil said, hugging Celeste.

"I wanna go to the Super Bowl," Kennedy pouted. "Does your friend need a date for the game?"

"He's in Hawaii for the Pro Bowl, with his girlfriend. So you two like athletes," Khalil said to Celeste and Kennedy.

"I prefer nerds . . . like you."

"Oh, I'm a nerd? I'm gonna show you the nerd in me," Khalil said, winking at Celeste.

"*Nerd* is not a negative label," Celeste defended. "Nerds are achievement oriented. *All needs met* is fun and sexy!"

"Same for athletes," Kennedy resisted.

"Nerds are smart. Not all athletes are smart," Celeste added.

"Athletes bring drama and insecurity," Bianca said. "Nerds provide security and peace of mind. They make intelligent life decisions and are capable of committing to them."

"Athletes and entertainers are attention whores, who generally have too many groupies to guarantee monogamy or longevity in a relationship," Celeste added. "Society keeps feeding their narcissism."

"You tripping!" Khalil laughed. "Not all, or even most, public figures are narcissists."

"There are plenty of celebrities committed to their spouses and careers," Kennedy added.

"I know not all famous people are narcissists," Celeste admitted. "I'm just saying that many of them are propelled to success because of their belief that they're the center of the universe."

"That sense of superiority is the mindset necessary for some people to excel to the top," Khalil conceded. "Just because I know I'm superior physically and mentally doesn't make me a narcissist."

"You'll have a better quality and longer life with a nerd," Celeste said to Kennedy.

"Single women statistically live longer than married women," Bianca added. "You'd better be careful who you marry. You might get the life sucked out of you."

"And married men generally live longer than single men because they have a woman taking care of them," Celeste replied.

"Taking care of them, how?" Khalil doubted.

"Clean home, balanced meals, proper sleep, unconditional love, and a place to rejuvenate and retreat from this crazy world."

"I'll acknowledge the importance of a nurturing home," Khalil replied. "And a woman can soothe a man's heart, mind and soul."

"Bad boys are for entertainment," Bianca said. "Nerds are for relationships."

"You ladies ready to go back to the hotel?"

"I'm ready," Celeste quickly responded.

"I need to get ready for my date," Kennedy said, standing up.

"With who?" Celeste asked.

"A guy who plays for the 49ers," Kennedy announced.

"Where did you meet him?"

"Online."

"Where are you going?"

"We're coming back here to watch the fireworks, get something to eat, and then go to a party at a teammates house in Atherton. I'm not really physically attracted to him, but he seems like a nice eligible dude."

"I'm ready to go," Bianca sighed, intentionally ignoring them. "I'm exhausted."

"Heard you started a women's empowerment blog. How's it going?" Khalil asked.

"Challenging but gratifying," Bianca said, getting up.

"We need more intelligent, strong Black women. What topics have you discussed?"

"Educational opportunities, trending careers for women, women entrepreneurs, and sexual discrimination and harassment in the workplace."

"One topic per week?" Khalil asked, leading the ladies out of Super Bowl City.

"Yes, and I have to write a blog post tonight."

"What's your next topic?" he asked, taking Celeste by the hand.

"I haven't decided. Maybe something about dating," Bianca said, making eye contact with both Kennedy and Celeste.

Khalil and the ladies weaved their way through the crowd back to the hotel. Bianca stood sternly, watching

Celeste gather her belongings. "When are you coming back?"

"Tomorrow before checkout."

"You ladies are welcomed to relax in my room until time to leave for the airport."

"Kennedy and I have spa appointments early afternoon," Bianca announced. "We'll come by afterward."

"Bye," Celeste said, as Khalil carried her baggage out the door.

"We've got two hours to relax before dinner," Khalil said, opening the door to his room.

"Where are we gonna eat?"

"Fisherman's Wharf," he said, putting down her luggage.

"We'll never get a table at Fisherman's Wharf or in Chinatown this weekend."

"I already have reservations," Khalil said, closing the door, pinning Celeste against it, and passionately kissing her.

Gentlemen held the sanctuary doors as Celeste, Bianca and Kennedy exited. A tall, dark, handsome guy gave Celeste a warm hug. "Hope you enjoyed *An Evening of Spirit*."

"I did!" Celeste beamed.

"Love your shirt," he continued, looking at Celeste dressed in a black long-sleeve tee with a white *Eye of Horus* graphic, black-and-white Nikes, and black Levi jeans.

"Thanks," Celeste said, heading towards the Agape Quiet Mind Bookstore.

"Oh, I see why you like coming here!" Kennedy teased, following Celeste.

"Here, we give people love. We like to hug," Celeste explained. "Good for your health."

"Isn't this one of your t-shirt designs?" Kennedy asked.

"Yeah. Daddy gave me a loan to get my business started. I spent the last week running around downtown getting t-shirts, screen prints and packaging."

"At least in L.A. you can get everything wholesale," Kennedy responded. "People need to take advantage of the resources around them."

"What's happening with your job applications?" Bianca inquired, following the crowd into the bookstore.

"Mainstream media is still not interested in my work," Celeste sighed. "I can't earn a living selling photos."

"Maybe it's not your work that's being rejected, but your skin color," Kennedy proposed. "You're a talented photographer."

"There aren't many female sports journalists," Bianca consoled.

"Women are not respected as sports analysts or reporters," Celeste complained, looking through a basket of crystals.

"There's no denying the quality of your work. You're being blocked by discrimination."

"What about applying to Black newspapers and magazines?" Kennedy suggested, looking at mandala coloring books.

"Nope. I don't wanna live in a Black world. I wanna be part of the global society."

"So, what are you going to do?" Bianca asked. "Sell t-shirts at the beach for a living?"

"Just focus on making money. I can't afford to chase dreams or be an activist right now."

"What about more model shoots?" Kennedy recommended.

"The agency rarely calls me for bookings. I think I'm being blackballed for turning down shoots last autumn when I was working on sporting events."

"Arrange your own shoots," Bianca suggested, looking at books on manifesting.

"I can't afford to rent studio time or get my own studio."

"Do location shoots. You love nature. Change the location weekly."

"You can advertise on Instagram," Kennedy advised. "I could do makeup."

"You two could easily start your own business. Experiment with a beach photo shoot."

"You could shoot each model on the sand or in the water," Kennedy suggested. "Just one swimsuit per model."

"Figure out how many models the two of you need to have a profitable day and the time to get amazing photos."

"I'm not confident that'll work either. Don't have the money or time to waste."

"You have to release past programming and start picturing a better life for yourself," Bianca demanded. "You could quickly build a following of models begging to shoot with you."

"I need to spend time meditating, changing my frequency, and allowing Source to direct me," Celeste replied, examining sound bowls.

"This must have taken forever," Kennedy intruded, leaning between them to pick up an orange candle decorated with crystals in a geometric pattern.

"This bookstore is great," Bianca said. "Everything you need for spiritual growth is here, including books by Wayne Dyer, Deepak Chopra, Eckhart Tolle, Marianne Williamson,

Louise Hay, Joel Osteen, Joyce Meyer, Neale Donald Walsch."

"The *Bodhi Tree* was an iconic New Age bookstore in West Hollywood that closed a few years ago. People from all over the world came there to hang out late into the night skimming the most popular books on spirituality, and some of the most difficult to find. The Agape bookstore is now the new *Bodhi Tree*."

"This bookstore has an eerie feeling," Kennedy said, shuddering as if she felt a ghost.

"You're just experiencing unfamiliar energy in here," Bianca explained. "Many geniuses and intellectuals believe there is more to reality than we are aware of through our five senses."

"Unfamiliar and spooky," Kennedy replied.

"Trust me, there's nothing to be afraid of," Celeste comforted. "People here are simply trying to expand their consciousness and improve their communications with Source."

"Einstein did mind experiments on himself," Bianca added.

"I don't smoke or drink, and I'm not interested in tampering with my mind."

"I'm an alchemist," Celeste stated, enjoying several deep breaths of frankincense and myrrh. "And I am working on changing my reality."

"Blackness is the condition you suffer from and the blueprint of your failures," Bianca alleged. "See yourself differently."

"Let's go buy some books and get in the signature line," Celeste deflected, leading them out of the bookstore into the bustling hallway swarming with clusters of people chatting.

"James Van Praagh was amazing!" Bianca said, walking towards a table covered with stacks of his books.

"I could feel Mama's presence," Celeste sighed. "I wish he could have connected us."

"We should see if it's possible for you to get a private session," Bianca suggested, looking over the books.

"If so, I probably can't afford it," Celeste moaned, reviewing the book choices.

"Don't focus on your limitations. Focus on your goals," Bianca advised. "You want to communicate with Mama, and she wants to communicate with you."

"I'm gonna get *Ghosts Among Us* and *Talking to Heaven*," Celeste said, grabbing the two books.

"I'll get *Adventures of the Soul* and *Watching Over Us*. We can exchange books when we finish reading them."

"I don't believe in psychics, clairvoyants or mediums," Kennedy stated, standing with her arms folded. "And I don't play with pagan rituals."

"What pagan rituals?" Bianca questioned.

"Crystals, candles, incense, chanting, ritual dance, meditation altars. All that ceremonial nonsense of Africans, Native Americans, South Americans and Islanders."

"Oh, the spiritual practices of people of color are nonsense?" Celeste resisted.

"Oh, sorry. And Hippies like you," Kennedy added, tossing her golden blonde shag.

"The spiritual practices of our ancestors are not pagan rituals. The truth about human capabilities is being hidden."

"Especially from us," Bianca added. "The Bible is not the origin of Truth. The Hindu scripture book, the *Bhagavad Gita*, which means *The Song of God*, is the oldest holy book."

"Are you Hindu?" Kennedy asked, studying Bianca.

"No. But if I were, that wouldn't change the facts."

"The Bible is older than the Qur'an," Kennedy defended.

"Only in book form," Celeste amended. "Prior to becoming a book, the Qur'an was revelation written on leaves, stones, leather, paper, and memorized by Hafiz. The spiritual practices of Africans, before organized religion, are the original practices of mankind and purest connection to Source."

"The word pagan has nothing to do with evil or the devil," Bianca explained. "It was a derogatory term first used by Christians to invalidate the spiritual practices, and beliefs in false gods, of people they considered peasants."

"African slaves were forced to give up their spirituality and adopt Christianity," Celeste said. "Christian Crusaders were the savages, not Africans."

"During slavery, we were not allowed in God's house. Now ignorant Black folks enthusiastically contribute to making churches and ministers wealthy," Bianca murmured.

"Even though we were kept out of churches, Christianity belongs to all people," Kennedy defended. "Where two or more are gathered, there's church."

"That should apply when only one person is present. We're never truly alone if God is omnipresent," Bianca responded. "What church do you attend?"

"I rarely go to church, but I was raised by my grandmother, who was a faithful Baptist."

"God did not make a mistake, when he created Black people, that he needs help fixing," Celeste declared. "You're not a real Christian if you're keeping anybody out of God's house."

"Religion is infested with hypocrites," Bianca added. "Nowhere in the Bible does it say that anyone or group of people should be prevented from entering the House of The Lord."

"We need to get back to our African roots spiritually and culturally," Celeste said, paying for her books.

"African Americans have no culture," Bianca complained.

"There's definitely Black culture admired and adopted by white youth," Kennedy resisted.

"And that culture is exploited financially by old white men," Celeste added.

"That *Black* culture is contributing to our oppression," Bianca said, purchasing her books. "African Americans don't even know who they are."

"We aren't Africans, and we certainly aren't treated like Americans," Kennedy said. "We're the black sheep of this country . . . literally."

"All African Americans need to get DNA testing and uncover as much as possible of their ancestral tree," Celeste stated. "There's even one specifically to trace your ancestral African roots . . . AfricanAncestry.com."

"Tracing our ancestral tree is problematic," Kennedy pooh-poohed. "During slavery, our lives were recorded with cattle and livestock."

"Slaves were included in census reporting, but initially accuracy and completeness were not of concern," Bianca excused.

"Less than one hundred years ago, the U.S. Constitution stipulated that slaves were counted as three-fifths of a resident for tax purposes," Celeste said in disgust.

"Southerners wanted them counted as whole people," Bianca added.

"Only so their apportionment of state delegates to the House of Representatives would increase, giving southern states political control to preserve their way of life . . . slavery."

"Everyone has a need to know who they are genetically," Kennedy said. "Kids with absentee fathers feel like they don't know part of themselves. Adoptees often feel incomplete, not knowing their birth parents."

"Understanding where we come from helps us understand who we are. Slavery intentionally shattered families to eliminate resistance, and that left our people alone, displaced and traumatized," Celeste said. "We have conditioned helplessness."

"We must know our conditioning and shortcomings to reprogram our minds," Bianca added.

"We are the descendants of slaves," Celeste declared.

"We've got to stop identifying with slavery," Bianca insisted.

"We suffer from Willie Lynch Syndrome," Celeste continued. "Slave mentality is in our bones."

"Who's Willie Lynch?" Kennedy asked.

"Knowledge is power."

"Knowledge is only potential power until used," Celeste amended. "Willie Lynch was a Virginia slave owner who gave an infamous speech to other slave masters about how to control slaves by setting them against one another. *Divide and Rule*. Distrust and rivalries would keep slaves from uniting and rebelling."

"Scholars believe that speech is a hoax," Bianca added.

"It really doesn't matter if the speech is a hoax," Celeste continued. "*Divide and Rule* was used by slave masters and continues to be used by white supremacists. The conditioning is still in our DNA."

Bianca and Celeste got their books signed, shook Van Praagh's hand, and quickly moved on. "He was too busy to ask about a private reading," Bianca said. "We can try to contact him later."

"Yeah, it would have been awkward," Celeste said, heading out of the building into the cool night air. "Should we get something to eat?"

"I'm hungry."

"Let's go to the marina," Bianca suggested.

"Okay."

"So, are you and Khalil officially a couple?" Kennedy asked.

"We're in a long-distance relationship," Celeste answered, walking towards her SUV.

"But are you a monogamous couple?" Bianca questioned.

"I don't know. How can I ask him to be monogamous when we've only seen each other twice since the Super Bowl."

"If you can share your body, he can commit to monogamy."

"So, you have an open relationship?" Kennedy continued.

"We haven't talked about it, and I wouldn't agree to that."

"He's not worried about what Celeste is doing. He knows she's not dating other guys. She's the only one in the dark," Bianca informed Kennedy.

"Oh my God! It's not that serious! I don't have time to date, and it's nice having a friend to spend time with occasionally."

"You're just trying to stay emotionally detached. You like this long-distance BS."

"Do Robert and Khalil like each other?" Kennedy probed.

"Yes, but Robert is a little possessive."

"What does your father think?" Kennedy asked.

"He's just elated that I have a boyfriend. Dad was impressed when Khalil sent me roses for Valentine's Day and gladiolas for the first day of spring."

"So he took the time to find out your favorite flower," Bianca said approvingly.

"You need a man in Los Angeles," Kennedy responded.

"She's still avoiding a real relationship. Khalil is her way of getting everybody off her back about finding a man."

"At least Khalil is loosening her up a bit."

"What's he up to now?" Bianca asked.

"He's finally following his passion to perform spoken word. He did a lot of writing while he was on the road with *Black Lives Matter*."

"How does he make money?" Bianca asked. "Does he sell drugs?"

"He sold weed in high school and undergrad."

"Been arrested?" Bianca continued.

"Not until he protested with *Black Lives Matter*."

"What does he do now?" Bianca pressed.

"He and his brothers have a couple rental properties."

"What other work has he done?" Bianca probed.

"He was a night club bouncer, before becoming a community organizer, while working on his master's degree."

"He has a master's degree?" Bianca questioned.

"He has a bachelor's degree in Afro-American Studies with a minor in Political Science. His master's degree is in Political Science."

"From Howard University?" Bianca asked in disbelief.

"He told you he played football at Howard."

"Doesn't mean he graduated from there."

"How's your love life?" Celeste asked Kennedy.

"I'm gonna meet my new beau in Vegas next weekend. He'll be there all week with his agent."

"The guy from the 49ers?" Bianca asked.

"No. I met Darius at the party in Atherton."

"Does he play football?"

"Yeah."

"What team?"

"He's a free agent right now."

"Unemployed," Bianca ridiculed.

"This must be serious for you!" Celeste teased. "Two months with the same guy!"

"I'm not interested in nobody else. Darius is the man of my dreams!"

"How many times have you seen him?" Bianca asked.

"He's come to L.A. once on business, and we turnt up. Crazy wild sex!"

"Have you met any of his family or friends?" Bianca questioned.

"We're keeping our relationship private for now. We don't want the hassle of building a relationship with paparazzi following us."

"Looks like he's trying to hide you," Bianca accused.

"Taking me on vacation is hiding me?"

"A business trip is vacation?"

"Does he have a girlfriend?" Celeste interrupted.

"If so, not for long. I'm gonna lock him down in Vegas."

"Have you told him about your twins?" Bianca asked.

"Not yet."

"He know about Pierce?" Celeste questioned.

"Nope."

"How's home life?" Celeste probed.

"Fine. I have no desire to go out. Pierce doesn't have a reason to be suspicious."

"Maybe he knows but doesn't care," Bianca offered, getting into the passenger seat of Celeste's vehicle.

"He cares, but thinks he has me trapped with twins," Kennedy replied, getting into the back seat.

Celeste climbed into the driver's seat. "Your blog is blowing up!" she interrupted, redirecting the conversation. "You could be the next *Dear Abby*!"

"And you could be the next *Ann Landers*!" Bianca chuckled.

"Who are they?" Kennedy asked.

"Twins who starting writing advice columns, under pen names, back in the 1950s," Bianca answered.

"What's does Wade think of your blog?" Celeste asked.

"He'd prefer I stick to L.A. lifestyle."

"Women empowerment will probably bring better sponsors than L.A. lifestyle," Kennedy presumed.

"Wade doesn't care if she makes money, as long as she's at home."

"I care. I'm applying to media outlets as a contributing columnist," Bianca announced.

"That would be an excellent career change for you," Celeste said approvingly.

"I intend to keep my job, and hopefully find a freelance columnist position that gives me some satisfaction."

Celeste, Kennedy and Bianca emerged from the showers into the spa area wrapped in large fluffy white spa towels. "You okay?" Celeste asked, putting her arm around Kennedy's shoulder.

"I'm just numb," Kennedy murmured, laying her head on Celeste's shoulder. "Finding out Darius got married, via the Internet, was heartbreaking."

"That was brutal," Celeste consoled. "He should've at least had the decency to tell you before it was all over social media."

"Thanks, Bianca, for treating me to a spa day," Kennedy whimpered, with tears running down her face. "I really need it."

"Yeah, thanks," Celeste added, wiping tears from Kennedy's eyes. "We all could use some rejuvenation."

"I'm grateful that I can pamper my girls. Sorry you had such a dreadful experience."

"You're gonna be fine," Celeste assured Kennedy. "We'll get you through this."

"Let's start in the Jacuzzi, and then go into the steam room and sauna for a few minutes. We have thirty minutes until our body scrubs. You'll feel better when they scrub that asshole off of you."

"Have you talked to him?" Celeste asked, slathering conditioner into her large cornrows.

"No. He hasn't called and has changed his number."

"Wow!" Celeste said incredulously. "He owes you a conversation. What a coward."

"He doesn't deserve to talk to you," Bianca countered, wrapping her hair in a white towel. "You can't trust anything he says. His life is based on playing games."

"I just wanna know why he lied to me for almost five months."

"It doesn't matter. He's a liar and a cheater. His word means nothing."

"I understand. You need closure," Celeste said, wrapping a towel around Kennedy's tousled blonde hair with dark brown roots. "Nothing he could say would make you feel better, and there's no reasonable excuse for hurting another human being in that way."

"I've scheduled hot stone massages for us after our body scrubs," Bianca announced, dropping her body towel on the side of the Jacuzzi and stepping in nude.

"After lunch, mani-pedis will be my treat," Celeste added, dropping her towel and joining Bianca in the hot bubbling water.

Kennedy stood on the side of the Jacuzzi momentarily staring at the steam rising from the water, before disrobing and quickly submerging her naked body. "I can't believe he cheated on me with a white girl and married her."

"Don't let that encounter lower your self-esteem," Celeste pleaded.

"You're not missing anything, and she didn't win a prize!"

"Why her, not me?" Kennedy sighed, sitting in front of the water jet between Bianca and Celeste.

"Maybe it's not about you being Black," Bianca proposed. "He was attracted to you. Maybe they've been together longer."

"He could've told me about her," Kennedy said, gazing into the bubbling water.

"You could've told him about your twins and Baby Daddy. Sometimes it's hard to determine the right time to share personal business with a new love," Bianca responded.

"I finally got up the nerve to tell him about my twins just before Mother's Day."

"What did he say?" Celeste probed, moving her hands and arms front to side on the surface of the water.

"He just asked their age and names. Me having kids didn't seem to bother him."

"Does he have children?" Celeste asked, changing to breaststroke arm movements.

"I don't know," Kennedy murmured, still gazing into the water.

"Well, what did you two talk about?" Bianca asked.

"We didn't do much talking."

"He was living the life of a playboy, and probably didn't want the drama of someone else's children," Bianca considered.

"That's a serious problem for women with children," Celeste added. "Men who wanna get married and start a family, usually prefer not to start with a ready-made one."

"Why do so many Black athletes marry white girls?" Kennedy pondered.

"Probably aren't many Black women to choose from at the predominantly white universities, from where most Black athletes advance to the pros," Bianca offered.

"Too many males aren't men," Celeste said. "They're looking for a mother figure, and white girls are willing to take on that role. Not much is expected of those Black men they view as handicapped. White girls pamper and spoil man-boys."

"So what do they want with them?" Kennedy asked, looking at Celeste bewildered.

"To piss off their fathers. Or to have wild animal sex. They view Black men as beasts."

"Black athletes probably think white girls validate their upward social climb," Kennedy said, laying her head back and looking at the tiled ceiling.

"Maybe they suffer self-hate and need a white girl to help wash away the black," Celeste added. "Those Niggas ain't woke! You don't want a weak ass man with self-esteem issues."

"So you're asleep and weak if you're dating or married to someone outside your race?" Bianca challenged.

"I'm specifically talking about Black men," Celeste defended. "The African American community loses when Black men partner with women who aren't Black. Most of the time, when Black men accumulate wealth, it just trickles back to white people. A Black athlete's white wife spends his money in white establishments. If they divorce, white wives take at least half of their husbands' wealth back to white neighborhoods. The lifespan of Black men is shorter than that of white women. Black husbands usually die first, so white wives often inherit Black wealth."

"An ex-wife or widow deserves to be compensated for her investment of time," Bianca countered.

"Successful Black men obviously prefer utilizing the services of white agents, managers, attorneys, accountants, financial advisors and realtors, who earn a good chunk of their money. Makes them feel more legitimate. Like they've arrived."

"Something wrong with hiring the most qualified people you can find and afford?" Bianca asked.

"No, but why don't wealthy African Americans take the time to find qualified Black people to provide services they need?" Celeste asked.

"Black women accumulate wealth. Aren't you concerned about their money going back to the white man?" Bianca challenged.

"No," Celeste answered. "Wealthy Black women don't marry broke ass white men. We only do that with Black men."

"So what is someone suppose to do if they fall in love with someone from a different race, religion, country?" Bianca asked, studying Celeste.

"If two people are in love, wanna get married and can legally do so, then they should," Celeste replied. "But Black folks have to build wealth and pass it down to future generations. Some of us are gonna have to make tough sacrifices to build a better world for our descendants."

"If you have faith in mankind, then you can choose love because you trust the world is evolving into a nondiscriminatory and kinder place to live," Bianca attested.

"Our choices affect the African American community and determine whether it's surviving, striving or thriving," Celeste said, turning sideways allowing the Jacuzzi jet to massage her thigh. "You can show people better than you can tell them who you are, what you stand for, and what you are capable of doing."

"Some of us would rather focus on the global community," Bianca responded.

"Our people need to get educated and share knowledge so that we can build the African American community," Celeste advised.

"Won't change the way white people view us," Bianca pooh-poohed. "They'll just destroy those communities like they always do."

"A solid foundation of truth is critical for every human being to build a meaningful life. Discovering who we really are builds self-esteem, self-respect and pride. We must intentionally counter all lies about us with the truth."

"White folks need to find out who we really are," Kennedy threatened.

"The ones running this country and the world know exactly who we really are," Celeste affirmed. "They're trying to keep *us* from finding out the truth."

"We were the first humans. White people came from us. We did not come from them," Bianca emphasized. "We carry the strongest DNA on this planet, which survived slave ships and slave masters."

"History, *his story*, is the white supremacy story of mankind which is full of lies and misrepresentations. Mystery is *my story*. Mystery is the hidden and forbidden truths that white supremacy toils to keep buried," Celeste clarified.

"The Truth and our power are concealed in cosmic and spiritual mysteries."

"Black kids need traditional education to compete in this world," Kennedy insisted.

"The mystery sciences need to be part of that formal education," Celeste added.

"They're not gonna get that in public schools," Kennedy informed them.

"We need our own schools, and we need to write truthful history and science textbooks," Celeste said, turning to her opposite side to massage her other thigh.

"Black folks need degrees, from respected colleges, and a way to get their careers started," Kennedy replied. "That's the only way for us to gain freedom."

"Unfortunately, we have to be much more qualified and impressive than our white counterparts to get jobs in our careers," Bianca explained.

"We've gotta create ways for our people to pursue careers," Celeste responded, turning her head with her back to them. "Neither a degree nor a career guarantee financial stability for African Americans," Celeste added. "When companies downsize, we're the first to go, without tenure or position."

"The *American Dream* does not apply to us," Kennedy sighed.

"We need positions of power," Bianca declared. "Institutionalized racism is everywhere. We must infiltrate all institutions."

"We need the education necessary to start somewhere other than at the bottom," Kennedy advised.

"Not just a bachelor's degree but at least a master's degree, and, if possible, a doctorate," Celeste said, facing forward allowing the water jet to massage her back.

"Some of us will have to endure emotional abuse, and break some rules," Bianca admitted.

"The quality of education in our neighborhoods must drastically improve," Celeste added.

"Inner-city schools need Black teachers committed to educating our kids."

"Nobody wants to spend time and money getting an education, and then get paid in the lowest salary range for enduring a job in an environment with limited resources like books and computers," Bianca scoffed.

"Then we need to get involved in local politics to increase salaries of teachers and improve the quality of our schools so that we can attract and keep brilliant and motivational teachers," Celeste directed.

"Have you been listening to what that obnoxious, ignorant, despicable Presidential candidate has been saying?" Bianca asked.

"That orange narcissist is clearly insane!" Kennedy said. "And incredibly childish!"

"These repulsive Neanderthals are trying to take over the U.S.," Bianca complained.

"Knuckle draggers are trying to take over this world. They can't keep up with evolution, so they use propaganda to beat intelligence out of people and maintain the status quo," Celeste said. "That moron reminds me of the cartoon *Pinky and the Brain*!"

"I'm horrified at the destruction of the Republican Party," Bianca continued. "There's no way I can support a chauvinist, misogynist, homophobic, racist candidate. He's a poor excuse for a human being!"

"I don't have much love for the Republican Party, but it's insulting to call that deplorable man-boy a Republican. It's no different than referring to the Taliban, Al-Qaeda, ISIS or Boko Haram as Muslims. Is the KKK representing Christians, Republicans, or the U.S. Government?" Celeste asked facetiously.

"Are you supporting another candidate or switching to another party?" Kennedy asked.

"I'm supporting Senator Sanders," Bianca announced.

"Come on!" Celeste whined. "How you gonna support Bernie, not Hillary? Help women breakthrough the ultimate glass ceiling in this country!"

"As important as that is to me, the U.S. is in financial crisis and I believe Bernie Sanders is the best candidate," Bianca countered. "He believes in social democracy, and is concerned about the wealth and income inequalities in this country."

"Bernie's an excellent candidate, but he'll never win," Celeste opposed. "We can't split our votes between two great candidates and expect to beat the Republicans with one asshole."

"I think as women, we have to vote for Hillary, just like we had to vote for Obama as Black Americans."

"Those are not justifiable reasons to vote for a candidate," Bianca replied.

"I've decided to volunteer for Hillary Clinton's campaign, and start a HuffPost political photojournal," Celeste announced.

"I definitely need a new project to distract myself from agonizing over Darius. Maybe I'll volunteer with you."

"Well, I don't know what I'm going to do. Doesn't look like this country is ready for an African American advice columnist," Bianca sighed.

"White folks don't believe you have any useful knowledge for them, and don't want you advising and waking up Black folks," Kennedy responded.

"I don't know where to go from here."

"Start your own podcast," Celeste suggested.

"The only place to be heard is through social media," Kennedy added.

"Neither unity nor education is enough to change our reality. We need political power," Celeste responded, leaning her head back and closing her eyes.

ROOKS

The ROOK moves in a straight line horizontally or vertically to any empty square, without jumping over another chess piece. The rook has also been known as the tower or the castle. A rook has access to the entire board, whereas a bishop has access to only half the board. The rook captures by taking over the square occupied by an enemy piece. Castling is a unique move involving a rook and king, both of which have never moved. The king moves two squares towards one of its rooks on its first rank, and the rook moves to the square the king crossed.

ROOKS

"Auntie, Auntie, look at that one!" Robert squealed, standing between Bianca and Celeste holding their hands.

"It's amazing! Fireworks are all around us!" Bianca replied, sitting Robert on the side of an elevated fire-pit. "That's Dodger Stadium over there, where Wade took you to the baseball game. There's a fireworks display going on there now."

"I can see everything!" Robert yelled, scrambling to his feet and throwing both hands in the air, flashing peace signs.

"There's Griffith Observatory, where your Mommy and I took you to the planetarium to learn about our solar system."

"I wanna go there again."

"We have to explore different places. Next time, your Mommy and I want to take you to the Jet Propulsion Laboratory. You'll love that place."

"What's there?"

"Robotic spacecraft and stuff about traveling to other planets," Bianca explained.

"Oooh!" Robert squealed. "When are we going?"

"I don't know. We have to find out when visitors are allowed."

Celeste leaned her head back, gazing into the clear night sky watching fireworks. "I'm not sure we should be celebrating the Fourth of July as African Americans."

"We're Americans," Bianca replied. "Independence from Great Britain applies to us too."

"When the original thirteen colonies gained independence from Great Britain, African Americans were still being enslaved."

"Racist, savage colonizers were our oppressors, not Great Britain," Kennedy added, holding her squealing twins by the hand.

"Well, we're not slaves now," Bianca announced. "We are citizens of the United States, the leader of the Free World."

"We're living in the Free World, but we're not free," Kennedy complained.

"Auntie, what are slaves?" Robert inquired.

"A long time ago, mean people made other people do work they didn't want to do and didn't pay them," Bianca explained, briefly glaring at Celeste and Kennedy daring them to say anything.

"That wasn't nice!" Robert condemned, furrowing his brow. "Did they do that to you?"

"No, Cupcake. That was before your grandparents were born."

"Well, fireworks are good 'cause people aren't slaves," Robert deduced.

"I agree," Bianca said, with a genuine smile.

Robert stared down at his mother, waiting for her response. "Agreed," Celeste conceded.

"We don't take our citizenship seriously," Bianca said. "African Americans fought and died for the right to vote, but now we don't value that right."

"Most Black folks don't see any point in voting," Kennedy replied. "Nothing changes for us no matter who is in political offices."

"That attitude is exactly why I decided to launch my podcast today, with the first topic being *The Right to Vote for Women and African Americans*," Bianca explained.

"Black folks make up less than twenty percent of voters in a Presidential election," Kennedy stated. "And white folks make up more than seventy percent."

"Our lives are endangered mathematically," Celeste scoffed. "Minorities need to make up at least fifty-one percent of voters; otherwise, we are at the mercy of white people for our safety and survival."

"Our lives are in jeopardy because we won't take responsibility for the changes we seek," Bianca replied. "We need somebody else to fix sh . . . stuff."

"More African Americans and women definitely need to register *and* vote," Celeste said, taking photos of Robert and the twins enjoying the fireworks.

"Every African American and every woman eligible to vote should get registered and vote," Bianca edited. "It is their duty to contribute to the advancement of our country."

"Voter registration is a major focus of the Clinton campaign," Kennedy divulged.

"Voter registration is the major focus of every Presidential candidate," Bianca amended.

"It's not just about registering people to vote," Celeste said. "We need to reach our generation, women and minority groups, with the truth and a vision for the future."

"What's the name of your podcast?"

"*Cali State of Mind.*"

"How did your first episode go?"

"Celeste was the perfect first guest. The conversation went smoothly."

"I enjoyed our late night debate," Celeste added. "Déjà vu of our teen years."

"Did you do an audio or video podcast?" Kennedy asked, trying to keep hold of her wriggling twins on the dimly lit rooftop.

"Video."

"Where did you shoot it?"

"In my suite."

"It was sophisticated and beautiful," Celeste recalled.

"How long did it take to edit?" Kennedy probed.

"All week."

"You're new at this," Celeste responded. "Give yourself time to learn this craft."

"You need to be branding with something unique," Kennedy stated. "What about video podcasting from this fabulous sun deck?"

"That's a great idea," Celeste seconded.

"Background noise would be a serious problem," Bianca overruled.

"Angel number ten-ten," Celeste contemplated. "Spiritual awakening, enlightenment, personal development."

"That's not what Wade had in mind for me when we moved here. I was supposed to cultivate our couple status, not become an activist concerned with civil rights and politics."

"You can keep developing your IG and HuffPost *L.A. Lifestyle*," Kennedy said. "Your involvement in social changes could be your brand, as a socialite and expert on L.A. lifestyle, and increase your following."

"My podcast will probably cause me to lose some *L.A. Lifestyle* followers."

"Not everybody is gonna like you, no matter what you do," Celeste replied. "Being involved socially and politically is part of the L.A. lifestyle. California is a progressive state."

"But I do want my husband to like the person I'm becoming and respect my work," Bianca said. "I need to know he's on my team."

"He loves you," Celeste assured.

"We're supposed to be having fun," Bianca announced, putting Robert back on the ground. "Let me show you around the pool area."

"The gym looks adequate, but the L.A. skyline must be the attraction," Kennedy said, noticing the exercise facility surrounded by large windows.

"That gym is high-tech," Celeste informed Kennedy.

"It's perfect for me," Bianca replied, holding Robert's hand. "Everything I need is right there, with an invigorating view." Bianca sashayed through the crowd, briefly chatting with neighbors and introducing her guests. Most people already knew Robert, and everyone was enamored by the twins.

"Glass outdoor sauna and steam room, with magnificent views! Wow!" Kennedy cried, taking a selfie.

"We also have an indoor sauna and steam room, in both the men and women's locker rooms. We've even got massage rooms."

"There's also a lounge and theater room," Celeste added.

"You can find *somewhere* up here to record your podcast," Kennedy uttered, spellbound.

"I'm liking this idea," Bianca responded, looking intrigued.

"Great views for taking Instagram photos," Kennedy smiled, standing against the railing taking another selfie.

"Let me show you the grilling area," Bianca said, leading the way.

"Nice Jacuzzi," Kennedy acknowledged, as they passed by.

"I love the Jacuzzi!" Robert grinned.

"You stay in the pool too long, and jump in the Jacuzzi to warm up," Bianca complained.

"Outdoor TVs!" Kennedy exclaimed.

"There are more TVs on the other side by the bar and buffet," Bianca replied. "Who wants something to eat?"

"I do!" Robert cheered.

"Cupcake, you're always hungry!" Bianca teased, heading towards the buffet.

"Me too!" the twins said in unison.

"This rooftop is incredible!" Kennedy uttered, following Bianca.

"*1010 Wilshire* rooftop is my favorite hot spot in downtown L.A.," Celeste announced. "Let me get photos of everyone before we start eating."

Kennedy wearing white shorts, China red shorts, India blue shorts, and the trio wearing matching American flag tees posed first for Celeste. Next, Bianca and Robert annoyed Celeste doing silly poses. "Please be serious! I'd like to get some good photos."

"Let me take some photos of you, Robert and Bianca," Kennedy suggested.

Celeste surrendered her camera and posed with Robert and Bianca for a few photos. Bianca stepped away so that Kennedy could get some photos of Celeste and Robert.

"Mommy, now you and Auntie take pictures," Robert directed.

Celeste dressed in jean shorts, red thong sandals, and a red, white and blue *Vote Like a Girl 2016* tee, and Bianca wearing blue shorts, blue leather flip-flops, and a *Bernie for President 2016* tee, posed like opposing warriors for Kennedy.

"You look like superhero twins!" Robert said, watching his mother's medium-brown long straight weave with bangs and his aunt's brunette long straight weave with center part dancing in the wind. Both of them flashed him a smile.

"Everyone should try the fresh squeezed organic lemonade," Bianca advised, walking up to the bar. "It is unbelievable. If you want something alcoholic, order whatever you want and give the bartender my suite number."

"I'm gonna have some lemonade," Celeste declined.

Bianca handed everyone large plastic cups of lemonade topped with a slice of lemon and mint. "Let's walk past the buffet and see what everyone wants to eat. We can get these cuties seated and come back for food."

"Good idea," Kennedy said, overwhelmed with the twins.

"I want tacos!" Robert sang.

"It's great that the building puts on this celebration free of charge," Kennedy said, looking over the massive buffet.

"Monday through Friday, there's a complimentary happy hour for residents here."

"Wow. Do you and Wade spend much time here?" Kennedy asked, following Bianca to the sun deck seating.

"I get a glass of wine from the bar and then sit in the Jacuzzi almost every evening during the week. Wade comes up here to play billiards with other guys in the building. On weekends he's up here watching football or some other sports."

"Where's Uncle Wade?" Robert asked.

"Visiting his Mom and Dad for the holiday," Bianca answered. "Let's sit on this lounge bed. I'll wait here with these fireballs while you two get food."

"What do you want me to bring you?" Celeste asked.

"Just some fruit and veggies."

Celeste and Kennedy went to the buffet, while Bianca entertained the children. Kennedy and Celeste returned with plates for everyone and sat down to eat. When they were finished, Robert and the twins laid back on the round lounge bed, staring mesmerized into the night sky. The ladies stood around a nearby fire-pit people watching.

"There's a good mix of people here," Kennedy stated.

"Trendsetters from all over the world live and work in this building."

"This scene is energetic, open-minded and innovative," Celeste added.

"How do we achieve this harmonious existence nationally?" Kennedy asked.

"Ignorant people can't handle this kind of environment," Bianca replied.

"We've gotta put progressive people on ballots for local, state and federal seats," Celeste advised.

"You can only count on African Americans to vote in Presidential elections, and they rarely get involved during the primaries. They let everybody else decide who'll be on the ballots," Bianca complained.

"Voter turnout for Black folks is less than white folks," Kennedy said. "But only by ten to twelve percent."

"You're getting into politics," Bianca said approvingly.

"She has a crush on her supervisor at the Clinton campaign office!" Celeste revealed, giggling with Kennedy.

"A political nerd?" Bianca asked bewildered.

"Yep. Can you imagine?!" Celeste whispered.

"He's a secret crush," Kennedy chuckled.

"Oh, he doesn't know?"

"No point. He's married," Celeste exposed.

"They're separated and filing for divorce," Kennedy justified.

"How do you know all that?" Celeste inquired.

"He told me."

"He told you? When?" Celeste probed.

"We had dinner one night last week after work," Kennedy disclosed.

"Wow. Have you slept with him?" Celeste whispered.

"No! We enjoy our conversations. He's teaching me about politics."

"I thought you were taking a break from dating," Bianca interrogated.

"We're not dating! He makes my heart flutter and keeps my mind off Darius."

"So, how is volunteering going for you?" Bianca asked Celeste.

"I love it."

"Is there someone you're interested in, at the campaign office?" Bianca teased.

"First Lady, United States Senator and Secretary of State Hillary Rodham Clinton. Photo journaling her SoCal campaign is the most exciting project I've ever undertaken."

"Her work is getting noticed around the office," Kennedy revealed. "Some of her photos have been enlarged to posters that are on walls in the meeting rooms."

"What's up with Khalil?" Bianca asked.

"He spoke at a gathering in Chicago today."

"About what?" Bianca inquired.

"Liberation of Black people."

"When are you going to Chicago?" Kennedy asked.

"The end of this month."

"Meeting the family?" Bianca queried.

"Yeah."

"Is he working with the Clinton campaign?" Bianca asked.

"He's doing voter registration."

"He has the personality and power of persuasion for the job," Bianca attested.

"There's no point in voting for a Presidential candidate if you're not gonna vote in the midterm elections for Congressional members who will support her," Celeste said, with dismay.

"Black folks don't vote for Senators or Members of the House of Representatives!" Kennedy scoffed. "In fact, they rarely vote for Governors or Mayors unless there's a Black candidate."

"Apparently quite a few people skipped class when U.S. government was being taught," Bianca said. "They don't understand that we have three branches of the federal government. The Executive Branch, administered by the President as Head of State and Commander-in-Chief, is responsible for enforcing laws. And he has a staff that participates in decision-making processes. Congress, the Legislative Branch, administered by the Senate and House of Representatives, creates laws. The Judicial Branch, administered by the nine members, justices of the Supreme Court, evaluates laws."

"The three branches ensure the separation of powers so that no individual or group can become a dictator," Celeste added. "We've gotta be involved in the selection of people in all three branches."

"It's difficult convincing Black folks to participate in the political process, without proving it can benefit them."

"If you want benefits, you'll have to participate," Bianca responded.

"You can't sit rooted in your misery, not take action, and expect anything to change. Do something!"

"You saw what happened to Vice President Al Gore," Kennedy said. "Our votes don't count."

"The election was stolen from him. He won the popular vote but lost the electoral vote."

"That was only the third time in history that the Electoral College voted to elect a candidate who did not win the popular vote," Bianca expounded.

"What happened?" Kennedy inquired.

"Apparently the electors did not represent their constituencies," Bianca said, taking a cup of lemonade from the hostess.

"Who are the members, and how are they selected?" Kennedy asked, declining another cup of lemonade.

"Usually, the electors are political party leaders, state-elected officials, or people closely associated with the Presidential candidates," Celeste responded, accepting the cup of lemonade offered by the hostess.

"Why do we have an Electoral College?" Kennedy asked.

"The Founding Fathers created the Electoral College to create a buffer between the population and the selection of a President, fearing a tyrant could manipulate public opinion and gain the power of the Presidency," Celeste said, studying her phone.

"Hopefully, the electors will shield us from the GOP frontrunning tyrant, if necessary."

"Actually, the electors are anonymous to average citizens," Bianca said. "But it's not difficult to find out who they are with a quick Internet search."

"That's ridiculous! For all we know, they're all Klansmen!"

"I'm sure there have been some Klansmen electors, especially in the South," Celeste said, sipping her lemonade.

"We can't just hand over political offices to dangerous sociopaths. We have to make them spend big money and bust their asses to steal elections," Bianca declared.

"This is our country, and we'll fight them to the very end," Kennedy pledged.

"Check out Hillary's first major campaign rally speech, at FDR Four Freedoms Park, on New York City's Roosevelt Island," Celeste said, searching the Internet for videos on her phone.

"Our voices will only be heard through our votes," Bianca added.

"We've gotta encourage everybody we see to vote. I'm doing it with my tees."

"To Hillary Clinton becoming the first female POTUS," Kennedy said, raising her cup to toast.

"To electing a populist, socialist POTUS, *Feel the Bern*!" Bianca toasted.

"To democracy and freedom," Celeste toasted. "The Clinton and Sanders camps will soon have to join forces to defeat the Grand Old Party."

Kennedy sat on the curb in a floral sundress, next to the JFK memorial plaque at Dealey Plaza, and placed a large mixed bouquet of yellow flowers on the opposite side. "How could the President be killed right out here in the open?" Kennedy pondered, while Celeste took photos.

"The conspiracy theories involving Vice President Johnson, Cuban President Castro, CIA, Mafia, and KGB are terrifying!" Bianca replied, looking at a website on her phone about the JFK Memorial Plaza.

"Political opposition is potentially dangerous and sometimes fatal," Celeste responded, continuing to photograph Kennedy.

"JFK was the *Great White Hope* for Black folks in the 1960s," Kennedy reminded them. "His assassination and the assassinations of his brother Bobby and Martin Luther King, Jr. shattered all hope in Black folks for freedom and equality in America."

"Federal, state and local governments are supposed to protect our basic human right to live," Bianca asserted. "They couldn't even do that for the President."

"Alton Sterling and Philando Castile were also denied the right to live," Kennedy sighed.

"If they'll kill the President of the United States in broad daylight, in front of a crowd of people, they'll kill your Black ass," Celeste warned. "Government and law enforcement allow intolerance to violate our human rights."

"Hopefully, tomorrow's protest will bring some compassion and understanding."

"The KKK is thriving in Texas," Kennedy cautioned. "*Hopefully*, they don't start any confrontations."

"I'm not confident law enforcement here in Dallas will protect us," Celeste worried. "We'll be safest staying close to Khalil and the stage."

"Take photos of me on the big white *X*," Kennedy requested, heading for the spot in the street where JFK was assassinated.

"Stand with your back to the former Texas School Book Depository," Bianca suggested.

"Why? What's over there?" Kennedy asked.

"The Sixth Floor Museum," Bianca replied. "It's the JFK museum located exactly where Oswald supposedly fired the shot that killed the President."

"The perfect background," Celeste added, looking through her camera.

"We should go there last," Bianca suggested. "Let's take photos at the Grassy Knoll and afterward go to the Kennedy Memorial."

"I wanna take some photos at the reflecting pools," Celeste said, adjusting her camera lens.

"The museum and reflecting pools are on our way out of here."

"I wonder how many Black folks were here when JFK was assassinated," Kennedy pondered.

"I doubt very many Black people would have felt welcomed or safe," Celeste speculated.

"Black folks don't have basic human rights in this country," Kennedy complained, somberly posing for Celeste.

"Our society tolerates the continuation of white supremacy."

"The federal government should classify all white supremacy groups as hate groups and immediately dismantle them," Bianca declared.

"But they don't," Celeste scoffed. "Isn't that interesting?"

"Clearly our government officials share at least some beliefs and objectives of the Klan," Kennedy said in disgust.

"I don't think the KKK is running our government, but we definitely have prejudiced government officials," Bianca said, joining Kennedy posing on the white X.

"White supremacy is of the utmost importance for too many politicians, and they are willing to allow programs to fail and citizens to suffer," Celeste replied, taking photos of Bianca and Kennedy.

"Capitol Hill politicians are trying to block the first Black President from accomplishing anything that might be historic," Kennedy criticized.

"Obama has been blackballed by a racist Congress," Celeste added, walking along looking through her camera lens.

"I hold African Americans responsible by not removing politicians who hold onto white supremacy views."

"Our government tolerates white supremacy, but not the *Black Lives Matter* movement," Kennedy said ironically.

"The government considers the *Black Panther Party* and *Black Lives Matter* hate groups. Loving and protecting ourselves translates into hate in their puny minds."

"They fear our hate for them is stronger than our love for self," Bianca added.

"Of course they fear retribution since they've been so vicious and inhumane towards us. Sorrowful fate is coming their way. We don't need to do anything to them."

"We must stop tolerating white supremacy," Celeste stated. "Speak up and take action every time you see that dumb shit."

"Apparently the U.S. government does not have our best interest in mind," Bianca sighed. "We're going to have to take care of ourselves."

"They don't even want Americans to have universal healthcare, even though it is successfully working in other countries. What kind of monster would deny people life-saving medical care?"

"They have no problem leaving us to die," Kennedy replied. "Look what happened when Hurricane Katrina struck New Orleans."

"Maybe the U.S. government didn't leave us to die, but instead intentionally caused those deaths by doing shoddy work," Celeste proposed. "The levees, designed as a flood protection system, had fatal engineering flaws. More than fifty levees surrounding New Orleans were breached. The *U.S. Army Corps of Engineers* knew a hurricane would eventually breach the levees and flood Black parishes."

"Louisiana was not the only state devasted," Bianca added. "Hurricane Katrina struck the U.S. Gulf Coast impacting Florida, Alabama, Mississippi and Texas, as well."

"Most of the devastation was in Black neighborhoods in New Orleans," Celeste insisted, taking photos of Kennedy and Bianca on the Grassy Knoll.

"The emergency response by the federal government was inexcusable."

"The emergency response by the state and the local governments was reckless. They should have been the first responders," Bianca criticized. "The Mayor of New Orleans and the Governor of Louisiana did not uphold their duty to protect citizens of the city and state."

"Of course a Black mayor and the first elected female Governor of Louisiana, both Democrats, are being blamed for the deaths due to their mismanagement," Kennedy scoffed. "There was plenty of warning that a massive hurricane was coming. A natural disaster of that magnitude should have been handled with the federal government leading, before landfall."

"Mayor Ray Nagin is now a convicted felon because of his business dealings in the aftermath of Katrina," Bianca revealed, getting up from the grass with Kennedy.

"People need to stop acting like he's some hardened criminal. He got in trouble over city contracts. Most politicians, most of whom are white, are involved in some illegal government contracts or other business relationships, with tiers of white supremacists to protect them."

"White people were enraged at the idea of a Black mayor profiting from Hurricane Katrina," Kennedy said. "That was supposed to be their cash cow."

"No one should have been profiting from a natural disaster that took people's lives, and devastated families and communities," Bianca protested.

"White folks always paint Black politicians as crooked and power-hungry," Kennedy scoffed. "We always hear about rampant political corruption in Black communities like Chicago, Detroit, Philly and New Orleans."

"Black politicians are novices at political corruption. That's why they get caught. White politicians are the most corrupt people on the planet."

"So you think the justice system should have been lenient on Mayor Nagin?" Bianca asked.

"White politicians get plea deals all the time," Celeste said. "Black politicians go to jail."

"White politicians protect themselves better and get top legal representation," Bianca responded.

"Criticism of FEMA's response led to the resignation of its director. The federal government should lead in responding to catastrophic natural disasters."

"New Orleans is still recovering from Katrina," Kennedy complained. "Many families were never able to return."

"The goal of the GOP was to change the voting demographic in Louisiana, by not rebuilding predominately Black parishes that traditionally voted Democrat," Celeste divulged.

"Is that what they're trying to do in Flint, Michigan?" Kennedy asked.

"I don't know what's happening there," Celeste replied. "Flint is predominately Black and Democrat. The auto industry has died in Michigan. It looks like the whole state is being erased off the map."

"The source of drinking water, for the bankrupt city of Flint, was changed to the Flint River because it was cheaper," Bianca explained. "Water treatment was inadequate, and the lead pipes leached lead into the drinking water."

"City officials knew the water was toxic and provided bottled water to government employees," Kennedy said. "They wouldn't even drink the water they were delivering to Flint residents, or warn them of the toxicity."

"Flint residents have been poisoned by their local government, without resistance by state and federal governments," Celeste said. "All of those Black children have lead poisoning and possibly face permanent brain damage."

"People died from Legionnaires' disease contracted from Flint drinking water," Bianca added. "Why are Black people anywhere in this country still drinking tap water?"

"There's crippling unemployment in Flint. Most families are struggling and can't afford to buy bottled water."

"Society doesn't have a problem with Black people being poisoned," Kennedy grumbled.

"And apparently neither do we," Bianca replied. "Local, state and federal governments have committed crimes and should be sued by Flint residents."

"What's going on at Standing Rock?" Kennedy asked.

"A U.S. Fortune 500 natural gas and propane company, here in Dallas, wants to construct a pipeline from North Dakota to Illinois, crossing beneath the Missouri and Mississippi Rivers," Bianca explained.

"It would also run under part of a lake near the Standing Rock Indian Reservation in North Dakota. Tribal members consider the pipeline a threat to ancient burial grounds and the region's clean water," Celeste said. "Our reputable *U.S. Army Corps of Engineers* did a study and found there would be no significant environmental impact."

"So now they're trying to kill Native Americans by poisoning their drinking water!" Kennedy sneered.

"They're not trying to kill them. They just don't care about them," Bianca clarified. "It's all about mega wealth."

"They don't care about indigenous people, their reservations or sacred burial grounds."

"And clearly they don't care about the environment," Kennedy added.

"Almost four hundred archaeological sites along the pipeline will be desecrated," Celeste said. "The U.S. government is allowing the destruction of the most cultural and spiritual areas for indigenous people."

"People from all over the country have gone to *Sacred Stone Camp* to support and protest with Native Americans," Bianca added.

"If I could afford it, I'd definitely be there," Celeste sighed.

"All of these human rights violations are unfortunate, but they're bring together people from all walks of life," Bianca acknowledged.

"Minority groups are becoming more tolerant and supportive of each other."

"It's white supremacists against the rest of us," Celeste said. "We've gotta stop letting them divide and conquer us."

"We've gotta stop letting them nullify our efforts for reform by distorting what we are saying or doing," Kennedy replied. "Let's go to the Kennedy Memorial."

"We've lost friends from high school and college for supporting the *Black Lives Matter* movement," Bianca revealed, following Kennedy. "They think we're ungrateful for our privileged childhood in predominately white neighborhoods and schools, and private university education."

"We've been ostracized in a feeble attempt to discourage us from addressing social injustices," Celeste added. "We're supposed to be refined ladies who engage in appropriate conversations that don't include politics, finances, religion or sex."

"I've even had classmates try to reprimand me about my points of view or the way I express those views," Bianca continued.

"They seem to feel compelled to silence and rock back to sleep their Blacks who have been awakened by some unruly Blacks," Celeste scoffed.

"I had poor judgment of character," Bianca reflected. "I didn't realize my *friends* were capable of discrimination."

"They're not my friends if they don't care about the lives of the Black men I love being threatened," Celeste declared. "And I consider them the enemy."

"Do you consider them white supremacists?" Kennedy asked.

"Yep," Celeste responded. "Based on their actions or lack thereof, obviously they consider our lives to be of lesser value."

"Most of them probably don't think they're racists," Bianca added. "Their racism is subconscious."

"White people get pissed when I speak the truth about the Republican frontrunner."

"Black people never have the right to criticize a white politician, even one who is infamous for acting like a middle-schooler whirling insults," Kennedy sneered.

"When Democrats win, Republicans want us to be humble to soften the pain of their loss. They think celebrating the first African American POTUS is retaliation against them," Celeste said. "We're celebrating progress, and not thinking about them. Republicans are bitter losers who have spent Obama's entire presidency sabotaging it."

"Well, Republicans will be red-faced enraged when women celebrate Hillary's victory," Kennedy avowed. "We'll be getting our party on!"

"Stand in front of the tomb," Celeste instructed Kennedy and Bianca, facing the JFK cenotaph.

"I'm thirsty," Kennedy grumbled. "Let's find somewhere I can get something to drink and a snack."

"I need retail therapy," Bianca announced, posing with Kennedy.

"Isn't that what you did yesterday, when you stormed into Wade's office with numerous designer shopping bags, after quitting your job?" Celeste inquired.

"I'm still in recovery. And shopping is a sport in Dallas."

"Why did you quit your job?" Kennedy asked.

"Racism and sexism. My request to take vacation time this week was denied. I took unpaid leave and gave my two weeks notice."

"Why wouldn't your boss let you take vacation time?" Kennedy probed.

"She said I needed to give her more notice. Several coworkers took the entire week off. There's hardly anybody in the building, and I'm not working on anything urgent or important."

"Did you tell her where you wanted to go?" Kennedy asked.

"Yes, I told her I was coming to Dallas for the protest. Her expression made it obvious she did not agree with my involvement in the *Black Lives Matter* movement."

"Massa thinks she's running a plantation," Celeste scoffed. "Her Blacks are not allowed to interact with rebellious Blacks."

"She has no right trying to influence the choices you make in your private life," Kennedy criticized.

"Well, congrats!" Celeste interrupted. "You're free of that repressive environment!"

"Thank you!" Bianca grinned.

"What did Wade say?" Kennedy asked.

"He's furious that I've thrown away my career for the *Black Lives Matter* movement."

"This has been looming for a while," Celeste revealed.

"I wasn't being recognized or promoted," Bianca explained. "And Wade waited for the perfect opportunity to link *Black Lives Matter* to my downfall and dissension in our relationship. Apparently, he's okay with my oppression."

"Your meltdown at the mall didn't help," Celeste counseled.

"I was shopping with money I earned! And I flew to Texas on my own tab."

"Alright, calm down!" Celeste said. "You'll be in an expensive boutique shortly!"

"What time does Khalil arrive?" Kennedy inquired.

"His flight gets in at 6:30. He should be at the hotel by 7:45."

"Great!" Bianca exclaimed. "We have time to shop. Let's start at the flagship Neiman Marcus store here in downtown Dallas. Then we should go to Highland Park Village to the Chanel and Christian Louboutin boutiques."

"Ooh, that sounds like fun!" Kennedy squealed.

"I'm in, even though I can't afford anything. That'll keep me from watching the clock, waiting for Khalil to get here."

"I guess you two are going to disappear at eight o'clock," Bianca teased.

"You know it!" Kennedy said, laughing with Bianca.

"No! We're not horny rabbits! Khalil is taking us to get some world famous Texas barbeque," Celeste announced.

"Yes!" Kennedy cheered.

"I guess I'll have to try some," Bianca said, fighting back a smile.

"No one is forcing you to eat meat. You can get a salad," Celeste prodded.

"You two better get some sleep," Bianca warned. "We have to be up early tomorrow."

"Khalil has to leave for the protest way before us, so we'll be going to bed early."

"At least you two have all day Friday to be alone," Kennedy reassured.

"Unfortunately, he leaves early Friday morning to attend the protest in Atlanta," Celeste sighed, staring at the ground.

"You'll see him again in a couple of weeks," Bianca consoled.

"I can't wait to get back to the campaign office," Kennedy uttered.

"You just saw Todd yesterday," Celeste pooh-poohed, stepping away to answer her phone.

"Does he know you're at this protest?" Bianca asked.

"Yes."

"What does he think about your involvement?"

"He was surprised to know I'm an active member of the *Black Lives Matter* movement."

"Does he support the movement?"

"Yes, but Todd doesn't attend protests. His focus is getting Hillary elected President."

"Does he know about your twins?"

"Yes."

"Does he know about your Baby Daddy?"

"Yep."

"Do you two talk on the phone?"

"Never."

"Do you flirt with him?"

"Nope. I avoid eye contact."

"Does he flirt with you?"

"No. He's very professional."

"But Todd is always looking at her," Celeste interjected, returning to the conversation. "You can see the heat between them."

"Stay away from married men. When they see a woman to amuse themselves, they always claim to be separated and getting ready to file for divorce," Bianca warned. "And they rarely leave their wives for side-chicks."

"I'm not his side-chick."

"Khalil is at O'Hare International Airport!" Celeste announced, grinning.

"Let's send him a quick video of you before he gets on the plane," Kennedy suggested.

"And I'll take some photos of you," Bianca said, seizing Celeste's camera.

"Give me your phone," Kennedy requested.

"You look radiant today," Bianca commended. "Your skin is glowing."

"All that is about Khalil!" Kennedy teased. "Her blood is rushing to the skin surface!"

"You're a tropical beauty in that yellow halter dress!" Bianca smiled, taking photos.

"Spin around so that the skirt floats in the air, and then send him a message," Kennedy urged, turning on the video camera.

Celeste spun around and stopped in a runway pose, with her hands on her hips. "Hey, Boo! I had trouble sleeping last night. Can't wait to be in your arms. Have a safe trip. See you soon!"

Kennedy returned Celeste's phone, so she could send the video to Khalil.

"Khalil just sent me a video."

"Hey, Baby. You look scrumptious! Love your long tanned legs. You're gonna have trouble sleeping again tonight. I suggest you take a nap. I'll be there shortly!"

"My father doesn't want me going to any more protests because of the shootings in Texas," Celeste grumbled, sucking her teeth and dropping her phone on the bed.

"I agree," Khalil replied, standing in the doorway of his master bathroom with a large gold towel wrapped around his waist looking like an African warrior. "I was alarmed searching for you in that panic-stricken horde of people."

"But we'd be together tonight," Celeste resisted, perched in the middle of Khalil's bed wearing one of his Howard University t-shirts.

"You were near me in Dallas. When chaos erupted, you vanished into the stampede."

"We found each other in less than two minutes."

"Seemed like five to me. That's not happening again," he vowed. "You came to visit me, not protest. We planned your first visit to Chicago before Paul O'Neal was killed."

"I wanna see you speaking in your hometown," Celeste protested.

"It's not safe," Khalil insisted, returning to the bathroom mirror.

"Then it's not safe for you. I don't wanna lose my man to the civil rights movement."

"I've gotta keep doing this working, and I can't do it worried about you. We have security measures in place, and I can take care of myself," he said, rubbing shaving cream on his five o'clock shadow.

"We need gun reform in this country," she said, getting off the bed. "That crazy dude shooting police officers damaged the *Black Lives Matter* message. Definitely scared off some supporters and protesters."

"Unfortunately, the movement is being defined by someone with no affiliation."

"That's all governments and white supremacists needed to denounce the movement," Celeste said, standing in the bathroom doorway watching him.

"We're not gonna let this movement be dismantled by one mentally ill person with a gun," Khalil said, looking in the mirror shaving his face. "They don't stop selling guns because of mass shootings by crazy white folks."

"The murders of those police officers were heartbreaking. Their families were expecting them home that evening. They were there to protect us," she said, taking off the towel wrapped around her head. "What kind of world are we living in where we can't disagree without turning into Neanderthals?"

"What kind of country are we living in where law enforcement blow up people with robots? Of course, the first time they do it to a mentally ill Black man, and then claim he made racial rants just before he was killed," Khalil noted. "Reminds me of when slave masters pulled disobedient slaves apart with horses, in front of Black and white women and children."

"At least Black people tried to help the officers. Nobody knew who was being targeted. Protesters risked their lives to save police officers. Black lives matter, but they're not the only lives that matter to most of us."

"Well, I'm gonna keep fighting for our liberation."

"African Americans have never been free," Celeste sighed, stepping to the other sink of the double vanity. "We're now enslaved mentally instead of physically."

"Oh, we're still physically enslaved," he rejected. "First kidnapping, next slavery, then sharecropping, and now incarceration."

"But what's worse is that our minds are in chains."

"We still have slave mentality. Our people are gonna have to wake up and *stay woke*."

"Are truth and knowledge enough to erase slave mentality?" she asked, taking out the three big braids in her hair.

"Nope. Each of us must uncover, confront and rise above our programmed limitations."

"We're programmed to maintain white supremacy," Celeste complained. "Today's slave masters don't have much work to do keeping us subjugated."

"We're instinctively driven to resist and fight oppression and injustice."

"The Criminal Justice System is criminal and unjust to people of color."

"The privatization of our prison systems is one of the biggest businesses in the U.S.," Khalil said. "They've gotta keep prisons full to make money."

"Most prisoners are there because they struggled to survive and pursue their dreams. The mental anguish of being constantly oppressed and racially profiled can lead to anti-social behaviors," she said, brushing her hair. "Most people aren't inherently wicked. Babies are born perfect, and their minds are clean slates. Family members and society damage them, and then blame them for developing personality disorders."

"If we spent money educating people, they wouldn't be struggling to survive."

"Do you know, it costs more to imprison a person in California than to pay one year of tuition at Harvard University?" Celeste asked, braiding one medium cornrow from her forehead to her crown.

"Our prison system is the new covert form of slavery. They've got Niggas on deck for war, free labor, experimentation, and even organ harvesting," he replied, rinsing his face.

"People laugh at the idea of clinical studies and organ harvesting of prisoners. They forget about the *Tuskegee Syphilis Experiment*, less than one hundred years ago."

"The U.S. Public Health Service allowed Black men with syphilis to go untreated even when penicillin was being used successfully to treat it and did not give them their diagnosis," Khalil said. "You can actually die from syphilis eating up your brain."

"They watched Black men suffer in the name of science, and they wanted syphilis to spread rapidly through the Black communities of Alabama. They tried to sterilize us."

"They tried to exterminate us like some roaches," he amended, splashing skin toner on his face. "Impoverished sharecroppers participated in what they thought was gonna be a six-month study because they thought free medical care, meals, and burial insurance from the government were godsends. The U.S. Public Health Service knew syphilis was gonna kill those Black men."

"*The Tuskegee Syphilis Experiment* was a 40-year infamous clinical study, that was unethical and malicious. The study employed Black healthcare professionals and educators associated with the Tuskegee Institute to lure study participants."

"There's debate over whether the healthcare professionals and educators knew that the real purpose of the study was to observe the natural progression of untreated syphilis in Black men. I find it hard to believe that Black doctors and nurses would have knowingly participated."

"The Black nurse, who was the main contact person for study participants, definitely knew what was happening. She was the only staff member working with participants the entire 40 years," Celeste contended, brushing her Cappuccino-brown hair into a shoulder-length ponytail.

"She allegedly felt the benefits of the research and free medical care outweighed the risks."

"Every time Black folks experience injustice by white supremacists, white folks wanna put the focus on any Black person involved to distract from what they've done. A few subordinate Black workers did not orchestrate that study."

"I loved your beard and mustache. Why did you shave?" she asked, gently stroking his smooth face.

"Less intimidating. Don't wanna make the Chicago Police Department feel threaten just by my appearance."

"You still look sexy clean cut."

"You look sexy wearing my t-shirt," he sighed, pulling her close to him.

"Love this silky hair," she purred, running her fingers through the thick wavy hair in the middle of his chest.

Khalil leaned over and put his nose against her neck, inhaling deeply. "You smell so good. You're addictive," he moaned, kissing her neck. "Baby, I've gotta get dressed," Khalil said, pushing away from her and walking to his closet.

"The police will be looking for a reason to arrest protesters," Celeste warned, following him out of the bathroom.

"They're always looking for a reason to arrest Black folks. What they really want is for us to get felony charges."

"Why?" she asked, curling up on the bed watching him get dressed.

"Felony charges for Black folks contribute to maintaining white supremacy," Khalil explained. "Convicted felons lose their voting rights."

"A predominately Black prison population means a large portion of the Black population does not have the right to vote. They're at the mercy of voters, and better hope American citizens have compassion for them."

"In most states, convicted felons can have their voting rights restored. Unfortunately, many felons don't know this."

"I'm sure that's not information readily shared with convicted felons upon their release."

"The right to vote is not a concern of most felons being released from prison. They have hostility towards law enforcement, the criminal justice system, government and politics."

"Prisoners have witnessed some of the worst injustices and experienced inhumane treatment. They know better than most people about corruption in our institutions. We need their help fighting for progress in our society and the evolution of mankind. They need to get involved politically just to protect themselves."

"It's tough reacclimating to society," Khalil replied.

"There should be real organizations established that have the resources to help them make the transition. They should have no problem finding decent housing, getting a job, going to school, or getting medical care. The system is set up for them to fail."

"In some states, felons can permanently lose the right to vote depending on the crime. But in Vermont and Maine, felons retain the right to vote, even while incarcerated."

"Senator Bernie Sanders is from Vermont. That must be a progressive thinking state."

"In most states, felons can regain voting rights after they are released, after they complete their parole, or when they are no longer on probation. In some states, felons have to apply to state officials for the right to vote. Felons in Florida must wait *five years* after their release to apply."

"The rules are so different from state to state."

"Former felons often don't vote because the rules are confusing, and it's not worth risking another felony conviction for illegally voting."

"Still scaring Black people away from the voting booths."

"Washington, D.C. is the only place in the continental U.S. that doesn't have voting rights in Congress," Khalil said. "D.C. residents, most of them Black, have no representation at the federal level."

"Why?"

"Our Constitution grants each state representation in the House of Representatives and the Senate. The District of Columbia, our nation's capital, was established as a federal district, not a state. And Congress has exclusive jurisdiction over Washington, D.C. granted by the Constitution."

"What does exclusive jurisdiction mean?"

"District residents are fighting for *Home Rule*, the ability to govern local affairs. Because Congress has exclusive jurisdiction, it can overturn or enact local laws. For instance, D.C. voters decriminalized marijuana, and Congress is attempting to repeal the referendum. And in fact, Congress can revoke the District of Columbia's elected government at any time."

"How do we change that?"

"An amendment to our Constitution or D.C. statehood."

"Does Puerto Rico have voting rights?"

"Puerto Rico and the other U.S. territories are not considered states, so they don't have voting rights. Unlike the *District* of Columbia, U.S. *territories* don't pay federal taxes."

"Is population size the issue?"

"D.C. has a larger population than Vermont and Wyoming, which both have two Senators and one Congressman . . . or Congresswoman. A large mostly Black demographic, providing the workforce for the federal government, is not represented on Capitol Hill."

"Do D.C. residents participate in the Presidential election?" Celeste inquired.

"They didn't have the right to vote in Presidential elections until 1964."

"They didn't vote for JFK?"

"D.C. residents loved JFK but weren't allowed to vote for him."

"What does Eleanor Holmes Norton do?"

"She is the D.C. Delegate to the House of Representatives but is a non-voting member. She can speak on the House floor and serve on committees but is not allowed to vote on the final passage of any legislation. Just another attempt to pacify Black folks."

"What's so hard about granting D.C. statehood or amending the Constitution?"

"D.C. would probably be a Democratic state, adding two Democrats to the Senate and one Democrat to the House of Representatives. Partisan politics apparently is sufficient reason to deny this fundamental right."

"Damn! Residents of the District of Columbia, tax-paying American citizens, have no voice in national debates on subjects such as taxation, war, treaties, Supreme Court nominees, or any other federal government decisions impacting their lives!"

"Residents of D.C. pay more than a billion dollars per year in federal taxes. That is more per person than residents of every other state in America. And those taxes are not coming from any of the state representatives on Capitol Hill, who vote and pay federal taxes in their home states. The predominately Black community is being enslaved."

"*Taxation without representation is tyranny!*" Celeste quoted.

"A slogan of the Revolutionary War. Even the United Nations sees this as a human rights violation."

"White supremacists will never allow the Constitution to be amended if Black people will benefit."

"Former Chief Justice Rehnquist, of the U.S. Supreme Court, believed an amendment to the Constitution should be made providing representation for the District of Columbia," Khalil said. "The Constitution was amended allowing Black men to vote, and later allowing women to vote, the 15th and 19th Amendments."

"Do you think D.C. residents will ever have voting representation in Congress?"

"Yes, when Democrats take back the House and Senate. And when we elect a President that cares about all U.S. taxpaying citizens being represented in Congress."

"That might not be possible with a right-wing Supreme Court," she worried.

Khalil took a box of Nikes out of his closet and sat on the foot of the bed next to Celeste. "I'm tired of waking up and going to sleep without you. Our living arrangements aren't working. You and Robert need to move here, or I need to move to L.A."

"Well speaking of D.C., I might get a job there after the election."

"Doing what?" he asked.

"Probably working for a White House leadership council, or possibly photojournalism for one of President Hillary Clinton's commissions."

"Damn."

"At least we'd be closer. And you're in D.C. often."

"I could probably find a great job there."

"Doing what?"

"Campaign Manager," Khalil aspired.

"Could you really leave what you've built here in your hometown and return to D.C.? You could just stay with us whenever you're in town."

"I want us to be together. I'd move back with you, and keep my condo in Chicago. This could be our getaway spot, which is what it has been for me the past two years."

"I'd love that," she sighed, fantasizing.

"I'll start networking and looking for a position with a Black politician."

"I'm afraid to dream that big. Is our reality changing? Is the universe aligning to manifest our dreams?" Celeste pondered.

"There are multiple realities. Every choice we make leads us down a different path to a different outcome. I choose a reality that includes you by my side."

"Then let me go with you to the rally," she pleaded.

"Nope," he said, standing up.

"What am I supposed to do while you're gone?" Celeste pouted.

"I suggest you rest and relax. There's some weed and rolling papers in the wood box on your nightstand. Don't you need a nap?" he joked, slapping her on the butt.

"Don't you?" she asked, rolling her eyes.

"I'll be ready to get back in bed when I get home," he threatened, running his fingers up her thigh.

"Are you trying to hide me, or hide something from me?" she asked, studying his eyes.

Khalil chuckled, looking behind Celeste at a black-and-white photo of her sitting on his nightstand. "Don't try to con me into taking you. I'm proud of you. And you're gonna meet my family and friends."

"I'll go find somewhere at the lake to sit and watch the sunset," Celeste sighed.

"Please don't go anywhere. I promise I'll be back as soon as possible."

"This isn't a bad place to be kept," Celeste smiled, looking at the colorful gold-framed African art on the walls. "Your house has a Zen atmosphere."

"I was going for an African vibe," Khalil laughed.

"The look is African, the feel is Zen. It's immaculate and peaceful in here."

"Thanks. I want you to feel comfortable and at home here."

"Looks like a woman did your decorating," she said, getting up and grabbing her black-and-white yoga pants.

"Why? Is it girly in here?"

"No, but it doesn't look like a bachelor pad."

"That's sexist! I'm a grown ass man, and I'm not gonna live like I'm still in a dorm."

"Don't be getting all sensitive!" Celeste laughed, putting on her yoga pants.

"Just to satisfy your curiosity, I did all the decorating myself. No female helped me, not even my mother!"

"I'm impressed," she said, changing into a *Huey P. Newton* black-and-white photo tee. "I'll do some yoga and watch the news. Maybe I'll get to see you at the rally."

"Later tonight, we're meeting some of my friends at a nightclub."

"Don't you have another commitment tomorrow?"

"Tomorrow evening I'm going to a protest at Millennium Park. It was organized by four *Black Lives Matter Chi Youth* teen girls. I'm not staying for the march.

Before the protest, we'll have an early dinner at my parents' house. They're looking forward to meeting you."

"I'm a little nervous," she said, sitting on the edge of the bed.

"No reason to be nervous. They'll love you."

"How long have they been married?"

"Twenty-nine years. When they got married, my mother had a one-year-old son, Elijah. We call him Eli. And my father had two sons while he was in the military."

"And you have a sister and a brother by your parents?"

"My younger brother, Talib, is my full brother. He's your age. Rain, my sister, was the result of an affair my father had that almost destroyed our family."

"Are you close to your sister?"

"Not really. I disagree with the way she leads her life. She's twenty-five with three kids by different dudes, no higher education, no career, and no direction. She definitely ain't *woke*!"

"So, who am I gonna meet?"

"Just my parents and Talib. My nosey sister will probably come by on Monday during the day, with her bad kids."

"I bet your family is really proud of you."

"My parents are proud I have a Master's Degree."

"What about your work?"

"I could've gotten a better paying job, but they're proud of the career path I've chosen."

"You're contributing nationwide, but staying committed to Chi-Town."

"We have an obligation to wake up as many Black folks as possible."

"How do we know we're awake enough to enlighten other people?" Celeste asked, walking to the bedroom picture window.

"We realize our people are still being oppressed, and are working towards liberation. We're shining light on oppression and confronting injustice. You don't have to be an authority, just care enough to keep educating yourself and make a difference."

"When we free our minds, we will have the power to free our people. Our generation will never allow society to regress."

"At voter registration events all over Illinois, I see young people getting involved more than any other demographic," Khalil said, gathering his keys, wallet and phone.

"I'm gonna get involved with voter registration in L.A.," Celeste vowed, gazing out at the lake. "I choose the reality where Hillary Clinton is POTUS."

"Bye, Baby," he said, giving her a kiss and pat on the butt.

"This election party is depressing," Celeste sighed, standing in the windowless ballroom of the Century City hotel wearing a Democrat blue *Hillary 2016* long-sleeve fitted tee, blue tailored trousers, and blue snakeskin loafers.

"Election results so far are mind-boggling," Bianca moaned, staring at CNN's election coverage being projected onto the screen backdrop on the stage.

"These people look defeated before the game is over. Damn, our polls just closed!"

"Everybody knows Hillary will win California," Bianca replied. "It might not matter by the time our results are in. Women let us down in other states."

"There are some surprising red states," Celeste responded.

"It's hard to stay positive. The situation looks grim."

"Makes you wonder about the minds of women and minorities in those repressive states."

"I wonder why they continue to live there," Bianca replied. "They aren't trapped."

"Why wouldn't every one of those Americans be at the polls trying to protect their lives and improve the quality?" Celeste pondered.

"Maybe there are more racist, sexist white men registered to vote than women and minorities combined."

"I doubt it."

"How was working the polls?" Bianca asked, fixing Celeste's unruly bangs.

"Bizarre! By noon we had run out of voter information guides in English! I had the only one at my desk, which I had to literally protect all day. English was not the first language of most of our voters, so I guess we didn't receive many English versions."

"I'm shocked at the number of bigoted Americans that showed up at the voting booths, and how compelled they are to *Make America Great Again*. This is not the United States I thought I was living in," Bianca said, taking a sip of her blue vodka martini.

"White supremacists came out of the woodwork for this one," Celeste replied, waving to Kennedy who was searching for them in the crowd.

"Sexism and racism are gaining power and momentum in this country," Bianca sighed.

"Any woman or minority who did not vote for Hillary, who was eligible and capable, is suffering from Stockholm syndrome," Celeste diagnosed.

"Women are being disrespected in this election," Kennedy said, greeting Celeste and Bianca with hugs. "Women will never accept Hillary losing."

"I refuse to believe that in the 21st century white supremacy can triumph in the United States," Celeste declared. "I have faith in Americans."

"Are Republicans against women in power, or for white supremacy?" Kennedy asked.

"White male dominance is apparently the top priority for too many Americans."

"They don't care what their candidate did in the past or does in the future, or how much he profits, as long as white supremacy advances," Celeste disclosed.

"Women in America are still being oppressed," Kennedy grumbled, shaking her head.

"Women's Rights are at stake in this election."

"Apparently there are white women who care more about white supremacy than the rights of women," Bianca replied.

"It's time for Yin energy, life force Chi, creative Prana, to restore balance on this planet!"

"Did women show up at the polls?" Kennedy asked. "Did Black folks?"

"Women showed up, but I'm not sure about Black people."

"African Americans did not show up for Hillary in the numbers they did for Obama," Bianca complained.

"Senator Sanders' supporters let us down," Celeste countered.

"Many had broken dreams about a new government concerned about the people," Bianca explained. "They lost faith in the political system."

"They let corruption win," Celeste condemned.

"Black folks might cost us this Presidential election," Kennedy said, taking a selfie with Celeste and Bianca who presented fake smiles.

"We just can't break the chains on our minds," Celeste sighed. "We're still putting our lives and future in the hands of white folks."

"When and how was America great, and for whom?" Kennedy asked.

"Nobody ever answers that question," Bianca scoffed.

"Why bother? Everybody knows the answer. In the minds of Republicans, America was great when white supremacy ruled without resistance," Celeste replied. "When the concerns of minority groups were irrelevant."

"You mean before the Civil War when southerners fought to protect their institution of slavery," Bianca expounded.

"The slogan should really be, *Make America White Again*!" Kennedy said. "Republicans are the Grand Old Party. Anti-slavery activists were members of the founding fathers of that party. How and when did it turn so racist?"

"Who knows," Bianca replied.

"Well now the GOP wants Blacks, Latinos, Asians, indigenous people, senior citizens, poor folks, sick people, the disabled, women, and LGBTQ to shut the fuck up and endure abuse by psychotic maniacs."

"Prejudice is growing, instead of tolerance," Kennedy sighed.

"What has Todd had to say about the poll results so far?" Celeste inquired.

"I've been calling him all day, but he's not answering," Kennedy grumbled.

"He's probably very upset about these poll results," Bianca said, nursing her cocktail.

"Don't bother him," Celeste advised. "You know he's busy. He'll call when he gets a chance."

"We had plans to celebrate Hillary's victory tonight. Now I don't know what we're doing."

"Doesn't look like there's going to be much celebrating tonight, maybe tomorrow."

"I'm not giving up until I hear Hillary Clinton give a concession speech," Celeste vowed.

"My podcast won't survive a rabid Republican in the Presidency, and the escalation of white supremacy and white nationalism."

"If Hillary loses women nationwide will revolt," Kennedy responded. "There will be plenty of material for your podcast and women interested in contributing to debates."

"I won't be able to get advertising sponsors, and therefore, won't be able to earn money."

"I refuse to even contemplate Hillary losing," Celeste resisted.

"Hillary losing would mean another L for me. Four months wasted focusing on politics. Wade will feel justified in not supporting my civil rights and political concerns and activities."

"Did he vote?" Kennedy asked.

"He voted for Hillary, but he doesn't really care who wins. The President of the United States has no relevance in the pursuit of his dreams."

"Well, I need this win," Celeste moaned.

"Religious intolerance started and is fueling racism and sexism worldwide," Bianca declared, finishing her martini. "It all began with religious beliefs that alienated groups of people and put women in a subservient position."

"We don't see female prophets who are leaders in the Bible or the Qur'an," Celeste replied.

"This is not about religion," Kennedy said baffled.

"But the belief that women are inferior to men physically, mentally and emotionally was founded in religion," Bianca insisted.

"Hate and fear have regained control in this country," Celeste added. "Discrimination is now in fashion for white people."

"This Presidential election has polarized the United States," Bianca complained.

"The GOP nominee intentionally caused the polarization."

"This country has been divided since President Obama was elected," Kennedy scoffed.

"Clearly, the Obama presidency has racists enraged."

"The GOP is infuriated by Obama's presidency," Celeste revised. "Their only concern is regaining control of our government."

"The Obama presidency hurt Republicans financially."

"That's not why they're angry. They're racists spinning out of control because we have a Black POTUS!" Kennedy replied.

"The Founding Fathers are turning over in their graves about a descendant of slaves holding the highest office in America and living in the White House!"

"People are afraid of change," Bianca said. "White people are fearful of a world that they cannot dictate."

"White supremacists fear the loss of their white privilege."

"White supremacists hate the fact that Black people are superior," Celeste added. "The Obamas are a class act, who make white supremacists look like cavemen."

"This election is not strongly contested because surprising numbers of white supremacists came out to vote," Bianca announced. "White nationalists turned out."

"They're like dinosaurs you read about but never expect to see," Celeste sighed.

"This is alarming. I had no idea white nationalism had so many followers."

"What's the difference in white supremacists and white nationalists?" Kennedy asked.

"White supremacists believe white people are superior to non-whites," Bianca answered. "White nationalist believe the U.S. is a white nation, their culture should be foremost, and the *white race* should maintain political and economic dominance and their majority in the population. They fear white genocide."

"White nationalists are undercover white supremacists," Celeste revealed. "White supremacists are low-class, uneducated white folks. White nationalists are the middle-class and upper-class, educated white people."

"Wrong," Bianca retorted. "The upper-class, educated white nationalists are our lawmakers . . . Congress."

"Our only safety net is the Supreme Court. The one place Americans rely on for justice and fairness," Kennedy said. "Justices aren't supposed to be swayed by public opinion."

"A conservative majority in the Supreme Court could maintain the status quo," Celeste cautioned. "Khalil's calling," she said, looking at her phone. "Hey. I'm in the ballroom. Hang on, while I go outside so I can hear you."

"Hey, Baby," Khalil smiled, FaceTiming Celeste.

"Hey, Boo," Celeste replied, looking despondent.

"You okay?"

"No," she sniveled, with tears rolling down her face.

"Baby, what's wrong?"

"Everything is messed up," Celeste whimpered.

"What's messed up?"

"My council position with Hillary's administration is evaporating in front of my eyes."

"Baby, please don't cry."

"The Grand Old Party is trying to steal this election promoting white supremacy and white nationalism. We are actually experiencing tyranny!"

"Looks like our fight against political corruption is just beginning. These white shape-shifters have been hiding in darkness, like the KKK, for decades pretending to have evolved, but now they're exposed."

"I'm never gonna get my career started mainstream! I was so close! And our dream of going to D.C. together as activists for political and social reform is dying!"

"Baby, calm down."

"How can I?! I can't be with you! I'm poverty-stricken! And my father is gonna have to take care of Robert and me forever!"

"Hold up, Baby! This political drama doesn't have anything to do with our relationship! Our future isn't dependent on you getting a job in D.C. with the Clinton Administration. We will make a difference in this world together in Chicago, Los Angeles, or wherever we choose to live. And your father is not gonna be taking care of you forever. Stop crying. We'll figure it out."

"Alright," Celeste sniveled.

"Baby, why don't you go home and watch the election results? You've had a long day."

"I'm gonna stay a little longer with Bianca and Kennedy."

"Take an Uber home. I know you're upset and have been drinking."

"Alright, Boo."

"I should be home in the next hour. Call me when you get in bed."

"Love you."

"Bye, Baby. Love you too."

Celeste went into the ladies room to wipe her eyes and freshen her face, and then returned to the gloomy gathering in the ballroom.

"What does Khalil think about the election?" Bianca asked.

"He's not surprised, and it is not gonna deter his fight for civil rights."

"Women aren't *good enough* to be President according to this society," Kennedy scoffed. "We are still fighting for respect in this country."

"We should have been one of the first countries to have a female leader, especially since the United States wants to be forefront in every arena."

"Look at all of these countries that have had female Presidents and Heads of State," Bianca said, scrolling through her Google search. "Canada, the United Kingdom, Ireland, Iceland, Israel, France, Switzerland, Norway, Finland, Denmark, Australia, New Zealand, India, Turkey, Pakistan, Sri Lanka, Ukraine, Kosovo, Latvia, Jamaica, Saint Lucia, Barbados, the Bahamas, Panama, Argentina, Chile, Brazil, Costa Rica, Nicaragua, South Korea, the Philippines,

Thailand, Senegal, Liberia and plenty other countries. Many of them have had more than one. Our country is a disgrace!"

"Wow!" Kennedy said, looking over Bianca's shoulder. "I never would have guessed there have been so many female Presidents."

"Women have no political voice in the U.S. Welcome to the Stone Ages."

"And women won't stand together to gain political power," Celeste sighed. "They trust the men in their lives to make decisions that impact their lives, while they sit in the parlor enjoying *high tea*."

"This is Todd calling now," Kennedy said. "I'll be right back."

"We'll be over there by the champagne fountain," Celeste said, watching Kennedy float away in her beautiful flowing maxi dress.

"Hey, Bae!"

"Hello, Kennedy. This is Todd's wife, Olivia. I know who you are and what you've been doing with my husband. Todd and I are back together, returning to the Bay Area tomorrow, and expecting a baby."

Kennedy was speechless for a few moments before replying, "Please ask him to call me."

"I strongly suggest you find some self-respect. You have a history of chasing men who are already in relationships. Your best bet is the father of your children. Please stay away from my husband. I won't be as pleasant next time I speak to you. He does not want to see or talk to you. Your little fling is over. Good day."

Kennedy froze staring at her phone, trying to fight back tears and rage. She ambled across the ballroom floor to the fountain and got herself a glass of champagne, while Celeste and Bianca watched in disbelief.

"How's Todd?" Celeste asked.

"Married and expecting a baby."

"What?" Bianca probed.

"That wasn't Todd. That was his wife using his phone."

"What did she want?" Celeste inquired.

"To tell me that they were back together and expecting a baby," Kennedy said, with tears welling in her eyes.

"Damn!" Celeste said, giving Kennedy a hug as she broke down.

"All men are liars and cheaters!" Kennedy wept.

"Not all men," Bianca consoled.

"I'll never trust another man."

"Give yourself time to heal," Celeste advised.

"You got into this relationship when you were vulnerable . . . before you were over Darius."

"Todd just blew up my life. I've broken up with Pierce, and he knows I was planning to move with Todd. Even the twins know because we had numerous fights about me taking the twins to live with another man. What am I gonna do now?"

"Can you salvage your relationship with Pierce," Bianca asked.

"I don't know," Kennedy cried, shaking her head. "I don't even know if I wanna get back with Pierce."

"He's the father of your children. Calm down and think things through," Celeste recommended.

"He's been going out the past few months. I think he has a new girlfriend."

"You still live in the same house," Bianca said. "You have the upper hand."

"I can't go crawling back to Pierce after Todd dumped me."

"You can't be homeless with the twins. It's not fair to put the girls through this upheaval because of pride. Maybe you two could get relationship counseling, for the sake of the girls," Celeste advised.

"And maybe he'll try to take the twins from me. I just feel cornered."

"Let's get her out of here," Bianca recommended. "These heels are hurting my feet, and this ballroom seems like it's closing in on us." The ladies quickly finished their drinks and fled the ballroom.

QUEENS

The QUEEN is the most powerful chess piece. Also known as the Lady, the queen can move to any unoccupied square in a straight line vertically, horizontally, or diagonally, without jumping over another chess piece. The queen's moves are a combination of the moves of the bishop and the rook. "The Dress Matches the Shoes" or "Queen Gets Her Color" means the white lady starts on a white square and the black queen starts on a black square. The queen captures by taking over the square occupied by an enemy piece. If a pawn avoids capture and reaches the opposite end of the board, it must be promoted to any piece of the player's choice, except a king. A pawn is usually promoted to the most powerful piece, the queen.

QUEENS

"Quentin and Robert, please stop the tomfoolery in public," Mrs. Sullivan requested, glaring at her son and grandson seated at the opposite end of the table.

"Alright, Mom," Quentin responded, letting Robert out of a headlock and tickling him.

"*Dr. Sullivan*, please try to be a positive role model for your nephew."

"Sorry," Quentin apologized, elbowing Robert.

"Sorry, Grandma!" Robert giggled while trying to kick Quentin under the table. "I'm gonna be a doctor, just like my uncle!" Celeste and Bianca stared across the table expressionless, visibly annoyed by the two of them.

"Of course you are!" Quentin responded, giving his nephew a high-five. "And you're going to be a Bruin!"

"No, he's not!" Bianca scowled. "He's going to USC!"

"He's going to UCLA," Bianca's father assured, in his deepest baritone voice, seated on the other side of Robert.

"We have an unending family feud between USC and UCLA alumni," Celeste explained to Khalil. "Dr. Sullivan, Bianca's father, is a cardiologist at the UCLA Medical

Center. Quentin and his father attended UCLA School of Medicine."

"Apparently, UCLA is only for male family members," Bianca admonished.

"USC Annenberg School of Journalism is one of the best in this country and the best in California," Bianca's father defended.

"It must get intense when the Trojans vs. the Bruins in football," Khalil surmised.

"All hell breaks loose!" Celeste replied. "Every family member goes to those games!"

"We hosted a lavish tailgate party, last Saturday night, at the Rose Bowl," Mrs. Sullivan added.

"USC won!" Celeste cheered.

"So, which side are you on, Mr. Alexander?" Khalil asked.

"I don't get involved in that feud!" Mr. Alexander cautioned. "I'm a Grambling Tiger."

"Robert has had USC and UCLA gear since he was a newborn," Bianca expounded.

"Robert was born at UCLA but left the hospital in a Trojans onesie and USC cap," Celeste chuckled.

"Did Quentin deliver Robert?" Khalil murmured to Celeste.

"No!" Celeste recoiled. "And Quentin works at Kaiser."

"Everyone have their plates?" Mrs. Sullivan inquired, as Kennedy and her twins returned from the buffet.

"Yes, Mom," Bianca confirmed, seated next to her mother.

Mrs. Sullivan stood up, at the head of the table opposite her husband, and tapped her coupe glass of champagne with her salad fork. "It is with great pleasure that my husband and I are once again hosting our Thanksgiving celebration here in Long Beach, on the *Queen Mary*. We are so pleased to have my dear friend, Mrs. Margaux Weaver, Kennedy and her lovely daughters, and Celeste's boyfriend, Khalil from Chicago, joining us. To family and friends!" Mrs. Sullivan smiled, raising her glass with everyone else. "Bon Appétit!"

"Should we be celebrating Thanksgiving?" Bianca questioned, turning to Celeste seated on her other side.

"I'm not sure Black people should be celebrating any U.S. holidays," Celeste pondered.

"We're not celebrating the colonizers' Thanksgiving," Mrs. Sullivan interjected. "Our Thanksgiving is a celebration of our lives, and the wonderful people we call family and friends."

"Thanks, Mom, for making it clear we're not celebrating the annihilation of Native Americans," Quentin said, cutting up the food on Robert's plate.

"Indigenous people," Celeste corrected.

"After Hillary's loss, family and friends are all we have to be thankful for these days," Bianca whined.

"I'm still heartbroken from the election," Celeste sighed. "We are powerless to change anything in this society controlled by white nationalists."

"The Presidential Election was a slap in the face to women," Bianca said. "White supremacists and white nationalists don't believe women are worthy of leading countries or companies."

"Women are not respected as equals," Kennedy added. "And Black folks definitely don't have influence in this country."

"Our government has taken over the U.S.," Bianca disclosed. "Instead of government working for us, American citizens are enslaved by the government."

"Women are invisible in this country," Kennedy sighed.

"Misogynist men are trying to keep women invisible worldwide," Bianca revised.

"I will never again get involved in politics," Kennedy vowed.

"You're gonna let a couple disappointments silence your political voice?" Celeste asked.

"I'll vote, but I won't be volunteering for campaigns or getting emotionally involved," Kennedy responded.

"I may never vote again," Bianca considered.

"I'll definitely vote in every election in which I'm eligible," Celeste pledged.

"Black folks uniting did not result in justice for those murdered by law enforcement or discourage the continuation of abuse," Kennedy complained.

"Waking people up led to enlightenment for some, but didn't lead to change in the status quo. Education is not enough," Bianca added. "And our political involvement was a joke."

"My career trajectory just disintegrated. Back to square one for me in a much more racist, sexist and dangerous country," Celeste despaired.

"A college degree, a loving and supportive family, the Internet, social media, human rights, civil rights, *Black Lives Matter*, nor politics benefit me because I'm a Black female," Bianca agonized.

"Take the lemons in your life and make lemonade," Mrs. Sullivan instructed. "You didn't waste your time protesting or volunteering. You gained vital knowledge, added valuable material to your portfolios, had impactful life experiences, and participated in society through protests and the political process."

"Your story of overcoming the unique challenges in your life will lead to your purpose, acknowledgment, and prosperity," Mr. Alexander explained.

"Whatever you are trying to hide from others or erase from your memory, is the secret to your success," Mrs. Weaver revealed.

"A day of pampering, that includes getting your hair done, might elevate your moods and clear your minds," Mrs. Sullivan suggested, eyeing Bianca and Celeste.

"Getting a weave won't fix my state of mind," Bianca resisted, wearing a medium-brown shoulder-length natural bob.

"My hair is already done," Celeste replied, wearing five dark-brown reverse cornrows gathered into a kinky afro puff crown.

"Well, I'm proud of my little sisters," Quentin announced. "You've invested your hearts and time into the election. There was nothing else you could've done. You contributed to the efforts to make this country a better place. Time to get back to *your* goals."

"I need to see your bright smiles and joy in your hearts again," Mr. Alexander requested. "The President should not determine the level of happiness in your lives."

"The President *does* affect my quality of life and the world I live in," Bianca refuted. "Even though Wade's life isn't impacted."

"If Wade's not impacted, you shouldn't be either," Mrs. Sullivan resisted.

"Enough you two. We don't quit or cry in this family because of gut punches from morons," Bianca's father said, glaring at Bianca and Celeste. "You can do or become anything you choose. No one is standing in your way."

"Discrimination is standing in my way," Bianca grumbled.

"And programming," Celeste muttered.

"What happened to our two fearless young ladies who were USC freshmen?" Bianca's father inquired.

"What happened to the wonder and awe in my baby girls' eyes?" Mrs. Sullivan asked.

"Reality," Bianca answered.

"Life," Celeste replied.

"Focus on possibilities, not your obstacles," Bianca's father recommended. "We're all here willing to support you."

"Khalil, what do you think?" Mrs. Sullivan investigated.

"I'm proud of Celeste's work, and admire her passion and commitment. This political climate might be perfect for her career. Her hard work could pay off."

"So, you believe in hard work?" Mrs. Sullivan probed.

"I believe in working smart, not hard."

"Do you think this political environment directly impacts your life?" Mrs. Sullivan asked.

"I won't allow it to be an obstacle in my life," Khalil responded. "Hillary's loss was a devastating blow to women. They need time to heal and regroup. From now on, women are gonna be very dangerous politically."

"Can *Black Lives Matter* contribute to eliminating racism, and abuse by law enforcement in America?" Quentin asked.

"Doesn't look like it," Bianca scoffed. "The movement seems to be fueling racism and abuse, and expanding outside of law enforcement to vigilantes."

"Maybe not, but I believe it's still important to shine a spotlight on abuse and injustice. I believe in karma. What you put out, good or bad, is coming back to you like a boomerang. We reap what we sow. These heinous crimes and corrupt politicians will suffer at their own hands."

"We must keep fighting," Kennedy said. "Black folks can't endure suffering forever."

"We've gotta be driven by a vision for a better future. We'll perish without one," Khalil warned.

"*Whatever you resist persists*," Bianca quoted.

"Unfortunately discrimination still persists even when we don't resist," Kennedy scoffed.

"*What you resist not only persists, but will grow in size*," Celeste quoted. "Carl Jung."

"Turn it over to Jesus Christ, our Lord and Savior," Kennedy suggested.

"Doesn't look like there's a God. Why would he tolerate centuries of oppression of any of his creations?" Bianca wondered.

"Are you an atheist?" Kennedy probed.

"I'm a person who doesn't have an invisible source of life support," Bianca responded. "My support system is here at this table. I grew up in a family where science and facts ruled, not religion and interpretations."

"I had no clue, especially since Celeste often goes to Agape," Kennedy explained.

"I'm spiritual, not religious," Celeste clarified.

"Do you believe in God?" Kennedy questioned.

"Of course. I believe we are all emanations of God, and that God is conscious formless energy, not a man."

"Celeste and I love to discuss quantum physics," Bianca added.

"Try to discuss," Celeste corrected. "The concepts are mind-boggling half the time."

"Anyway, those conversations led me to believe in a superior organizing intelligence, The Universe, but not a white man in the sky, who gets lonely, demands everyone's attention, and has anger management issues," Bianca continued.

"Agape reminds me of Unity Church which taught that each of us is a unique expression of God, sacred, and worthy," Mrs. Weaver said. "They believed the teachings of Jesus Christ could be lived every day."

"*What I Believe*, by Ernest Holmes, is an excellent read," Mrs. Sullivan added. "He's the founder of Religious Science."

"Unity Church and Religious Science are branches of the New Thought movement. Even Christian Science originated from New Thought," Celeste clarified. "Reverend Beckwith, of Agape International Spiritual Center, is a New Thought minister."

"What is New Thought?" Kennedy asked.

"God is omnipresent, we are all divine beings, and our minds have the power to heal," Celeste explained. "It's about universal spiritual principles, positive thinking, law of attraction, personal power, creative visualization, metaphysics, life force energy."

"Foundational beliefs trace back to Plato. It's actually not new," Bianca added.

"What's the difference in spirituality and religion?" Kennedy asked.

"Religion is following a communal belief system," Celeste answered. "Spirituality is experiencing God consciousness one-on-one."

"Religion is for people seeking heaven," Bianca added. "Spirituality is for people who've been through hell."

"There are Truths in the foundation of all religions, hidden amongst personal opinions and analyses by the authors of scriptures and revelations," Celeste continued.

"Are you religious or spiritual?" Mrs. Sullivan asked Khalil.

"I'm spiritual, but was raised in an AME church. The Creator is how I refer to God."

"What do you think of Minister Louis Farrakhan?" Mrs. Sullivan queried.

"Nothing but respect," Khalil responded. "He's a leader and warrior for our people."

"Don't you think some of his rhetoric is extreme and divisive?" Mrs. Sullivan probed.

"He is not concern about being politically correct. Minister Farrakhan is trying to save Black folks by teaching males what it means to be a man, and teaching females how precious they are to our men and families."

"I think we need to stop telling others what to believe about creation and learn to COEXIST!" Celeste professed. "That's gonna be my next t-shirt design."

"Alright, that's enough politics and religion for today," Mrs. Sullivan smiled.

"Robert tells me you like football," Quentin said, studying Khalil.

"I'm a loyal Raiders fan," Khalil responded.

"You play ball in college?" Quentin asked.

"I played football. Did you play?"

"No, I was a nerdy pre-med student and loyal UCLA Bruin," Quentin replied. "As an athlete, your college years must have been wild."

"Team spirit is huge at Howard," Khalil answered.

"Must have been a lot of beautiful Black girls on campus to choose from," Quentin snooped.

"The *Real HU* is known for having beautiful and intelligent Black women. Celeste would've fit right in."

"How did you stay focused on academics?" Quentin asked.

"African American history," Khalil responded. "When my professors woke me up, it was no longer playtime for me."

"Celeste tells us you have a Master's Degree from Howard University in Political Science. What was your goal in earning that degree?" Mrs. Sullivan asked.

"To change the world. African American studies led to my involvement in the civil rights movement. My ambition was to work for campaigns of Black politicians nationwide."

"What about human rights?" Mrs. Sullivan inquired.

"I'm concerned about human rights, but civil rights are my priority," Khalil responded.

"Is there a difference?" Kennedy asked.

"There's some overlap. Human rights are the most fundamental rights you have as a human being, such as the right to life, the right to a fair trial, and freedom from discrimination, slavery, and torture. Those rights are defined by the United Nations, and other international organizations and conventions," Khalil responded. "Civil liberties are the basic freedoms legally granted by a government, such as freedom of speech. Civil rights are rights based on citizenship. For example, freedom from unequal treatment based on protected characteristics such as race, gender, sexual orientation, religion, disability."

"Civil and human rights work is dangerous, challenging, and not very profitable," Mrs. Sullivan pooh-poohed.

"It's not about making money for me. It's about creating a safe world for Black folks."

"Financial security is critical for survival and safety, and necessary to fight discrimination," Mrs. Sullivan scoffed.

"When I have a family to protect and provide for, I won't be on the road as much. And I know how to get what I need to take care of myself and my family."

"So, how do you earn your money?" Mrs. Sullivan asked, perched on the edge of her seat scrutinizing Khalil's every move.

"My brothers and I own some rental properties," Khalil responded. "My long-term goal is real estate development in Black neighborhoods."

"Interesting," Mr. Alexander said, redirecting his attention away from Mrs. Weaver. "I'm in the real estate business."

"Celeste told me," Khalil replied. "Hopefully, we'll have a chance to discuss real estate while I'm here."

"Do you remodel your properties?" Mrs. Sullivan asked.

"We did for the first two, but I'll never do it again," Khalil revealed.

"Okay," Celeste interrupted. "Let's take a break from Khalil's interrogation."

"Mom, please leave him alone," Bianca chuckled. "He's a great guy for Celeste."

"I'm not harassing him!" Mrs. Sullivan scowled. "I'm trying to get to know him!"

"You can ask me anything," Khalil offered. "I want my lady's family to be comfortable with us dating."

"Let's find the powder room," Bianca whispered to Celeste, removing her small black vintage crocodile handbag hanging on a jeweled table hook.

"Bianca and I will be right back," Celeste announced, picking up her gold Kate Spade clutch in front of her plate.

"I wanna go," Robert requested.

"You're not going anywhere!" Quentin said, putting Robert in a headlock. "I keep telling you to stop following those girls around!"

"Robert, you're in charge of making sure no one questions or gives Khalil a hard time."

"Okay, Mommy, I won't let anybody talk," Robert giggled, putting his hand over his uncle's mouth.

"Leave Khalil alone," Celeste demanded, as her family laughed.

"Excuse us," Bianca said, standing up dressed in a classic LBD.

Celeste wearing an emerald green knee-length satin cocktail dress and matching Jimmy Choo slingback heels followed Bianca out of the *Grand Salon*. "Slow down."

"I need a joint," Bianca fretted, leading Celeste outside.

"I didn't bring a joint, but I brought my weed pen," Celeste smiled. "Khalil and I shared a *medible* brownie before we left home."

"Let's find a secluded area on the deck where we can smoke and talk," Bianca suggested.

"What's wrong?" Celeste asked, handing Bianca the pen.

"I think Wade is having an affair," Bianca revealed.

"What?! I don't believe it!" Celeste replied.

"I didn't believe he was capable of it either," Bianca sighed.

"Do you have any idea who it is?"

"I think he's having an affair with his secretary."

"What makes you think that?"

"She calls at all times of day and night, and on weekends. They're always on the phone, often laughing. When I go to his office, she is standoffish and has a strange vibe."

"I doubt he'd mess with a white girl. There must be another explanation," Celeste said. "Where is Wade?"

"Spending Thanksgiving with his family."

"Why didn't he join us, or you join them?"

"He felt we each needed to spend time with our families. I thought we were a family," Bianca said, taking a drag from the pen. "He's distancing himself from me physically and emotionally. We're basically just roommates."

"Don't make any assumptions, or take actions based on anything but facts."

"I will find out what's going on. I'm getting a private investigator. If he's having an affair, we're done!"

"There's been tension in your relationship ever since you quit your job. Maybe he's not having an affair."

"My lack of employment is not causing us any financial difficulties," Bianca insisted.

"You two were supposed to be a power couple. He could be frustrated with your efforts."

"He shouldn't have asked me to marry him if he couldn't afford a wife! I have no career or source of income," Bianca fretted, with tears welling in her eyes.

"Don't cry!" Celeste pleaded, hugging Bianca.

"My life has fallen apart. I'm just a coon and fucking housewife!" Bianca sobbed.

"Don't say that!"

"I'm totally dependent on a probable adulterer!"

"So, what do you wanna do?"

"I don't know," Bianca sniveled.

"Do you still love him, or do you need him?"

"I still love him, but I won't disrespect myself by staying with a cheater. If you love someone, you don't get with other people and disrespect them. Men don't tolerate wives who cheat. They can't live with the sacred bond that has been broken."

"What if he's not cheating?"

"There's some problem."

"Focus on strengthening the bond between you."

"Why should I do all the work to save our marriage?"

"Because he doesn't know what to do other than retreat."

"I need a man, not a coward."

"Are you two still taking a vacation next month?"

"Yes. We're going skiing in Switzerland."

"While you're in Switzerland, try to remember why you fell in love with Wade."

"You're right," Bianca said, taking another puff.

"Table all of this until the new year. We'll figure out our lives when you get back."

"I definitely need a job. Hopefully, one with growth potential."

"Follow your joy," Celeste advised. "Why don't you get back to *Cali State of Mind*? It's gonna be a different world with the incoming emotional POTUS. Use your podcast as therapy for yourself, women and Black people dealing with the aftermath of the Presidential Election."

"I don't want to think about or discuss that misogynist asshole!"

"Hit the pen again," Celeste urged. "Let's go back before they scare away my man!"

"Mom will never believe anyone is good enough for you!"

"You remember how she tormented Wade for over two years?" Celeste chuckled, smoking weed.

"Yeah," Bianca smiled nostalgically.

"You know Wade loved you! Mom couldn't run him off! He wasn't going anywhere!"

"Don't forget, it took his family longer to accept me."

Celeste led Bianca back into the *Grand Salon* and got a second serving of food. "I love the harp!" Celeste said, returning to her seat. "Makes this setting feel regal and dignified."

"I'm glad you're not one of those women afraid to eat in public!" Khalil teased.

"Can anybody afford to keep you alive?" Mrs. Sullivan asked, gawking at Celeste's plate.

"This is a world famous buffet! I'm sampling!" Celeste justified.

"Most of us just got seconds," Khalil smiled. "Don't worry. I like a thick woman!"

"Ugh!" Celeste cringed, in response to the table erupting into laughter. "Can I enjoy this day and my meal in peace?"

"I don't know how you all can eat so much," Bianca said. "I'm waiting for dessert."

"Me too!" the twins said in unison.

"I doubt I could eat anything else, including dessert," Kennedy said, leaning back in her chair.

"At least Celeste hasn't lost her appetite," Mrs. Sullivan smiled. "There are still signs of life in you ladies."

"This dinner was extraordinary," Kennedy said to Mrs. Sullivan. "Thanks for including India, China and me in your celebration."

"We're delighted you joined us!" Mrs. Sullivan replied.

"We needed something uplifting," Bianca sighed.

"This looks like the perfect time for each of us to share one thing we have to be thankful for in our lives. No repeats. Say something different. There's plenty for all of us to be grateful for," Mrs. Sullivan said. "I'll start by saying that I am thankful for my family and friends."

"I'm thankful for my husband," Bianca said, looking at Celeste.

"I'm thankful that Khalil is here," Celeste beamed.

"I'm thankful that Celeste is my lady," Khalil professed.

"I'm thankful for my health," Mrs. Weaver declared.

"I'm thankful for meeting Margaux," Mr. Alexander said, smiling at Mrs. Weaver.

"I'm thankful for abundance in my life," Dr. Sullivan stated, looking into his wife's eyes.

"I'm thankful for Zeus," Robert grinned.

"I'm thankful for my nephew," Quentin said, winking at Robert.

"I'm thankful for India," China giggled.

"I'm thankful for my twins," Kennedy affirmed.

"I'm thankful for Mommy," India smiled, gazing at Kennedy.

"To transform your life, find something to be grateful for every day," Mrs. Sullivan advised. "The perfect time to practice thanksgiving is when it's difficult."

"Wish African Americans could use the *Law of Attraction*," Bianca sighed. "We are traumatized people who can't generate enough positive vibrations."

"Universal laws should apply to everyone, everywhere and at all times, just like gravity," Khalil challenged.

"Disenfranchised minority groups are not working the *Law of Attraction* to their benefit," Celeste said. "We are focused on discrimination and injustice, instead of tolerance and fairness."

"How can we ignore what's happening and just think positive?" Kennedy wondered.

"More thought, passion, and action must go into what we want rather than what we don't want," Celeste maintained. "We're creating an energy vortex around this chaotic hateful world."

"We're definitely witnessing more of the racism and sexism that we fear," Bianca added.

"All Black people are potential criminals. All white people are potential racists," Celeste said sarcastically. "We've gotta start seeing people differently. I'm giving spirituality a try."

"So you think we can chant away racism?" Kennedy doubted.

"You think we can pray away sexism?" Bianca scoffed.

"Nothing we've tried has been successful," Celeste said. "Our only hope is faith in a Higher Power . . . God, Allah, The Creator, The Universe, Source or Science."

"That Higher Power is capable of changing anything," Mrs. Sullivan ministered.

"We have to be the instruments of love working for God," Celeste stated. "I've heard *Agape Love* defined as the Love of God operating through the human heart."

"The challenge is connecting to Universal Consciousness, Source Energy, the Akashic Records, the Matrix, or whatever you believe in," Bianca acknowledged.

"The only thing stopping us is the negative chatter running rampant through our heads," Celeste said. "Our power is in getting control of our thoughts and focus."

"What are you doing?" Kennedy inquired, startling Celeste who was gazing into the pool smoking a joint.

"I was fishing palm leaves out of the pool," Celeste answered, seated on a lounge chair wearing green elf pajamas.

"The kids are up and getting ready to come downstairs," Kennedy announced, standing in the patio doorway wearing matching elf pajamas.

"Okay, I'm coming." Celeste took one final deep draw, before putting out the joint, and grabbing her camera from the patio table.

"Santa came here!" China yelled, from the top of the circular staircase, looking down at the colorful Christmas tree surrounded by exquisitely wrapped presents.

"Of course, he did!" Celeste replied, photographing the children.

"We got bikes!" Robert shouted, scrambling down the stairs.

"Santa found us!" India squealed, following Robert and her sister.

"Merry Christmas, Sweethearts," Celeste smiled, hugging each of the children.

"Merry Christmas!" the children squealed in unison.

"Merry Christmas," Kennedy responded, helping the twins get on their bicycles.

"Merry Christmas," Mr. Alexander said, sitting in his recliner enjoying a cup of coffee.

"Merry Christmas, Grandpa!" Robert replied. "I got a bike! Can you take me outside?"

"Why don't you open your other gifts first?" Mr. Alexander suggested.

"Okay," Robert sighed, climbing onto his bicycle.

"Here's something from me to get you started," Celeste said, handing Robert a gift.

"Here are some gifts for you," Kennedy smiled, handing the twins matching boxes.

Robert sat on his bike, ripping the snowman wrapping paper. "A remote control car!"

"That's a Tesla!" Celeste clarified.

Robert got off his bike and took the car to his grandfather. "Show me how it works!"

"Merry Christmas," Celeste said, answering her phone.

"Merry Christmas, Baby," Khalil responded.

"Robert and the twins just got up. We're just getting started here."

"Did Santa come through?" Khalil asked.

"I sure did!" Celeste laughed. "Let me get my tablet, so I can call you back on FaceTime."

"Merry Christmas," Khalil answered, FaceTiming.

"Merry Christmas!" Robert yelled. "Santa bought us bikes!"

"Brought, not bought," Celeste corrected.

"Technically, both are correct," Kennedy whispered.

"Wow!" Khalil replied. "Do you know how to ride a bike?"

"Yep. Grandpa taught me."

"What else did you get?"

"Mommy got me a red remote control Tesla. She wants a real one!" Robert giggled.

"Looks like you're having a wonderful Christmas."

"I have more presents to open!"

"Here's a gift from Khalil," Celeste said, handing Robert a box.

Robert quickly removed the Kwanzaa wrapping paper. "Chess!"

"It's electronic. You can play against the computer anytime you feel like it."

"Thanks!" Robert said sincerely.

"Did you open your gifts from us?" Celeste asked Khalil.

"Not yet. I was waiting to open them with you."

"Alright, I'll get my gift from you," she said, searching under the Christmas tree.

"Okay, this one is from Robert," Khalil said, removing Santa Claus wrapping from a box. "This tie is very classy. Thanks, Robert."

"You're welcome," Robert giggled, watching Khalil.

"What's this? Cufflinks, with my initials? I love them! Thanks!"

"You're welcome!" Robert said proudly.

Celeste carefully unwrapped a small box from Khalil, with Kennedy and Mr. Alexander curiously observing. "Oh my God! Diamond stud earrings! Thank you, Boo!"

"Those are for the second holes in your ears."

"I'll wear them always," Celeste vowed.

"Those are so beautiful," Kennedy said. "Are those princess cut?"

"Yes," Khalil confirmed.

"Alright, open your gift from me," Celeste urged Khalil.

Khalil removed the gold wrapping from the present and opened the box. "Baby, this is too much," Khalil protested, admiring a wide gold bracelet.

"I really wanted you to have it," Celeste beamed.

"Thanks, Baby," Khalil said, putting on his bracelet.

"We're gonna finish opening gifts. I'll call you back while I'm cooking."

"What are *you* cooking?" Khalil joshed.

"Breakfast," Celeste chuckled. "What time are you going to your parents' house?"

"Around three o'clock. My mother wants to open presents and relax before dinner."

"Call me after you exchange gifts, so I can wish your family a Merry Christmas."

"Okay, Baby. But you be sure to call me while you're *cooking*."

Celeste ended the call and continued handing out gifts. "Daddy, this one is for you from all of us."

Mr. Alexander sat his *#1 Dad* coffee mug on the side table next to his chessboard and opened the present. "An Amazon Firestick and Apple TV?! Thank you, ladies and gentleman."

"We wanted the guardian of the mighty remote to have access to every sporting event and anything else you desire!" Celeste teased.

"Perfect," Mr. Alexander smiled.

"Come on, Grandpa," Robert pleaded. "I wanna ride my bike."

"In your pajamas?" Mr. Alexander asked incredulously.

"Yep."

"Okay," Mr. Alexander agreed. "We'll have to go out back since you're not dressed."

"Yea!" Robert cheered, skipping out the back door with Zeus trotting beside him.

"Can we go?" India asked Kennedy.

"Sure," Mr. Alexander answered. "This is your home too."

"I'll bring their bikes out back," Kennedy said, following the twins. She returned to the living room, to find Celeste laying on the floor on her back in the middle of gifts and torn wrapping paper. "Well, we pulled that off," Kennedy sighed.

"We always find a way to bring joy to our children's hearts."

"I've gotta take the twins to their father's house this afternoon. Pierce wants them to spend Christmas with him since they spent Thanksgiving with me."

"How do you feel about that?"

"Not happy. They'll be meeting his new live-in girlfriend, and eating Christmas dinner for the first time without me."

"I know the situation is tough."

"As difficult as it is, I must make sure they maintain their relationship with Pierce. They're not gonna experience the longing I've felt for my father."

"Why don't you have him pick them up here? Or I could take them."

"If you'd just ride with me, I'd really appreciate it. I need to do this myself."

"I got you."

"Evidently, dreams only come true for kids," Kennedy scoffed. "Wish I was still a kid."

"Me too!" Celeste laughed. "The problem with growing up is that we stop dreaming."

"Maturing is about letting go of fantasies and facing reality."

"The secret to life is dreaming! Everything begins as a thought. Everything!"

"Dreaming is not enough," Kennedy sighed.

"We're taught not to dream, so we don't discover our power to create the life we desire. Try to maintain a child-like, not childish, nature."

"Do we really have the power to create the life of our dreams? Black women face racism, sexism, rejection by Black men, self-esteem issues, colorism, and our femininity questioned by society."

"We're creating our lives every day with our thoughts about ourselves, other people and the kind of world we live in."

"I've been dreaming all my life, but my dreams never come true."

"Creative visualization is an excellent technique for perfecting dreams and goals."

"How does that work?" Kennedy asked.

"You dream in the present tense as if you are experiencing whatever you want right now, using all five of your senses...sight, scent, sound, taste, touch. And you've gotta add as much emotion as possible."

"Dream or daydream?" Kennedy probed.

"Meditating or daydreaming," Celeste replied. "And according to Neville Goddard, before you fall asleep."

"Who's Neville Goddard?"

"A 20th century author, lecturer and, some say, prophet. He believed that conscious manifesting requires us to feel what we desire before it can materialize."

"Did he start the practice of creative visualization?"

"No, he was before creative visualization. Check out Lisa Nichols and Shakti Gawain, the masters of creative visualization, on YouTube. I have Shakti Gawain's first book, back when she was our age, from my mother's book collection. And Lisa Nichols, my pretend celeb BFF, has been a guest speaker at Agape."

"I'm not sure about all this *Law of Attraction* stuff," Kennedy questioned.

"There are many approaches to manifesting and no magic formula. Just find what works for you. Get on the vibrational frequency of that which you seek; however you can do it."

"I don't think dreaming, chanting or burning candles can repair my circumstances."

"You don't need to believe in creative visualization. Use it as a peaceful break from your daily grind to rejuvenate your mind, body and soul. Your mind doesn't know the difference between reality and fantasy."

"I do need a mental break from all this stress."

"Your mind works on manifesting your predominate thoughts driven by emotions. If you fear getting sick, you'll get sick. If you believe you're wealthy, your mind will find a way to make that happen."

"Let's exchange gifts and see what we've manifested," Kennedy suggested.

"Alright," Celeste agreed, sitting up to find a box and then handing it to Kennedy.

"*The Power of Intention* by Wayne Dyer," Kennedy nodded approvingly, unwrapping the book. "I watched this PBS special once, and kept trying to catch it again but never could. I believe in setting intentions. Thanks. This is a great reference book."

"Here's another little something," Celeste said, handing Kennedy another gift.

"A DNA ancestry testing kit," Kennedy pondered, removing it from a small gift bag.

"I also got one for myself," Celeste added, attempting to lighten the atmosphere.

"Thanks. Maybe I'll find out more about myself . . . or possibly even my father."

"This one is from Santa," Celeste said, handing Kennedy a large box with a big red bow.

Kennedy eagerly ripped the candy cane wrapping paper. "Oh my God!" she squealed. "Who got me a MacBook?"

"That's from my father, Bianca, the twins, Robert and me," Celeste grinned.

"Thanks! Here's something from Bianca, Robert, China, India and me," Kennedy smiled, handing Celeste a box with Christmas tree wrapping paper and a green bow.

Celeste carefully unwrapped her gift. "An Apple watch! Thanks! I've wanted one for a while."

"We know. You're welcome!" Kennedy grinned. "Have you heard from Bianca?"

"No," Celeste said, trying on her watch. "She and Wade have agreed to no Internet, news or work, and have turned off their phones."

"Sounds romantic."

"I'm hoping the majestic and enchanting Alps ignite passion back into their marriage."

"What time is it in Switzerland?"

"I think they're nine hours ahead of us."

"How long are they gonna be there?"

"Through the first week of January."

"What a fabulous escape from the holiday season," Kennedy chuckled.

"Can you call your brother on the army base in Afganistan?"

"Yes, but he's twelve hours ahead. I'll call him after the girls come back inside and finish opening their presents."

"You should FaceTime or Skype with him on your new laptop."

"For sure. I never imagined I'd get a laptop for Christmas, but I really needed one."

"I didn't expect to ever get an Apple watch. We didn't have the audacity to dream of what we wanted. Fortunately, our loved ones believed for us!"

"It's difficult to dream when all of my time is consumed with survival. I just pray that I can make a decent life for us. Hopefully, I can give the twins tools to achieve their dreams."

"First, you must be able to see it in your mind, then you have to clear limiting thoughts so that you are in a *state of allowing*."

"What's that?"

"Not being in conflict subconsciously with your intentions. Our subconscious minds define everything about us," Celeste said. "That's where our programming lives."

"What type of programming?"

"Our internal limiting blueprints about love, money, success, health, beauty, race, gender, sexual orientation, worth, etc. Brainwashing from our childhood and teen years."

"Can we change blueprints?"

"Past programming must be cleared before we can manifest our dreams."

"How do we do that?"

"Research it on YouTube. There are numerous methods. And many religions have practices aimed at removing programming. If you prefer the help of a professional, try a psychologist or psychiatrist."

"I won't be manifesting any major changes in my life anytime soon," Kennedy whined.

"Not necessarily. Depends on where your blocks are and how hard you hold onto them. Yes, we prepare and position ourselves for change, but change happens instantaneously."

"The American Dream lured me away from a good man. Black women can't be choosy. If you find a Black man willing to work with you, you'd better keep him."

"Black women aren't so desperate we need to engage in relationships that are abusive, disrespectful, unfulfilling or disempowering."

"Prince Charming is not looking for me."

"Our emotions are simply a record of the past," Celeste said. "For health and longevity, we have to replace negative emotional molecules with positive ones."

"I've given up on love. I'm focused on myself and the twins."

"Traumas and strong negative emotions get trapped in our bodies and cause most, if not all, of our physical and emotions ailments," Celeste warned.

"I've gotta figure something out. The twins and I can't live here forever. I don't know how I'm gonna qualify or afford to pay for my own place. My only option is welfare."

"Welfare is bullshit!" Celeste scoffed. "You can't live a decent life on welfare."

"I have to file for child support. I'm broke."

"Do what you gotta do. I don't believe in that."

"Don't believe in what?"

"Filing for child support. You're putting another Black man in the white man's system of control over the Black family."

"Don't you get child support from Robert's father?"

"Nope. I'm not chasing him down or begging him to contribute to the care of his own flesh and blood. The Universe, Source, God will decide the cost of making that choice."

"I need some certainty in my life, and I'm not getting that as a makeup artist or stylist," Kennedy declared. "I can't keep doing the same thing expecting different results."

"I'm not gonna keep sitting here destitute turning into a zombie. I've decided to start the new year building my own business doing location photo shoots," Celeste announced. "Would you consider partnering with me? You'd be responsible for makeup, hair, and set design."

"Sounds like a great plan considering we're both in a financial crisis," Kennedy replied. "But I'm gonna need an education to create the life of my dreams."

"What do you wanna do?"

"Early childhood education."

"What's gotten into you?" Celeste asked in shock.

"I'm taking responsibility for educating my twins, and would like to contribute to the education of other Black kids."

"Do you wanna be a teacher?" Celeste asked stupified.

"I'd like to start off teaching and then get into administration. I'm gonna study elementary education or early childhood development."

"Wow, you've really thought about this."

"I don't know how, but I'm going to college. I was thinking about selling Donovan's low-rider to help pay for my education. Plus Pierce wants me to get it out of his driveway."

"Your brother would approve of that decision. But check into admissions for the Cal State Universities around here first. You might be eligible for a scholarship, grant or loan. There might even be student housing for students with families. You could always attend Santa Monica College in the spring just to get started with a couple of classes."

"I really miss my baby brothers," Kennedy said, with a solemn smile.

"Try to reminisce about heartwarming experiences with your brothers . . . images that make you smile," Celeste advised, putting on the *Christmas Interpretations* album by Boyz II Men.

"Ooh, my favorite Christmas carol is *Let It Snow!*"

"Wouldn't that be beautiful?!"

Khalil stretched out on the king-size bed of their Luxor Hotel pyramid suite, with a large white towel wrapped around his waist, and searched on his phone before playing *I'm Here*, by the Temptations. "Baby, we have a nine o'clock dinner reservation."

"Oooh, I absolutely love this slow jam!" Celeste squealed, emerging from the bathroom with her arms in the air swirling her hips, wearing a gold *Victoria's Secret* bra and panties set.

"I love to watch you dance," Khalil uttered, mesmerized by her undulating hips.

"Hey, how come you get to use your phone? Give me my phone, so I can call home."

"No phones! I'm just playing music. Everyone's fine at home. We're off the grid."

"I've gotta write my new year's resolutions by morning," Celeste fretted, separating her dark-brown natural curls.

"I don't know when you'll have time to do that."

"I'm gonna have to write my resolutions tonight, as I think of them."

"Can't you work on that tomorrow?"

"I have a three-way call at noon tomorrow, with Bianca and Kennedy, about our goals for the new year."

"I thought Bianca was in Switzerland?"

"They're still there. She'll be calling at nine o'clock at night her time."

"I doubt you'll be up by noon."

"I'll definitely be awake and ready to start the new year off right," Celeste declared, picking up her makeup bag laying on the desk next to a green vase full of gladiolas, in an assortment of colors.

"Please don't wear makeup tonight," Khalil requested, watching her.

"Why? You don't like the way I put on makeup?"

"That's not true. I just prefer your natural beauty."

"Is lipstick okay?" Celeste asked sarcastically.

"Oh, hell no! I'm not trying to kiss lipstick!"

"Whatever," she said, walking over to Khalil and kissing him. "I hate wearing makeup."

"Have you always written new year's resolutions?" he asked, pulling her on top of him.

"Bianca and I have been writing resolutions since elementary school."

"What made you start doing that?"

"Bianca's mother taught us to set goals and work towards them."

"What sort of goals did you set as a child?" Khalil inquired, rolling her onto the bed and throwing one leg over her legs.

"Things I wanted, places I wanted to go, experiences I wanted to have," Celeste said, playing in the hair on his chest. "There's something supernatural about writing down your dreams, in your own handwriting. Thoughts are things. Form follows thought. Your thoughts are beginning to materialize when you write them on paper."

"Do you tell Bianca and Kennedy all of your dreams?"

"I've always told Bianca all of my dreams. I share most of my goals with Kennedy. Verbally sharing your goals somehow helps you commit to them. Subconsciously, you need to keep your word."

"You're very introspective."

"I believe we create our own reality."

"*Reality is in the eyes of the beholder*," Khalil quoted.

"If we want conditions in our life to change, we must change the way we perceive those conditions," Celeste advised. "*Change the way we look at things.*"

"Our viewpoint is formed by our experiences. Black folks experience continuous discrimination, so our perspective is a lack of freedom and persecution."

"I believe reality is determined by what's happening internally," Celeste said, getting off the bed.

"But what's happening inside is a result of what's happening in our environment," Khalil countered, getting up and walking to the closet. "Family, friends, your work, where you live, and how you love, determine the quality of your life."

"Our thoughts are putting out vibrations that are attracting back to us those same frequencies amplified. What manifests as our lives is an out-picturing of what's happening inside. The goal is to change our minds so that we can change our lives."

"Protecting women and children in this society is challenging and stressful for Black men. We've always gotta be on guard. How can we change our minds about that?" Khalil asked, handing Celeste a garment bag.

"Reduce the stress by including women and children in education and training to help protect our people. And then find a way to change our focus," Celeste said, stepping into a muted gold evening gown.

"What's your reality?" Khalil asked, putting on black pants.

Celeste was quiet for a few moments. "I'm powerless and totally dependent on others," she responded, while Khalil zipped her gown.

"Damn, Baby! I hate that you feel this way," Khalil said, holding her in his arms. "I see you as a powerful woman fearlessly pursuing her dreams."

"I'm sick of being poverty-stricken, and terrified my life will be this way forever," Celeste said, resting her head on his chest.

"If you believe that your thoughts determine your reality, then we've gotta find a way to convince you of your value and what's possible for your life. I want you to start the new year with optimism."

"I'm optimistic. That's the only way I can keep surviving and striving."

"Your life will drastically change this year," Khalil avowed, handing her a shopping bag.

"What's this?" Celeste grinned, removing a shoe box. "I love them!"

"A little something to match your dress," Khalil said, adjusting the chain on the cartouche resting between her breasts.

"Thanks, Boo!" Celeste said, sitting down to put on her new gold Manolo Blahnik sling-back heels.

"Have you thought of any resolutions?" Khalil asked, putting on his shirt.

"The same as every year since I graduated from college, *independence*. My main focus is developing my career as a freelance photojournalist and publishing a coffee table book."

"Those sound like solid achievable goals. You've done the work, and now it's time to reap the rewards."

"I need to come up with a few more resolutions," she grumbled, putting on gold Egyptian earrings. "Kennedy and I are starting a small business doing location photo shoots."

"Logical. I love your entrepreneurial spirit."

"Have you ever made new year's resolutions?"

"I set goals in my mind all year long, not just at the beginning of the year."

"Do you ever write them down?"

"Nah," Khalil responded, putting on the tie Robert gave him for Christmas.

"You should try writing down a goal, and keep it in your wallet. Just see what happens."

"Okay, I'll try it tonight."

"What's your reality?" Celeste asked, looking into his eyes.

"I don't like conducting a long-distance relationship with the woman I love."

"Hopefully, we can move together next year, after I figure out my life and start making some money."

"Please make that one of your resolutions."

"Each of us is the creator of our universe! Change is all up to us!" Celeste said, making the final adjustments to her big curly afro.

"We've gotta take actions that get results, regardless of our reluctance."

"What people will do is quite different from what they're capable of doing."

"*Personal Power*, Anthony Robbins."

"I wanna go to a Tony Robbins retreat, with you, to one of those exotic locations."

"Maybe," Khalil said, putting on his suit jacket. "Baby, you ready?"

"Yes, Boo," Celeste responded, walking towards him.

"Baby, you're gorgeous! You look like a bronze goddess!"

"Thank you, Mr. Sloane. You're looking debonair and seductive in that suit," Celeste smiled, giving him a kiss. "And your cologne is irresistible."

"After you, my queen," Khalil said, holding the door for Celeste.

The couple strutted across the colossal lobby looking like the King and Queen of Egypt, exited the Luxor Hotel, and disappeared into a black limo. "A limousine, Mr. Sloane?"

"Only the best for my lady," Khalil replied, giving her a quick kiss on the lips.

After enjoying a romantic dinner, the couple returned to the Luxor. "That was an amazing five-star dining experience!" Celeste said, strolling hand-in-hand with Khalil along the path passing under the Great Sphinx. "I'm gonna have trouble staying awake until midnight. You can go to the casino while I'm sleeping if you like."

"I'm not leaving you! Instead of joining the thick crowd out on the strip, let's watch the fireworks from the tram platform, and then go back to our suite," Khalil suggested.

"Perfect," Celeste replied. "Where's that music coming from? It's beautiful."

"I have no idea."

"Wow, a Black harpist!" Celeste whispered, stepping onto the platform where a beautiful young woman wearing a green velvet evening gown sat playing her harp. "How romantic! That Sonata is by Bach."

Khalil stood with his arms wrapped around Celeste watching the harpist, with other tourists. "Umm, I love your scent," Khalil said, kissing her neck.

"This is magical, with the Great Sphinx in the background!" Celeste beamed. "I hope to vacation in Egypt one day."

"Egypt is on the top of my list of travel destinations."

"I should have brought my phone and camera," Celeste complained. "A photojournalist should never be without her camera!"

"I'll ask that photographer if he can take some photos of us," Khalil suggested. Khalil approached the photographer and had a short conversation before returning to Celeste. "Okay, the photographer is gonna take some photos of us and send us the file."

"Let's stand with the Great Sphinx behind us," Celeste suggested, leading him by the hand. The couple posed with Celeste on Khalil's left.

"Turn this way," Khalil said, turning sideways to face her. "Celeste, you are my best friend and soulmate, a devoted mother and daughter, a humanitarian and gentle spirit, and the love of my life," he said, gently taking her left hand and dropping to one knee. "I wanna spend the rest of my life with you and Robert. Celeste Alexander, will you marry me?" he asked, presenting a beautiful marquise cut engagement ring.

Celeste stood immobilized by shock and blinded by flashing cameras and cell phones. The Vegas skyline began to spin around her, as her vision blurred with tears welling in her eyes. Gazing down at him momentarily she finally replied, "Yes, Khalil Sloane, I'll marry you." The small gathering of bystanders applauded, as Khalil put on her engagement ring. No longer able to fight back her tears, she wept.

Khalil stood up, kissed Celeste, and wiped her tears. "I love you, Baby. And I promise to take you on a cruise up the Nile River by our tenth anniversary."

"I love you too! I can't believe this!" Celeste whimpered.

Khalil handed Celeste a piece of paper from his wallet. "You're right! Writing down goals is powerful," Khalil smiled as she silently read, "Get Engaged to Celeste."

"This doesn't count! You had already planned your proposal when you wrote this, and you knew what my answer would be!"

Khalil laughed. "Let's go back to our suite. We can watch fireworks while relaxing in the soaking tub, drinking champagne."

"Good idea. I've gotta call Daddy and Robert," Celeste said excitedly.

"They already know," Khalil disclosed.

"What the hell?!"

"I asked your father for your hand in marriage Thanksgiving Day."

"I can't believe he kept that secret for over a month. Anybody else know?"

"My parents, Talib and Eli."

"Robert knows?" Celeste questioned, recoiling. "He can't keep a secret!"

"Your father talked to Robert about us getting married after you left for Vegas, and he's okay with it."

The couple floated through the lobby oblivious to other people and caught an elevator back to their corner suite where Khalil carried Celeste over the threshold.

"I love this hotel. This is the only place I wanna stay when we come to Vegas," Celeste declared. "There's some kind of energy vortex in this pyramid."

"Here," Khalil said, handing Celeste her phone out of the safe.

"Hello, Robert. Hello, Daddy," she said FaceTiming, holding up her engagement ring.

"She said, yes!" Khalil interrupted.

"Congratulations," Mr. Alexander beamed.

"Congrats!" Robert cheered.

"Both of you were wrong for not telling me! What if I was looking a mess? I would've chosen to prepare for my engagement!"

"We all wanted you to be surprised, and knew you would look beautiful, Princess," Mr. Alexander grinned. "Enjoy your evening!"

"Happy New Year!" Celeste cheered.

"Happy New Year, Mommy! Happy New Year, Khalil!"

"Happy New Year, Robert and Mr. Alexander."

"When are you coming home?" Robert inquired.

"Khalil and I will be there in two days. Let me call the Sullivans and Kennedy, with the good news!"

"Did you tell Auntie?" Robert asked.

"Not yet. I'll have to tell her tomorrow when she calls. She and Wade are still skiing."

"Okay, bye, Mommy!" Robert yelled.

"Goodbye, guys! See you soon!" Celeste said, ending the call. "Let me call Kennedy."

"Congrats!" Kennedy cheered, answering the phone. "Robert told me this morning!"

"I can't believe it! I'm engaged! I didn't have on any makeup, and I was ugly crying!"

"Where did he propose?"

"Outside on a platform with the Luxor Hotel Great Sphinx in the background. He hired a Black harpist, a photographer and a videographer. It was beautiful and romantic. We're getting ready to watch fireworks from our hotel suite."

"The twins, Robert and I have been watching the New York Times Square celebration. Your father just ran off to the Sullivans' party, trying to make it before midnight, probably eager to see Margaux Weaver."

"I think they like each other. They were so cute Thanksgiving."

"He might be trying to kiss her at the stroke of midnight!" Kennedy laughed with Celeste.

"Well, enjoy your evening!"

"Girlfriend, I'm getting ready to write my new year's resolutions and go to bed. These kids are about to pass out. Are you still gonna make our noon conference call?"

"Definitely. Bye. Love you."

"Love you too."

"Boo, I wanna make a video to send Bianca. She'll freak-out tomorrow when she turns on her phone to call us! Can you play *Love All Over Me*, by Monica, for my audio?"

"Sure, Baby," Khalil said, pulling it up on his phone.

"I'm just gonna make a video of my fingers dancing wearing my engagement ring!"

KINGS

The KING is the most important chess piece. The object of the game is to capture your opponent's king. He moves like the queen, but only one square at a time. Therefore, the king controls the squares surrounding him. The king captures by taking over the square occupied by an enemy piece. Castling is a unique move involving a rook and king, both of which have never moved. The king moves two squares towards one of its rooks on its first rank, and the rook moves to the square the king crossed.

KINGS

"Where are we meeting Bianca and Mrs. Sullivan?" Kennedy asked, standing in front of The Grove *Apple Store*.

"Bianca's meeting us here. She just parked," Celeste replied, looking at her phone.

"I need to stop in *American Girl Place* to get the twins a dress for each of their dolls."

"Let's take them there soon for tea and lunch, while their dolls get ears pierced and hair done in the doll salon," Celeste suggested.

"They'll love that!" Kennedy smiled.

"A girls day would be fun for them . . . for us. Try to get doll salon appointments and a lunch reservation for next Saturday."

"Celeste!" Bianca called out. Celeste and Bianca squealed when their eyes met, dashed into each other's arms, and exchanged double kisses. "Oh my God!" Bianca shrieked, inspecting her ring. "You're engaged!"

"I still can't believe it!" Celeste grinned, looking at her quivering left hand.

"How many karats?" Bianca asked. "Wade and I were shocked at the size."

"Three," Celeste proudly answered. "One karat each for me, Khalil and Robert."

"How romantic!" Bianca smiled. "Did you pick this marquise cut?"

"We never talked about marriage, no less wedding rings."

"That's crazy!" Bianca said. "Your favorite cut."

"He picked this cut because he thought it would look good on my long fingers."

"It's a unique design," Bianca acknowledged. "Beautiful!"

"Khalil designed it and made sure I'm not wearing a blood diamond."

"I'm so glad you're not moving to Chicago!" Bianca beamed.

"Me too! Robert and I would've been sad to leave."

"Hey, Girlfriend!" Bianca said, giving Kennedy a big hug.

"Welcome back!" Kennedy smiled. "How was your vacation?"

"Magnificent! Let's take photos by the water," Bianca suggested.

"Okay," Celeste agreed, sashaying towards the dancing fountains dressed in a royal blue Coco Chanel style jacket and skirt, white silk blouse and royal blue designer pumps.

"My makeup job is flawless!" Kennedy bragged, taking Celeste's phone.

"Is my hair okay?" Celeste asked, handing Bianca her camera.

"Everything is perfect!" Bianca said, picking Celeste's massive afro puff with her fingers. "You look stunning!"

"Thanks," Celeste smiled, striking a supermodel pose featuring her ring finger on her hip.

"You and Khalil have renewed my faith in love and Black men," Kennedy proclaimed.

"I'm thankful that Source brought Khalil into my life."

"These tourists are trying to decide if you're a celebrity!" Kennedy chuckled, while people walked by watching them. The ladies ended their photo shoot by asking a young lady to take pictures of them together.

"We'll meet Mom outside the Farmers Market in about fifteen minutes," Bianca said. "Too bad we don't have time for a drink. You know she's going to drive us crazy planning your wedding."

"I've got my weed pen!" Celeste revealed.

"Perfect!" Bianca smiled.

"And I'm not letting her take over my wedding!"

"How long is Khalil going to be here?" Bianca asked, leading the ladies next to the trolley car tracks.

"Two more weeks."

"What's he doing today?"

"House hunting with Daddy and Robert."

"Where are the twins?"

"With their father," Kennedy replied, astonishing Bianca. "We're co-parenting. They'll be with him on the weekends."

"What?!" Bianca asked.

"Pierce is a good father. I've gotta do what's best for the twins, even if it hurts."

"You've really switched stuff up for the new year," Bianca admired.

"And she has already registered for college," Celeste announced.

"Where are you going?"

"Santa Monica College, in the spring."

"Congratulations!" Bianca smiled. "When is the photo shoot business starting?"

"Damn! I just got back too!" Celeste complained. "We'll dedicate three hours per day to developing our business. Starting Monday, we'll be working on our business plan."

"How is Khalil going to qualify for a mortgage without a job?"

"He's gonna continue working in Chicago as a Campaign Advisor."

"Is he going to be in Chicago most of the time?" Bianca asked.

"Every other week. His boss knows that we're getting married and he's moving to L.A."

"Is he selling his condo?" Bianca inquired, stopping to look in the *Michael Kors* display window.

"No. We need somewhere to stay when he's working in Chicago."

"Then, how's he gonna afford another property?" Bianca probed.

"His brothers are selling one of their houses as a wedding gift. That should cover at least half the cost of our new home."

"How long is he gonna work in Chicago?" Kennedy asked.

"Through the 2018 midterm elections. Khalil wants to finish what he started in Chicago. Local and state elections are critical nationwide."

"Then, what?" Bianca asked, heading back down the street.

"He'll find a job working on a political campaign here in California."

"So, you're comfortable staying here while he's working in Chicago?" Kennedy asked incredulously.

"Absolutely, but Robert and I will often travel with him."

"How's Robert going to attend school, traveling all the time?" Bianca complained.

"We're homeschooling him next year."

"Oh my God! Have you told your father or my parents?"

"Told Daddy we were considering it."

"You know that's never going to fly! They want Robert attending UCLA by twelve!"

"Well, homeschooling is the fastest and easiest route to that goal!" Celeste snickered.

"That's not going to be a strong enough argument!" Bianca laughed.

"Homeschooling is the best way to be sure Robert develops a strong academic foundation. In addition, it will give Robert more bonding time with his new step-father."

"Getting stronger!" Bianca chuckled. "But you'll need much more than that! Print some studies to give them in a packet!"

"I'm not going through all that anymore!" Celeste chuckled.

"How does Robert feel about you getting married?" Bianca asked.

"He seems neutral about it, but you need to talk to him alone. I'm gonna get Robert some children's books about step-families. Probably should also get a book about alternative families. Might as well explain all the possible family structures."

"He's handling it well, but needs something fun to do," Kennedy recommended.

"Good idea," Bianca said. "I'll take him shopping for video games, and then home with me. And I'll tell Quentin and Wade to take Robert somewhere enjoyable so they can talk to him. Maybe a Lakers or Clippers game."

"How are we gonna develop our photo shoot business while you're traveling?"

"The same way you're gonna go to college and work on our business. All of our shoots will be on weekends, at least at first. I'll be home weekends, and you won't have classes."

"Let's find somewhere to smoke," Bianca requested.

"Do you mind if I make a quick stop in here?" Kennedy asked.

"Alright. Meet you back here," Celeste replied, standing in front of *American Girl Place*.

"We should walk around to the back side of the mall going towards the garage," Bianca recommended, leading the way.

"Definitely," Celeste said, following Bianca.

"Is Kennedy okay?"

"She's fine. Just trying to make positive changes in her life."

"I was flabbergasted when she vowed celibacy!"

"We'll see how long that last!" Celeste chuckled.

"Has she been going out?"

"Nope."

"Her eyes look sad."

"It can't be much fun for her watching my wedding plans."

"We'll find ways to keep her spirit uplifted."

"So, how was your vacation?" Celeste asked, taking a drag of the weed pen.

"Started off dreadful but turned out wonderful."

"Why did it start off dreadful?"

"I insisted Wade fire his secretary before we left. He felt I was unfair, especially during the holiday season, since they were not having an affair."

"Well, at least you confirmed that he's not cheating on you," Celeste said, handing Bianca the vape pen.

"The private investigator gave me photos of Wade leaving her house numerous times."

"Damn!"

"I confronted him. He frantically gave me excuses and lies, desperate to keep me from leaving him immediately."

"So, did you two work it out?"

"I guess," Bianca said, exhaling weed. "He worked hard to win back my heart!"

"I'm glad to hear that!" Celeste smiled.

"He's trading in my Prius and buying me a Tesla!"

"Oh, hell no! I'm so envious, I'm nauseous!" Celeste said, putting her hand on her chest.

"And he's building a studio for me in our loft, right now! You know he has been doing something wrong!" Bianca continued, taking a second hit and then handing Celeste the pen.

"Does he actually support you continuing your podcast?!"

"Yes! He thinks I have a great concept and need creative freedom. He says he just wants me to be happy."

"Wade was a great catch!"

"Are you sure Khalil's the right man for you?"

"He's perfect. I'm just overwhelmed," Celeste said, inhaling weed.

"How is he perfect?"

"He's street smart and book smart, trustworthy, kind, humorous, sexy, strong, protective and responsible. And what I love most about Khalil is that he is a *woke* Black man."

"Those are great characteristics, but what about his accomplishments?"

"Character is more important to me than accomplishments."

"Character is not enough," Bianca insisted.

"Why do Black men need to prove their worth through accomplishments rather than character?" Celeste asked, taking another drag.

"Because that's how we gauge success in this society."

"The playing field is not level. We're never on offense, where most points are made. Always on defense in response to the aggressions or actions of white people."

"Too bad. It's survival of the fittest. African American females need alpha males."

"Black women must stop determining a Black man's worth by evaluating his monetary value, and accomplishments in this discriminatory environment."

"African American men must be held to a higher standard. People rise to expectations."

"Black men are the most important resources of the Black community but rarely get recognition for their value," Celeste complained, handing Bianca the pen.

"African American men are key to thriving communities, strong marriages, healthy families and well-adjusted children," Bianca acknowledged, walking back towards the store to meet Kennedy. "They need accomplishments."

"Black men rarely get recognition for their accomplishments."

"Black men rarely do anything warranting recognition."

"Often when they do, the credit goes to someone else who's not Black."

"I know that feeling," Bianca replied. "But Black men must overcome obstacles."

"Khalil has plenty of accomplishments. He has never been in prison, is college educated, not addicted to anything, and still alive."

"Don't get all defensive about your man!" Bianca teased, exhaling weed.

"Significance is more important than recognition. Khalil matters to me and Robert," Celeste said sincerely. "And his work is significant in the pursuit of a better world."

"I've got to make sure you've thought this through. And you know Mom is going to cross-examine you."

"I hate having to defend Khalil."

"He's lucky to have found you."

"I've got a child, no job, and live with my father. I'm a real catch!" Celeste scoffed.

"Yes, you are! You're beautiful, smart and devoted."

"Oh, so all I need is good characteristics, but he needs to acquire shit."

"Don't get the game twisted. Females are the prize, the prey. Males are predators. Their identity is tied to conquests."

"Black men are kings. Unfortunately, most of them don't know it," Celeste complained.

"They suffer from PTSD."

"Every Black person that goes to see a doctor for a medical marijuana recommendation should automatically get one just for being Black. All Black people are dealing with trauma."

"We're going to have to find a way to heal our traumas instead of medicating them," Bianca said, taking one last drag of the pen and passing it to Celeste.

"We've gotta uncover our emotional traumas and acknowledge the damage."

"I don't consider myself damaged," Bianca declared.

"How can a person be Black and not be psychologically damaged by this society?"

"We've all been harmed by others, but some of us keep it moving just to spite bigots."

"Black men are often unproductive because they're alpha males."

"Then they are too alpha to survive," Bianca mocked.

"It's practically impossible for any alpha male to accept domination, for any length of time, to earn money or pursue goals."

"Some men are desensitized to our society. They're outsiders with no value, and their efforts are pointless."

"So you think Black men should learn to assimilate, so they can participate?" Celeste asked, choking on smoke.

"They need to play the game well enough to survive. Thriving in the game leads to freedom."

"Woke Black men find it difficult to submissively play the racist games of this society."

"They will never be recognized as worthy human beings if they don't," Bianca warned.

"Worthy of what?"

"Worthy of being seen and treated as equal Americans. They need to bring something to the table."

"Which table? The Black family or white society?"

"American Society."

"My first concern is survival of the Black family."

Kennedy emerged from the store carrying an *American Girl* shopping bag. "Where to?"

"Mom is meeting us by the Farmers Market entrance," Bianca replied, leading the way.

"There are no appointments available until the first week of February and nothing on the weekends," Kennedy said. "I should have booked salon appointments when I bought the dolls."

"We should have known the salon would be busy after the holidays," Celeste moaned.

"I'm disappointed," Kennedy sighed, watching giggling children board the trolley car.

"There's Donovan's low-rider!" Kennedy squealed, spotting her brother's car amongst the floats and vehicles preparing to start the parade.

"Which one?" Bianca asked, holding the twins by the hand, while they jumped and pointed at their uncle's car.

"The purple convertible with the dancers around it," Kennedy said, waving to the troupe.

"Let me take some photos of you with the car and dancers," Celeste requested.

"Okay," Kennedy replied, joining the dancers for some animated photos with the twins, sitting on the car.

"Donating his car to the dance troupe was a great idea," Celeste smiled. "Keeping his spirit alive in the neighborhood, and supporting your passion for dance."

"It feels good contributing to the community. I'd like to get more involved with the dance troupe."

"Your brother would be proud of your decision," Bianca said, holding Robert's hand.

"Donovan would have been honored to see his beloved low-rider in the *Kingdom Day Parade*," Kennedy said, gazing at the car with her twins in hand.

"How do you feel seeing it back on the road?" Celeste asked.

"My heart aches. I miss my brother."

"Sorry for your loss," Celeste replied.

"Too many folks in the hood don't respect life," Kennedy agonized.

"Because they don't believe their own lives matter," Bianca responded.

"Being Black is potentially deadly," Kennedy sighed. "Law enforcement *and* Black folks threaten our lives."

"Let's head towards the judging area," Bianca said, leading the way.

"People living in ghettos are probably targeted much more often by law enforcement than in other areas," Celeste considered.

"There's more crime in ghettos, attracting more law enforcement and surveillance of people. Maybe they aren't actually being targeted, but rather being protected," Bianca offered.

"How do we ensure the survival of Black people, without violence?" Kennedy asked.

"Move out of ghettos or transform them," Celeste stated. "Location, location, location!"

"It doesn't appear safe outside the ghetto either," Kennedy argued. "We're racially profiled in white neighborhoods. Remember that Harvard professor? He was harassed and arrested for trying to break into his own house!"

"Henry Louis Gates, Jr.," Celeste identified. "He's also a literary scholar and the host of the PBS special, *Finding Your Roots*."

"That's how Black guys, with nice cars, use to be treated!" Kennedy said. "White folks automatically assumed they were drug dealers or auto thieves!"

"They still are, just not in Cali," Celeste reported. "Too many wealthy Black celebrities, athletes, entertainers, doctors, lawyers, and entrepreneurs here."

"There are no safe zones for African Americans of any social status," Bianca complained. "The belief that wealth will increase our safety is an illusion for our people."

"Ghettos are the most dangerous places for Black people," Celeste insisted. "More racial profiling in ghettos, and abuse by law enforcement without accountability. Thugs and hoodlums don't have the balls, brains or resources to go into neighborhoods where they could actually steal something of value. They victimize their own people, not those hurting them."

"If all Black people move out of ghettos, wherever they end up will shortly become ghettos. They bring down property values," Bianca replied.

"People living in ghettos have no investment in their environment. They think of their domiciles as grungy properties owned by slumlords, and treat them that way," Celeste explained. "We've gotta clean up ghettos and turn them into Black Wall Streets."

"The slumlords, who are rarely Black, usually don't live in the neighborhood."

"Black people don't understand the value of homeownership," Bianca sighed.

"Black people living in ghettos can't afford to purchase homes, or do the necessary upgrades to make them decent places to live and raise families."

"There's no fixing ghettos," Kennedy persisted.

"White people do it all the time," Bianca enlightened. "It's call *gentrification*."

"We must stop allowing white people to steal our neighborhoods, and start building our own communities of wealth and abundance," Celeste said. "We need at least one Black Wall Street in every state."

"Who's going to build them?" Bianca questioned.

"Rich Blacks need to invest in the renewal of our neighborhoods," Kennedy declared.

"Affluent African Americans did not fight their way out of the ghetto to return with money," Bianca scoffed.

"They don't have to live there!" Kennedy replied. "Just don't be slumlords, or desert your people."

"We can't clean up ghettos until we clear our minds of the propaganda for white supremacy," Celeste insisted. "We've gotta wake the fuck up!"

"Ooh, Auntie! You said a bad word!" China reported.

"Stop snitching!" Kennedy reprimanded.

"Stop cursing around the kids!" Bianca scolded, pulling Robert close to her.

"Sorry, everybody! I got a little upset," Celeste said, holding up her hands defensively, wearing a black and white *I'm a Superhero, Not a Princess* tee, with black Levi jeans and Nikes.

"You're looking real combative right now! Stop frightening my nephew and the twins!"

"Especially with your afro bursting from that African headwrap!" Kennedy teased.

"Where's Khalil?" Bianca asked.

"In Atlanta speaking at a *King Day* celebration."

"What's he speaking about?"

"Revolution."

"Mommy, who's the king?" Robert asked.

"Martin Luther King, Jr.," Celeste replied. "This parade is to celebrate his birthday."

"Where is he?" China asked, looking around.

"He's not here," Kennedy said. "Somebody killed him."

"Somebody killed my uncle," India sulked.

"Why do people kill people?" Robert asked.

"Because they're afraid," Celeste answered.

"Afraid of what?" Robert wondered.

"People they don't know and things they don't understand," Celeste explained. "They're afraid someone might try to hurt them or take something away from them."

"Why were they afraid of the king?" Robert probed.

"Because he wanted people to stop hurting other people," Celeste replied.

Robert stood there looking at his mother, clearly confused.

"Only mean people kill people!" Bianca interrupted.

"Hurt people, hurt people," Kennedy added.

"Are mean people trying to kill us?" Robert inquired.

"No! No one wants to hurt us!" Bianca exclaimed. "Let's go get your faces painted and some balloons before the parade begins."

Kennedy and the twins, with Celeste trailing behind, followed Bianca and Robert. Bianca got the children seated with face painters and joined their mothers in the waiting area.

"Chill around those sweet innocent babies!" Bianca demanded, shoving Celeste gently.

"Alright! But they need to know the truth."

"You getting ready to tell them about Santa Claus, the Easter Bunny and the Tooth Fairy?" Bianca inquired.

"What can they do with the truth?" Kennedy questioned. "We've gotta fight for their childhood innocence."

"Black children must be able to detect danger in this bigoted society," Celeste warned. "No different than teaching them about *stranger danger*."

"Technology is crippling children's development of skills to detect dangerous people or situations, by limiting their face-to-face interactions," Bianca added. "There are small changes, we notice subconsciously, in the facial muscles and body language of people who aren't being truthful and are possibly dangerous. All newborn animals learn to analyze faces."

"I guess our kids are only safe at home, in this racist country," Kennedy sighed.

"Learn how to interact with bigots, without exciting them to violence," Bianca suggested.

"Sounds like the Willie Lynch playbook for training slave wenches to teach pickaninnies obedience to the white man," Celeste scoffed.

"It's a shame we have to teach our children how to speak and behave, in order to stay alive, when dealing with law enforcement, regardless of the situation," Kennedy despaired. "White kids can do whatever. Rich white women can curse out the police and assault them with their purses!"

"Start with survival, and then strive for a better life," Bianca advised.

"Make our neighborhoods safe havens."

"What about surviving Black on Black crime?" Kennedy asked.

"Happens mostly in Black neighborhoods," Bianca informed them. "Get out!"

"The Black community is responsible for protecting our people," Celeste declared.

"We need more organizations like *Black Lives Matter* and the *Black Panther Party*."

"Law-abiding groups that can't be obstructed or tainted, not vigilantes," Bianca amended.

"Any gathering of *The Blacks*, to converse instead of play ball or sing and dance for Massa, must be examined and is consider a possible threat to white supremacy," Celeste scoffed. "Just like back during slavery!"

"All Black people should know their legal rights," Kennedy affirmed.

"Are you prepared for law school?!" Bianca questioned.

"Our rights as citizens of this country should be clear, consistent with the rights of others, and upheld by our government," Celeste stated. "We shouldn't need to take classes, but we do."

"Knowing your legal rights won't stop you from being killed by police," Bianca warned.

"Learning to be compliant with law enforcement and non-threatening doesn't ensure survival either," Celeste countered.

"We've gotta be compliant, but we should at least know when our human and civil rights are being violated," Kennedy insisted.

"We cannot adapt to abuse," Celeste warned. "I don't have Stockholm syndrome."

"For now, we are dependent on our oppressors," Bianca replied.

"Black people must learn to support and depend on each other and our community, if we are ever to experience harmony and peace in our lives."

"We've gotta get back to village mentality," Kennedy added.

"We've gotta start believing in ourselves," Celeste stated.

"We need skills to defend ourselves," Kennedy responded.

"Everyone including toddlers, children and the elderly should be learning Capoeira," Celeste suggested. "You can't always reach a weapon. Make your body a weapon."

"What's that?" Kennedy asked.

"An Afro-Brazilian style of martial arts used by slaves. It combined music, dance and acrobatics to conceal their development of martial arts skills."

"We shouldn't teach or promote violence," Bianca opposed.

"Skills in martial arts should be developed for self-defense not attack," Celeste explained.

"Understanding and being able to use psychology and sociology to avoid confrontations is also a necessary skill," Bianca added. "Make your mind a weapon."

"We can't do that until we change our minds about who we are," Celeste said. "Warriors."

"Black people need leaders," Kennedy grumbled.

"The number one tactic of white supremacy is eliminating Black leaders."

"They are either killed, discredited or scared into becoming reclusive," Bianca added.

"We've gotta protect our men," Celeste said. "We hold the power."

"How are we suppose to do that?" Kennedy asked.

"Create a rejuvenating environment that keeps our men strong, motivated and believing in their abilities. Make sure they get proper nutrition, sleep, exercise, and unconditional love. Be their refuge from this racist world, supportive, encouraging, and grateful for their presence in our lives."

"Who's gonna protect Black women?" Kennedy inquired.

"Strong, intelligent, *woke* Black men," Celeste declared.

"Martin Luther King, Jr. was the most important leader of the civil rights movement," Kennedy stated. "Who do we have like that now?"

"MLK, Jr. was the most visible spokesperson, but the civil rights movement didn't end with his death," Bianca clarified.

"Leaders from our generation are starting to emerge in all Black communities," Celeste revealed. "Conditions will improve."

"I'm going to get Robert and the twins," Bianca said, leaving them in the waiting area.

The twins skipped along in front of Bianca holding hands, while Robert and Bianca strolled behind them. A man approached Bianca, looked her up and down seductively, and greeted her. Robert stuck out his tongue, and Bianca rolled her eyes as they kept walking.

"You two are so mean!" Celeste scolded. "Why were you rude to that guy?"

"Auntie has a husband!" Robert shouted, holding a blue balloon.

"He needs to be more respectful of African American females!" Bianca complained. "Coming at me like I'm a piece of meat!"

"Wow, Black males and females still have a long way to go," Celeste fretted.

"At least he was open to a woman with three kids!" Kennedy joked.

"Yeah, right!" Celeste laughed.

"Be careful what you tolerate. You're teaching people how to treat you."

"I've never bothered to come to this celebration before," Kennedy said. "It's great for the community. Have either of you been here before?"

"Nope," Celeste replied.

"Me neither," Bianca responded.

"I hope to get some great portfolio photos," Celeste said, taking photos of Robert and the twins with their faces painted.

"Our Crenshaw District celebration is supposed to be the best in SoCal."

"How is your coffee table book coming?" Bianca asked.

"Being printed. It has been hard keeping it a secret from Khalil!" Celeste chuckled.

"Khalil doesn't let her out of his site for more than a few hours!" Kennedy laughed. "He wants to know everything she's doing!"

"Because he thinks I'm only working on wedding plans. He's trying to be supportive and involved."

"Luckily, you started working on your photobook before Christmas."

"Let's find our seats," Bianca suggested.

"I'm glad Mom got us this hookup. We'll have a birdseye view of the parade, and all the floats will stop right in front of us."

"Looks like the parade is about to begin," Bianca said, taking India's hand.

"Okay," Kennedy replied, following behind, holding China's hand.

"Stay together," Celeste warned, taking a firm hold of Robert.

The ladies and children made their way through a multicultural sea of dancing Angelinos, as the grand marshal, Congresswoman Maxine Waters, began the parade.

"My homegirl, Congresswoman Maxine Waters was great," Celeste stated. "In fact, all of the speakers have been eloquent."

"Let me take some pictures of my snow bunny," Khalil said, backing up to take photos of Celeste, in the pink swarm of women on the National Mall.

"Take one with the National Monument behind me," Celeste requested, dressed in a pink *Women's March on Washington* tee, black ski pants, pink ski jacket, black scarf, and pink *Pussyhat* covering her two afro puffs.

"Smile, Baby."

"I don't feel like smiling!" Celeste pouted, slumped over looking at her pink Ugg boots destroyed by mud. "The election was stolen from Hillary!"

"Don't look so miserable, Baby!" Khalil pleaded.

Celeste forced a quick smile. "This place is haunted. Slaves were traded right here."

"Come here, Baby," he said, pulling her close to him, tucking her cartouche under her tee and hugging her.

"I can't believe I live in a reality were racism and sexism are still in power," she sighed, resting her head on his chest.

"As you can see, bigotry is no longer gonna be tolerated," Khalil said, looking around.

"I just wanna scream and go berserk on bigots! I wanna see groups of women physically, mentally, emotionally and financially stomp out all unevolved men. Fuck this dumb ass shit!"

"You can't bug out," he cautioned, leading her by the hand. "We've gotta stay calm, and execute strategies and tactics to disarm the enemy."

"This turnout is incredible. We must have broken some record."

"Women know how to organize and rally together. Don't provoke them."

"The Million Man March must have been spectacular and inspiring."

"My father brought me, and my brothers, here to the march. I'll never forget all the Black men holding up dollar bills. We were actually looking at over one million dollars."

"Everybody held up dollar bills?"

"Every man held up at least one dollar. And if a brother didn't have a dollar, another brother gave him one. Solidarity."

"I'm thrilled to see women of all ethnicities and religions gathered here in solidarity, but where are our male supporters?"

"Many men have no idea what y'all are protesting. They think this is some girly stuff."

"Oh . . . my . . . God! How is that even possible? Women are just white noise to men!"

"Not all men."

"We're here advocating policies and legislation regarding human rights, not just women's rights. We're fighting for healthcare, environmental issues, racial equality, religious freedom, immigration reform, and workers' rights, all of which also impact the lives of men."

"Most men didn't know they were wanted or welcomed at this march."

"That's no excuse for Black men not standing beside us, supporting and protecting us. They should've cared enough about us to at least ask."

"Many Black men don't understand that Black women are our most powerful assets," Khalil offered. "And most Black women aren't aware of the power they possess."

"Are Black people loyal to anyone or anything, or did slavery and centuries of oppression edit that from our genome?"

"Black folks are faithful to white supremacy," Khalil declared. "They spend all their time and money trying to prove their white worth."

"Black women deserve the loyalty of Black men simply for birthing them. How can you hate that which you come from, that which you are?"

"*Woke* Black men not only have an allegiance to our women but love and cherish them."

"Too many of our men don't respect us. We are not the help! We're queens supporting kings and raising children in a menacing world."

"Black women are for *woke* Black men."

"We need *all* of our men. Black men are critical to the survival of the Black family."

"Black women, nurturing the next generation, are critical to the evolution of our people."

"I really wanted to work here making a difference," Celeste complained, entering a vendor area.

"We can still move here," Khalil considered.

"I would never live here, now that Rome is falling."

"I want you and Robert to stay near your father."

"I want you to be happy and inspired where you live," Celeste said, giving him a kiss.

"I like California."

"Can we make a significant difference living in Cali? Californians are so progressive. We need to reach people in other repressive states."

"We can make a difference wherever we live, or join a national campaign. There's work to do everywhere."

"What should we do in L.A.?"

"When I finish with my political commitments, I wanna get involved in the renovation of old and construction of new Black neighborhoods."

"In addition to homes, we need schools, libraries, grocery stores with healthy food, free outdoor public areas and playgrounds surrounded by nature, medical facilities with the latest technologies, and professional office buildings."

"And we've gotta attract Black doctors and mental health professionals, counselors, educators, and mentors. Most importantly, we need Black-owned banks."

"Sounds like you've been listening to Dr. Umar Johnson again," Celeste chuckled.

"That brother is trying to liberate our black asses! People hate on him because he's harsh with the truth."

"White folks are offended by him, but he also be hurting Black people's feelings!"

"We think we're woke, but we're still asleep in most areas. Our oppression and white supremacy is insidiously weaved deep into this society. Black folks shouldn't be offended by a strong, intelligent Black man enlightening us."

"Do you agree with everything he says?"

"Don't need to. I support anybody Black trying to enlighten and liberate Black folks."

"He alienates Black people in interracial relationships. We need to bring folks back to our community, not drive them further away."

"They'll be back. White folks will eventually remind them that they're still just Niggas."

"Dr. Umar Johnson also ostracizes the LGBTQ community."

"I don't care about the sexual preferences of other people, as long as my children are heterosexual. I intend to have grandchildren."

"Oh my God! You're ridiculous!"

"Whatever!" Khalil replied. "Let's find something to bring Robert, that's not pink!"

"I also wanna get tees for Kennedy, the twins, Bianca and Mom."

"Let's get some hot chocolate, and then pick up our souvenirs."

"Okay," Celeste said, following Khalil. "Will Black people ever understand the necessity to be loyal to our community?"

"Injustice and abuse are waking folks up. Our survival is at stake."

"Black people didn't understand that not voting for Hillary Clinton was a vote *for* the continuation of our oppression."

"Hillary Clinton couldn't have helped Black folks, no matter how much she wanted to. Strong support for white supremacy and white nationalism was revealed in the election. Folks need to listen to the Prince of Pan-Afrikanism explain why all elected U.S. officials are controlled by white supremacists."

"This sea of activists gives me hope that human beings are learning loyalty to the only race, the human race."

"This openly racist and bigoted society is actually strengthening the loyalty of Black folks to each other and our community."

After spending almost an hour shopping, Khalil followed Celeste as she photographed the event. "Are you shooting color or black-and-white?" he asked.

"Definitely color. You know I'm a Pink Princess!"

"What are you gonna do with these photos?"

"Maybe a photo essay or include them in a photobook," Celeste contemplated.

"You can probably sell them immediately to news outlets."

"Not interested."

"Mainstream media should be more receptive to women's issues than it was to racial injustice."

"I doubt it. Mainstream media is plagued with sexism. Let's move closer to the stage," Celeste suggested.

When the mothers of African Americans slain by law enforcement were acknowledged on stage, Celeste and Khalil joined the crowd chanting each of their names. "Baby, you okay?" he asked, wiping tears from her eyes.

"Women are the creative power on this blue planet. Men are the destructive force."

"Destruction clears space for something new. You need both destruction and creation."

"Yin/Yang. Dichotomy."

"Matter is neither created nor destroyed. Only the form changes."

"Women are God expressed in human form. We bring forth life."

"Men are also God expressed in human form, here to handle the dirty work."

Celeste turned towards the stage when she heard Angela Davis being announced as the next speaker. "My idol!" she squealed, as the crowd erupted into cheers. "I am a Black

Revolutionary Woman!" Celeste avowed, looking into Khalil's eyes.

"I am a Revolutionary," he responded, studying the joy in hers.

"Fred Hampton," she smiled approvingly.

"This is your last protest. You're gonna be a wife, mother and homemaker soon!"

"You best believe I'll be at every national women's protest against this administration!" Celeste vowed. "You'll be home babysitting!"

"You're so fiery!" Khalil chuckled knowingly, standing behind her in his black leather car coat holding her in his arms. "I'll be with you."

CHECK

The object of the game is to capture your opponent's king. A king that is attacked, and consequently in danger of being captured on the next move, is said to be in CHECK.

CHECK

Khalil and Celeste were sitting up in bed nude, with the white top sheet covering them from the waist down and the comforter balled up at the foot of the bed. Celeste, with her light-brown natural hair on top of her head in a large afro puff, was lying back between his legs against his chest full of wavy hair. Khalil relaxed against the headboard with his arms wrapped around her breast. "Happy Valentine's Day, Baby," Khalil said, kissing Celeste on the cheek.

"Happy Valentine's Day, Boo!" she responded, turning her head to kiss his lips.

"Where would you like to go for breakfast? Or would you rather order room service?"

"What are we doing today?"

"Having lunch in the Grand Canyon."

"Really?!" Celeste asked, grinning from ear to ear in disbelief.

"Yes, Baby."

"How are we getting there?"

"We're going on the *Grand Canyon Super Deluxe Airplane and Helicopter Tour*," he said, reading a pamphlet from his nightstand. "We'll have lunch on a Native American reservation."

"How big is the plane?"

"Seats 20, including the pilot," Khalil said, handing Celeste the pamphlet.

"Aerial views of the Hoover Dam and the Grand Canyon! I'm gonna get some magnificent landscape photos! How exciting! Let's order room service so we can relax before our flight."

"Sorry for keeping you up so late. A shower will rejuvenate us," he suggested.

"Let me call home first. I've never missed a Valentine's Day with Robert, and Kennedy is probably feeling lonely."

"Okay," Khalil said, handing Celeste her phone.

Celeste made a call home. "Happy Valentine's Day, Sweetheart!"

"Happy Valentine's Day, Mommy! I love you!"

"I love you too!"

"Are you in the pyramid?"

"Yes. We're staying at the Luxor Hotel again."

"Where's Khalil?"

"Right here. I'll put you on speaker phone."

"Hi, Khalil."

"Hey, Robert. Happy Valentine's Day."

"Happy Valentine's Day."

"Do you have a girlfriend?"

Robert was silent for awhile. "*Hello?*" Celeste asked. "You better not have a girlfriend!"

Robert began giggling. "He can have a girlfriend! Obviously, girls are gonna like him," Khalil protested. "He's handsome, smart, athletic and fun."

"Do you have a girlfriend?" Celeste insisted.

"Yeah," Robert admitted, giggling.

"What? Who is she?" she demanded.

"Leave him alone!" Khalil insisted.

"We'll talk about this when I get home!"

Robert continued giggling.

"Where's your Grandpa?"

"Right here."

"Happy Valentine's Day, Daddy!"

"Happy Valentine's Day, Princess. Are you and Khalil enjoying your vacation?"

"Yes. He's taking me to the Grand Canyon today!"

"Wonderful!"

"Hey, Mr. Alexander."

"Hello, Khalil. You enjoying yourself?"

"I'm always good when I'm with Celeste."

"You two have a great day. I'm getting ready to take Robert to school. He's got a gift for his girlfriend and cards for his classmates."

"What gift?" Celeste asked.

"A heart-shaped box of chocolate candy and a candy bracelet."

"When we get home, we'll be having a family meeting. All three of you guys are crazy. Robert is not having a girlfriend!"

Robert, Khalil and Mr. Alexander laughed.

"Talk to you later. Love you!" Celeste said, hanging up.

"You can't keep Robert to yourself forever!" Khalil teased.

"Whatever!" she said, elbowing him. "Let me call Kennedy."

Celeste got out of bed and walked across the room, with Khalil watching her every move, put on a robe and plopped down on the sofa to make her call. Khalil got out of bed, with Celeste watching him, and disappeared into the shower.

"Happy Valentine's Day!" Celeste said when Kennedy answered the phone.

"Happy Valentine's Day," Kennedy responded. "Thank you for the card and purse."

"How are you? How are the twins?"

"The twins are fine. I just dropped them off at school. Their class is having a party this afternoon. Robert and the twins were up late making cards for their classmates."

"What about you?"

"I'm really depressed. Everybody in our house is enjoying Valentine's Day but me. Even your father has a date."

"What?! Who?"

"I don't know. He asked me to babysit Robert this evening because he's going out."

"Oh, shit! I just talked to him, and he didn't mention anything about that to me!"

"Your father found a few apartments for me to look at in Westside."

"When are you going?"

"Thursday and Friday."

"I can go with you on Friday if you like."

"Definitely."

"Then, I can catch you up on my vacation."

"Is Khalil coming home with you?"

"Yes. He'll be staying ten days to look at houses and take care of some business."

"How's your day going?"

"We just got up and are getting ready to have breakfast in the room."

"What did Khalil get you for Valentine's Day?"

"Nothing. This trip to Vegas."

"Maybe, he'll surprise you later."

"I don't need anything. I've got him."

"Did you give him his gift yet?"

"No. I'm getting ready to put it on the bed while he's in the shower."

"Did you wrap it?"

"Nope. Let's see how long it takes for him to realize it's my book."

"He's gonna be stunned when he finds out you're an author."

"I can't wait to see his face. Please put Robert's copy on his bed before he goes to sleep. And put Daddy's coffee table book on his nightstand while he is out on his date."

"Okay," Kennedy replied. "Have you talked to Bianca?"

"Not yet. I'll call her after we have breakfast."

"What are y'all doing today?"

"Not much. Going to the casino. Sitting by the pool."

"What are your plans?"

"I'm getting a massage and mani-pedi."

"What? *You* . . . getting a massage?"

"Girl, I'm stressed!"

"That's right! Pamper *yourself* for Valentine's Day! Get yourself some candy and flowers for your room."

"Later, I'm taking the twins and Robert out to dinner."

"Where are you taking them?"

"The Spaghetti Factory."

"Oh, they'll love that."

"Then I'll come home and watch *The Notebook* . . . and cry myself to sleep."

"I promise you'll find true love. Please don't be sad!" Celeste pleaded. "I love you!"

"Love you too."

"I'm gonna jump in the shower, but I'll check on all of you later."

"Okay, bye."

"Hey, Boo," Celeste said, dropping her robe outside the shower.

"I've been waiting for you," Khalil replied, moving aside so she could join him.

"Kennedy is having a tough day. I feel so bad about not being there for her. She has never been single on Valentine's Day."

"I'm sure she wouldn't want you to miss Valentine's Day for her," he responded, allowing Celeste to get under the shower head.

"You're right," she said, turning around to wet her whole body.

"Kennedy will meet the right guy when she least expects it."

"Love is pain," Celeste replied, putting her face in the stream of water.

"For me, love is peace. You find our love painful?" Khalil asked, perplexed.

"It is when we aren't together," she answered, putting on body scrub gloves. "I ache for you."

"I miss you too. Now, it's hard for me to sleep without you," he said, washing her back. "I redirect that energy towards creating a life with you."

"If we get divorced, we will experience heartbreak. If we stay married, when one of us dies, the other one will be in pain."

"We're not getting divorced, and gonna take this life journey together. When it ends, I'll be thankful for the precious time we spent together . . . with no regrets."

"Losing my mother, and my failed relationship with Robert's father are still painful."

"Do you still have anger towards Robert's father?" Khalil asked.

"No, but I don't respect him because he is not a man of his word. The heartache is about Robert not having a father. My disappointment is for Robert."

"Robert is not missing that *fuck boy*! Robert has your father."

"I know Robert is blessed to have my father, Dr. Sullivan, Quentin and now you as positive Black male role models, who love and invest time in him."

"I'll provide everything you and Robert need, including love," Khalil vowed, spanking Celeste, before stepping out of the shower. "I'm gonna order breakfast, Baby. What do you want?"

"An omelet and hash browns. What are you having?"

"Waffles," Khalil replied, exiting the bathroom.

"And a mimosa, please!" Celeste yelled.

Khalil was gone for several minutes before returning to the bathroom. "Baby!" he shouted, joining her again in the shower. "Wow! You got published!" he continued, holding her in his arms, kissing all over her face. "The only problem is the last name!"

"I started publishing that photobook before we got engaged! At least I'll have one book in my maiden name to honor my father and son."

"What did your father and Robert say about your book?"

"They don't know yet. They'll find out tonight."

"This photobook should be on the coffee table of every *woke* Black family."

"Wouldn't that be wonderful."

"Do Bianca and Kennedy know about it yet?"

"They've been involved from the beginning. Everything was kept in Kennedy's room."

"Oh, that's why you kept hanging out in her room! I thought you were running off to get a break from me!"

"Ain't nobody scared of you!"

"Let's get the celebration started!" he said, getting out of the shower.

"I'll be finished in a few minutes."

"I'm so proud of you, Baby!" Khalil smiled, looking in the mirror about to shave.

"I'm so thankful for you and my father, who provide stability in my life allowing me to pursue my dreams."

"We love you!"

"Stability is more important than love," Celeste said, stepping out of the shower. "Stability is certainty, predictability, all needs met."

"Security, being safe and risk-free, is more important than stability, but not more important than love," Khalil countered, handing her a towel.

"Safety is a component of stability," she replied. "You can't feel stable without being safe."

"As a Black man, my number one priority is the safety of my family."

"Should a Black woman choose a man who she loves, one who can protect her, or one who can provide stability in her life?"

"Black women deserve it all. A Black woman can find a man who loves her, will protect her with his life, and one who will find a way to provide all of their necessities."

"Sounds like a fantasy world," she replied, gazing at the towel wrapped around his waist.

"Black women have to stop wasting time with worthless brothers."

"Black women can see the king trying to emerge from our oppressed and depressed men. We believe in them, and they constantly let us down."

"Have I let you down?" he asked, looking into her eyes through the mirror.

"Never."

"Are you confident that I love you and would do nothing to damage our relationship? That I can and will protect and provide for you and Robert?"

"Of course."

"There are plenty more Black men just like me. I'm not a unicorn."

"You might not be a unicorn, but you are an endangered species," Celeste responded, wrapping her towel around her body.

"The *Black Lives Matter* movement is spreading throughout the Black community."

"Black people must first learn to love themselves before meaningful, loving changes can be made to family, community, country, species, planet," Celeste said, taking her hair down and picking out her afro.

"I actually see the number of *woke* Black men rising. Everybody needs unconditional love, and more Black men are starting to find peace in the arms of a Black woman."

"Love is desirable, but not necessary."

"Not necessary for what?" Khalil asked, following Celeste out of the bathroom.

"For survival."

"Love is necessary to feel alive. You've taught me that love is all that matters."

"I'm lucky to have found you. Unfortunately, most Black women will never experience a committed relationship with a Black man. We have the lowest marriage rate in this country."

"Hopefully, that changes soon . . . to save the Black family and our community."

"Black men don't commit to Black women. They commit to women of other nationalities. They impregnate Black women, and either cheat on them or leave them, but rarely marry them."

"I've committed to you, and I'm gonna marry you. As a Neanderthal, I definitely intend to get you pregnant," Khalil declared, picking Celeste up and throwing her onto the bed.

"Stop playing!" she giggled.

"You my Baby Mama!" Khalil insisted, laying on top of Celeste, trying to bite her neck.

"You're so silly!" she said, laughing and squirming. "Get off of me!"

"Remove this towel!" he replied, pulling her towel open.

"I thought you were taking me to the Grand Canyon?"

"Alright, alright," Khalil said, rolling off her.

"You ready to have a baby?" Celeste asked, re-wrapping her towel.

"Naw, Robert and I need at least a year to develop our relationship. I wanna give him my undivided attention. But I'm ready whenever you are."

"I haven't really thought about it. But no time soon. First, we've gotta get settled into our life together."

"You've turned my life into an adventure," he said, staring at the ceiling. "Love feels good."

"How do you define love?" she asked.

"Love is the merging of the emotions of pleasure and trust."

"Love is joy in my heart and faith in my partner. I'm gonna keep following my joy."

"Love is peace in my mind, body and soul," Khalil said, playing with the golden-brown ends of her afro curls.

"Love is a verb, not a noun. It's an action, not an object."

There was a knock at the door. "Room service is quick this morning. Can you get the door?"

"No, you get it! I'm not dressed, either."

"Here. Put on my robe. I'm gonna finish up in the bathroom so I can eat with you."

"Okay, Boo," Celeste said, heading for the door. "Oh my God!" she squealed, opening the door to several bouquets of flowers and a card from Khalil.

"Oh my God! This place is amazing!" Kennedy exclaimed, turning around looking in every direction.

"Another hidden Malibu treasure," Celeste said, leading Kennedy along the meandering path through the beautiful meditation garden of blooming flowers, at the Self-Realization Fellowship Lake Shrine.

"Spring has sprung!"

"The first day of spring is tomorrow."

"These flowers are so fragrant!"

"Some of Gandhi's ashes are buried here," Celeste announced, taking photos. "How do you and the twins like your new apartment?"

"I finished setting up the rooms. The girls love the bunk beds your father bought them."

"How are you doing?"

"Nights were hard the first week, so I was up late organizing our stuff. I'm just now starting to enjoy having my own place."

"How's school?"

"Demanding but I'll survive. The twins and I like doing homework together. Hopefully, I'll teach a free weekly ballet class, this fall for young girls, at the community center in my old neighborhood, and include the twins."

"You and the twins should come spend next weekend with us. We have a lot of wedding errands. Daddy and Khalil can babysit and have a barbeque contest."

"I'm sure the twins would love that. They miss Robert, Zeus, and the pool. How is the house hunting going?"

"Today, Khalil, Daddy and Robert are going back to the two houses they like best."

"Have you seen either of them?"

"No. I'm not gonna see our house until we move in."

"Do you at least know the area?"

"Nope."

"This is crazy! What if you hate the house or the neighborhood?"

"I trust my father and Khalil."

"Obviously, you won't be in your house before the wedding."

"Khalil vows we'll be in our house on our wedding night. He's gonna make an offer on one of those houses tomorrow."

"That's a lot to do in a month."

"I agree, but Khalil is determined to make it happen. His focus is on our house. My focus is on our wedding."

"What about a honeymoon?"

"We're going to Jamaica! It's our gift from the Sullivans."

"Hedonism?"

"You know it!"

"At least we don't have to shop for your honeymoon! You two will never have to put on clothes!" Kennedy giggled with Celeste.

"I just need a couple of new bikinis. You know Khalil ain't gonna be sitting around outside naked. And he's already told me he doesn't want me running around topless!"

"Well, he don't know you!"

"Looks like I'm gonna have to clean up my act!"

"How's your book doing?"

"Sales are picking up, but I'm not making any real money yet. I have a few local book signings before the wedding. Khalil booked a couple speaking engagements for me early June."

"What's up with you?"

"I got back my DNA results. Devastating."

"Why? What did you find out?"

"My father is white!"

"Wow!"

"I can't believe everyone lied to me about my father!"

"I'm sorry you had such a shocking revelation. I thought learning about our ancestry would be entertaining and enlightening."

"It was definitely enlightening."

"I never would have given you the DNA testing kit if I thought there was any possibility of the results causing you pain."

"I'm glad I finally know the truth. No one loved me enough to be honest."

"I think everyone was scared and confused about what to do for themselves and you."

"I wondered about my father my entire life! Did my father ever wonder about me?"

"Of course he did. You're a parent. You know he has wondered about your life."

"I can't even look at my mother. And I wanna find my father and punch him in the face."

"Punch him in the face? For what?"

"Abandoning me because my mother is Black!"

"How do you know he willingly abandoned you?"

"A real man wouldn't let anyone take their child."

"You have no idea what happened. You need to forgive your parents."

"I don't know if I can."

"You've gotta let go of real *or perceived* injustices or wrongdoings."

"Just let folks off the hook?"

"You're not giving them a pass. You're freeing yourself from them and the experience."

"How?!"

"There's this thing called the *Sedona Method*. You answer three questions.

1. *Can I let this go*? You are physically capable and have done it many times before.

2. *Will I let this go*? Are you really gonna carry this to your grave?

3. *If so, then when*? If eventually, you'll let it go, then you might as well do it now."

"I could try it," Kennedy said, hesitantly.

"After getting my DNA results and delving further into my ancestry, I discovered that my ancestors were slave owners!"

"Oh my God! Which side of the family?"

"Obviously, my mother's."

"Creole," Kennedy replied, nodding her head to the revelation. "I don't wanna know anymore about my ancestry. I'm scared of what I might find."

"I felt filthy because the blood of rapists runs through my veins."

"I don't know if I still feel Black or if I'll identify as mixed. I feel different inside."

"My ancestry made me vomit. It was hard to live in my own skin."

"Did your *Sedona Method* help you deal with it?"

"Yes, but it took quite a few sessions. *Ho'Oponopono* is the method I prefer."

"What's that?"

"It's a New Age twist on an ancient Hawaiian practice of forgiveness and reconciliation. You chant four phrases repeatedly. *I'm sorry. Please forgive me. Thank you. I love you.* You can change the order of the phrases."

"How does that help?"

"The premise is that everything you see and experience is an out-picturing of the reality you create internally. If you see war, you brought it into existence."

"I'm not gonna take on that guilt!" Kennedy protested.

"The bad news is that you created the world you live in. The good news is that you are the only person who can change it, and you have the power to do so. You should read about Dr. Ihaleakala Hew Len. He cured criminally insane prisoners using *Ho'Oponopono*, most without any interaction or counseling, simply by reviewing their files and meditating on a positive image of them. It is really fascinating!"

"Hard to believe, but I'm willing to try anything."

"You should first use *Ho'Oponopono* on yourself. Forgive yourself for harming yourself, due to your own confusion. I had to forgive myself for picking the wrong person to be Robert's father."

"How did you finally let that go?"

"I really couldn't let it go. I tried everything. One day I realized it had just disappeared. And then Khalil walked into my life, the man who was supposed to be Robert's father."

"So these methods don't work!" Kennedy laughed teasingly.

"I think they do by slowly destroying negative energy. Let's go sit on that bench and try it," Celeste said, leading Kennedy.

"Which method should we try?"

"First decide what you need to forgive yourself for doing, thinking or feeling. You don't have to tell me what we're working on."

"I don't need to hide anything from you. I need to forgive myself for chasing men and neglecting my daughters," Kennedy stated.

"Either method is fine. Which do you wanna try?"

"The *Sedona Method*."

"Okay, just relax and hold your hands in this healing mudra. Close your eyes and take some deep breaths. Just focus on your breathing. Breathe in for a count of four. Hold that breath for a count of four. Release over a count of four. Leave your lungs empty for a count of four. Keep repeating this breathing pattern at your own pace. Just continue breathing. Relax. Can you forgive yourself? I know you're capable because you have forgiven yourself for mistakes you've made in the past."

"I'm capable of forgiving myself," Kennedy whispered, in a meditative state.

"Will you forgive yourself, or do you plan on taking this guilt with you to your grave?"

"I will eventually forgive myself."

"If so, when? Why not now? Every second that you hold onto that guilt, negative toxins are poisoning your body."

"I'm letting go of the guilt now."

"You are not that same person. You are unfolding like a beautiful rose."

"The weight of that guilt is lighter," Kennedy confessed, opening her eyes.

"You have to keep using the technique."

"It does bring some peace."

"You're just trying to quiet your mind, analyze negative thoughts and release."

"I have trouble meditating."

"The goal is silence and calm for a few seconds at a time. Those seconds will turn into minutes and then an hour. Answers to life questions are found in the silence."

"Can you keep your mind silent for an hour?"

"Not yet, but I can keep my mind quiet for minutes at a time. And I enjoy those few moments of inner peace."

"I'm gonna try meditation in the evening before I go to bed."

"Meditation is also good for children and great for teenagers."

"Is it easier to forgive yourself or others?"

"I don't know. But I do know that forgiveness frees us, not those who harm us."

"You forgave yourself, but can you forgive Robert's father?"

"I've already forgiven him. I'm thankful for the gift he gave me, my amazing son. Robert's father was engulfed in negative energy, and it's a hidden blessing that he left us."

"Good genetics but definitely weak mentally. Robert gets his smarts from you."

"Obviously!" Celeste smiled.

"Love heals all. You're blessed to have Khalil."

"You're fortunate to have the twins."

"They're definitely healing my heart and filling it with love."

"Self-love is what's healing your soul."

"You and Khalil's love lets me know the quality of relationship I desire is possible."

"Are you grateful for your life?"

"Yes."

"Your parents made that possible. Don't they deserve some credit?"

"I'm grateful that my parents found each other and were together long enough to create me. I will try to forgive them."

"Maybe there's nothing to forgive. Maybe this was actually the best scenario."

"My whole world is upside down."

"Your life is evolving. A new understanding of yourself, a new relationship with your daughters, and a new home."

"I'm trying to embrace all of these changes as a new birth for me."

"Everyday is a new beginning," Celeste said, picking up two purple flowers that had fallen on the grass, putting one in Kennedy's hair and the other in her afro. "Everyday is an opportunity to wake up and see the truth."

"What a beautiful Easter program! Robert did great!" Bianca announced, proudly.

"I can't believe he learned the sign language for that song," Kennedy said bewildered.

"That's one of the congregational hymns we sing every Sunday," Celeste replied, stepping into the aisle wearing a purple Egyptian goddess maxi-dress, and flat purple and gold leather gladiator sandals.

"I love the energy of Agape International Spiritual Center! I'm definitely coming back with you and Robert," Bianca declared.

"The highest form of love, the love of God, is *Agape Love*," Celeste stated, hugging one of the choir members passing by. "It's a great feeling at the cellular level."

"I can feel it in my bones."

"I'm gonna start bringing the twins. Sounds like they'd enjoy the summer camp."

"They'll develop life skills in a healthy and encouraging environment. Robert is going again this summer, giving Khalil and I some time alone."

"The twins would love to go with Robert. I like the way all religions are embraced."

"All paths lead to the light," Celeste proclaimed, shaking hands and sharing hugs with her brethren. "There's nowhere else to go."

"Isn't it crazy that we are ultimately made from photons of light?" Bianca pondered.

"And those photons all came from the same star that died to give everything on earth life," Celeste added. "Our sun is our step-mother, and we are all made of stardust!"

"There's a lot more science here than mysticism. The science supporting some religious beliefs is intriguing. Let's go in the bookstore," Bianca suggested.

"No way! The bookstore is jam-packed! It's the hotspot after services and extra crazy on Easter and Mother's Day," Celeste replied, leading them out of the sanctuary. "Let's go outside and check out the vendors."

"I want to get a book," Bianca whined.

"Let's go after we pick up the kids. I want the twins to get a couple books."

"Alright," Celeste agreed.

"Agape even embraces the LGBTQ community," Kennedy whispered in amazement.

"We embrace all people, even atheists."

"Most people lack compassion for people with conflicting belief systems," Bianca said, before receiving a hug from a complete stranger.

"They only notice the few differences instead of their countless similarities," Celeste added, leading Bianca and Kennedy outdoors.

"Religions have been hijacked by power fiends, and hold many secrets," Bianca replied. "It's not about me or we, but Thee."

"Religious fanatics disgrace their religion. They don't act like they believe in or respect the god they preach about," Kennedy said, shuffling close behind Bianca in the crowd.

"Many people believe some traditional religions are based in devil worship," Celeste murmured. "And there are people who believe secret ceremonies in extremely remote locations still occur."

"Agape is accused of being a cult where people engage in pagan rituals," Kennedy whispered. "What a shame so many people won't even take the time to find out for themselves."

"Traditional religions clearly don't want you to have a personal relationship with God. Here, our goal is to each have a personal revelation and relationship with Source."

"I need some decorations for my meditation area," Bianca said, heading for a vendor.

"I'm gonna have a meditation room in our new home. I should start getting some stuff."

"A whole room just for meditation?" Kennedy inquired.

"No. It will be *my* room, for meditation, exercise and relaxation. My private retreat."

"Where's Khalil gonna workout?" Kennedy asked, looking at crystal earrings.

"He'll join a gym. He needs free weights."

"I know you ain't gonna let him go to the gym by himself, especially in L.A.," Kennedy said, studying Celeste.

"I'm not concerned about other women. That's my man. He doesn't have to be with me, he *chooses* to be with me."

"You better go with him sometimes," Bianca advised. "Make sure the vultures know he has a wife."

"I'll probably join the gym with him, so I have access to a steam room, sauna, Jacuzzi."

"Yeah, I bet you will!" Bianca chuckled. Celeste gave Bianca a mischievous grin.

"What color is your meditation room?" Kennedy asked, looking at mandala posters.

"Khalil painted the walls flat antique gold. I wanna have an Egyptian vibe."

"If you see something you want, I'll get you an early house-warming gift."

"Let's ask someone to take some pictures of us," Kennedy suggested.

"Ask that guy who keeps watching us."

Celeste approached the man, "Would you mind taking some photos of us on my phone?"

"Sure," he said, with a hospitable smile.

Bianca, dressed in a lavender crochet A-line dress, with her dark-brown hair braided into two afro puffs, stood between Celeste and Kennedy, who was wearing a pink floral jumpsuit. "Wait a minute," Kennedy said, running her fingers through her curly black pixie. Bianca took the opportunity to adjust the curls in Celeste's afro being held up by a purple silk headwrap knotted on the side. After posing for numerous photos, the ladies thanked the gentleman and continued shopping.

"This place is an oasis from the ignorance of religious intolerance and hate," Bianca said, admiring a small Buddha statue.

"Love and fear are the only two emotions. Hate is just a form of fear. Cowards hate. We all make a choice to live our lives loving or fearing."

"Do we destroy hate with violence or love?" Kennedy questioned.

"At Agape, our weapon of choice is love."

"Violence is negative energy drawing more negativity," Bianca stated, purchasing the Buddha and a bundle of sage.

"Clearly we need to fight sometimes," Kennedy contended.

"The question is, fight with what . . . brain or brawn?"

"You can't beat up everybody," Bianca explained. "And beating people won't change their minds."

"What separates us from the rest of the animal kingdom is our ability to reason," Celeste replied. "We must dominate mentally, not physically."

"This is why any experimentation into spirituality is discouraged for African Americans," Bianca said. "When human mental capabilities expand, we'll be the last to develop the skills and our very existence will be threatened."

"That's already happening," Celeste disclosed. "There are people much further along the path of enlightenment than most Black people, and for that matter most Americans."

"We need more compassion in this world," Bianca declared.

"Men lack compassion for women. They can't understand our struggle."

"Compassion starts with each of us," Celeste advised. "We need to have empathy for someone else's lack of understanding. Men are afraid of yin energy. They recognize female power and magic. They know what it is. We are God-like. We can create life."

"Can you imagine Neanderthals when females were having babies?" Bianca laughed. "They didn't have a clue how a baby was made. Magically females could create life, and males could not."

"That's probably how homosexuality began . . . males trying to make babies with males!" Celeste joked.

"Neanderthal males probably thought any hole would work!" Kennedy snickered.

"Y'all are so wrong!" Bianca scolded, laughing with Celeste and Kennedy.

"But seriously . . . sexism is negatively impacting this world more than I realized. It's possible my twins could grow up in a world where they are oppressed because of their gender."

"Women have been oppressed by men since the beginning of time. Society is not progressing, it's regressing," Bianca replied, looking at a Himalayan salt lamp.

"There are a lot of perverts in the world. I'm thinking about homeschooling the twins, not just for a solid academic foundation, but for safety from weirdos."

"The Catholic Church protects homosexual pedophile priests, yet is against the LGBTQ community, denounce sex outside of marriage, and is concerned about the rights of *unborn* children," Bianca condemned.

"We often hear the homophobic rhetoric and rants of ministers and politicians, only to discover they're gay or engage in some anti-social behavior," Celeste scoffed.

"Real alpha males aren't sexist. They aren't threatened by women . . . or for that matter other men," Bianca said. "Unlike our President, they don't need to grab women. They spend most of their time fighting them off."

"That vicious, deceitful racist is not *my* President," Celeste proclaimed. "This is the United States of America, and it's the 21st Century!"

"I'm starting to wonder if he's the Antichrist," Kennedy contemplated, trying to choose rosary beads.

"He's not smart enough to be the anti-Christ," Celeste sneered. "He's some kind of social deviant."

"He's the puppet of white nationalists," Bianca said, looking at Mala beads with Kennedy.

"Well, I'm gonna fight sexism through education. I'm gonna make sure my daughters don't feel or operate like the weaker sex. They will know their power."

"Khalil and I are dedicating our lives to fighting racism."

"Biologists, geneticists and anthropologists will tell you there's no such thing as race," Bianca informed them.

"There is no classification or division of the animal kingdom below species."

"We realize race is a fake system to divide the human race," Celeste replied, heading for the yoga gear.

"Racism will eventually die as more mixed babies are born," Kennedy added, searching through the yoga pants.

"Pretty soon they'll be no one in America who is full blooded anything," Bianca replied.

"That's what white nationalists fear," Celeste said, looking at the yoga tees.

"And why they wanna keep Black men from making babies with white girls," Kennedy said, selecting a pair of leggings.

"In nature, genetic diversity always wins. It's necessary for our genetic evolution as humans, and creates unique beauty," Bianca educated them.

"Black genes are dominant. We are genetically threatening to others," Celeste explained.

"We're like Pit Bulls physically intimidating all other dogs," Kennedy added, looking for a matching yoga tee.

"Black people are not dangerous unless you threaten or impede our lives," Celeste warned, moving to the yoga pants.

"Pit Bulls are not vicious unless you threaten their family or territory," Kennedy responded. "But they still get labeled as violent and out of control, and handled that way."

"Well, at least we have plenty of opportunities to practice compassion," Celeste announced. "We can have compassion for people who fear their own extinction. We can have compassion for uneducated people who can't comprehend that we are all the same."

"We can have compassion for men who don't respect women or our power," Kennedy said. "We can have compassion for our men who don't recognize they're kings."

"We can have compassion for people misguided by religion to hate others. We should have compassion for all human beings. We must learn to *love period*," Bianca declared, holding up a purple t-shirt with the word *LOVE* and period punctuation in black.

"That's nice. I really like that one. Here are some yoga pants that match," Celeste said, holding up purple leggings.

"Those definitely won't be fitting me anytime soon," Bianca said, putting both hands on her abdomen, flattening her dress to reveal her baby bump.

Celeste and Kennedy froze momentarily, staring at Bianca in astonishment, before bursting into squeals of joy.

CHECKMATE

A king that is attacked, and consequently in danger of being captured on the next move, is said to be in check. A king cannot castle to avoid check. If on his next move, the king cannot move out of check, it is CHECKMATE, and the game is over.

Roberta Roberts

CHECKMATE

Celeste stood in front of a full-length mirror, while Mrs. Sullivan zipped her off-white Alençon lace strapless wedding gown. Her eyes scanned the vanity cluttered with makeup and hair care products searching for the gold-framed photograph of her mother on her wedding day and kept her eyes fixed on it. Bianca and Kennedy helped each other zip their antique matte-gold bridesmaid dresses, before slipping into matching sling-back sandals. Mrs. Sullivan stepped back to look at the ladies altogether. "You girls are stunning!"

"*WOW!*" Bianca exclaimed, throwing her hands out towards Celeste.

"Look how great her body looks in that wedding dress! I didn't know you could look so sexy!" Kennedy admired, rubbing body cream with a slight gold glimmer on Celeste's arms, shoulders and chest.

"You did an amazing job on her makeup!" Bianca acknowledged.

"Thanks. You know I'm gonna do my best work on my girl."

"I'm glad you decided on reverse cornrows. You look like an African Queen!" Bianca said, placing the pearled veil on Celeste's golden-brown braided bun.

"Fabulous!" Mrs. Sullivan cried with tears in her eyes. "My baby is getting married!"

"Gift time!" Bianca announced, gathering around Celeste with her mother and Kennedy.

"You are my best friend, and I am so happy for you. Thanks for including me and the twins in your wedding party," Kennedy smiled, handing Celeste a blue box. *"Something blue."*

Celeste opened the box, removed a blue lace garter-belt and put it on, never speaking a single word.

Bianca handed Celeste an identical blue box. "Ever since we were five years old, you have not only been my best friend but also my sister. When we were little girls, we dreamed of this day. Life happened, and you gave up the dream. My heart sings today because I get to witness a dream come true for you."

Celeste opened the box and found the charm bracelet she had given Bianca for her thirteenth birthday.

"Something borrowed," Bianca smiled, removing it and putting it on Celeste's right wrist.

Celeste, expressionless, froze in the mirror gazing at herself.

"I am an agent of your mother. Please see me standing here as her. *Something new,*" Mrs. Sullivan said, handing Celeste an envelope. "I love you. You are a beautiful young lady inside and outside. We are all so proud of you. I'm not ready to let you and Robert go! But you've found a wonderful young man. Wishing you a lifetime of romantic love and happiness."

"Khalil is gonna go crazy when he sees you!" Kennedy said, putting on her gold pearl necklace and drop earrings.

"I hope you didn't tell him anything about your gown," Bianca added, putting on her gold pearl earrings, while Mrs. Sullivan fastened her matching necklace.

Celeste burst into tears. "What's wrong, Sweetie?" Bianca asked, extremely concerned.

"Don't mess up your makeup!" Kennedy demanded.

Celeste dropped her head and arms crying uncontrollably. Mrs. Sullivan sent Kennedy to get Mr. Alexander.

"What's wrong, Princess?" Mr. Alexander said, entering the *Bride's Parlor*. Celeste just kept crying. "You're beautiful! As captivating as your mother was on our wedding day." Celeste laid her head on her father's shoulder with his arms around her. "Talk to me, Princess."

"Daddy, I don't know if I'm making the right choices," Celeste whimpered.

"I thought you were in love with Khalil?"

"Khalil *is* the love of my life," she sniffled. "My soulmate."

"So what's wrong?" Mr. Alexander asked, dabbing her tears with his handkerchief.

"It's just the wrong time."

"Wrong time?"

"I've never been independent and self-sufficient. If I get married, I'll never know if I can survive on my own."

"You're a talented photojournalist and published author. Your book sales and photo shoots are growing. Financial freedom is coming."

"I'm excited about my career growth and believe I'm contributing to a better world. I've got all facets of love, go interesting places, and often enjoy new experiences. But am I enough?"

"You're enough for Robert. You're enough for Khalil."

"Am I enough to keep Robert and me alive?"

"Sounds like you want to be sure you'll have enough . . . not be enough."

"It's not about having things. It's about knowing I'm capable of providing all of my needs and some of my wants. Can I survive, strive and thrive on my own?"

"Marriage doesn't stop you from knowing that. There are countless successful married women."

"I just wanna be happy and at peace. Is that possible not feeling fulfilled?"

"Sometimes . . . most times, we need to compromise in at least one area of our lives. Are you willing to sacrifice a thriving family for a winning career? You can have an amazing family life and a gratifying career."

"Khalil and Robert are the supreme blessings of my life, but they do compromise my career goals."

"The goal is not money. The goal is the quality of life your money can buy. There's no quality of life without someone to share it with. Everyone seeks fulfillment, not just happiness and success. Do that with Robert and Khalil."

"Alright, Daddy."

"You haven't given up on developing your career. You've changed your priorities."

Mrs. Sullivan gave Mr. Alexander a black velvet jewelry box, which he then handed to Celeste. "I've been saving this for your wedding day."

Celeste opened the box and found an elegant triple-strand pearl necklace and matching pearl drop earrings.

"*Something old.* I bought these for your mother. She wore them on our wedding day."

Celeste fought the tears flooding her eyes. "Thank you, Daddy. Thanks for making sure Mama was part of this day." Mr. Alexander removed the necklace and placed it around Celeste's neck.

Robert bolted into the *Bride's Parlor* towards his mother. Celeste smiled as she watched her little prince through the reflection in the full-size mirror. She stood there, hoping she was making the right choice. Would this union provide him a carefree and happy childhood and the tools to find that same happiness as an adult?

"Mommy, you okay?" Robert asked, studying her face.

"Yes, Sweetheart," Celeste smiled, putting on her mother's pearl earrings.

"Why you crying?"

"I'm happy. Grandpa gave me a gift from my Mama. Look at these beautiful pearls!"

"You look like a mermaid. You're pretty."

"Thank you. What are you doing in here?"

"Khalil said to check on you."

"Tell him I'm fine."

"Come here," Robert said, pulling his mother to the door. "He's right here."

"He can't see her!" Bianca protested. "Robert, *get out*! And don't tell Khalil anything about how she looks."

"Go finish your chess game with Khalil," Mr. Alexander instructed.

"Please don't beat him on his wedding day!" Celeste requested.

"I'm Black. I let him go first."

"But are you gonna let him win?"

Robert giggled, "Okay, Mommy!"

Celeste stood behind the door and opened it for Robert to exit. Robert held her hand as he exited and Khalil gently grasped her hand as she sent Robert out the door. "I don't know what's going on in there, but I'm not leaving here without you," Khalil whispered through the cracked door. "Don't you ever be afraid. I've got you and Robert."

"I love you. I'll see you in a few minutes," Celeste replied, closing the door.

Family and friends were seated on the Malibu West Beach Club deck facing the ocean, enjoying the sun and gentle breeze. Robert and Khalil, with matching haircuts, and his brothers Elijah and Talib stood right of the altar in traditional black tuxedos waiting for Celeste. The venue was decorated in white and gold. A large gold bow holding a bouquet of fragrant white flowers adorned each row. The wedding procession began with the flower girls, Kennedy's twins, charming the crowd wearing matte-gold dresses, and throwing red and white rose petals along the aisle. Next appeared Bianca and Kennedy enchanting all, with their *Black Girl Magic*. Mendelssohn's *Wedding March* began just before Celeste appeared in the doorway on the arm of her father, carrying a cascading bouquet of white flowers.

Celeste was in a trance until the smell of the sea-salt awakened her. Everything was so bright. There wasn't a cloud in the sky. She kept her eyes fixed on the rolling waves as she walked towards her future.

Most of the guest were clearly stunned by her beauty. Everyone quickly turned to Khalil who appeared ready to pass out. His younger brother, Talib, elbowed him in the side and smiled. Eli held Khalil by his upper arm to ensure he remained upright. Robert fidgeted while watching his mother and grandfather. When Celeste reached the wedding arch, Mr. Alexander and Khalil stared into each other's eyes momentarily before her father offered her hand to Khalil.

The men nodded, and Mr. Alexander took his seat next to Dr. and Mrs. Sullivan.

Under the wedding arch draped with gold flowing fabric and covered with white roses, Khalil faced Celeste gently caressing both hands, standing in front of the minister. Khalil squeezed her hands and whispered, "You are gorgeous."

Celeste looked at Khalil and whispered, "You're so handsome."

"We are gathered here today in the sight of God, and in the presence of beloved family and cherished friends, to witness the union of Khalil and Celeste in sacred matrimony," the minister said, beginning the wedding ceremony. When it was time for their wedding vows, they shared ones they had written.

Khalil spoke:
Illuminating the darkness, I was drawn to you in a trance
I am glad I was persistent, you hardly gave me a glance
A cunning sweet voice sparked my curiosity, in retrospect
I am grateful celestial bodies aligned, for our lives to
intersect

Celeste spoke:
From red roses and heart-shaped chocolate, I once ran
I am now comforted, by the gentle touch of your hand
You've restored my faith in love and confidence in a man
I am thankful beside you, until the end of time, I will stand

Khalil spoke:
Fighting for freedom and peace on earth, to my surprise
I feel heaven on earth, gazing into your sparkling eyes
Visions of amber sunsets, our spirits must have shared
I feel liberated, traveling through time and space paired

BLACK CHESS

Celeste spoke:
Spiraling anxiously through the cosmos,
                              peace was revealed
I feel paradise, in the eye of storms that your arms shield
You are a perfect role model, of what a man can be
I feel free to blossom, soar, and be uninhibited me
   Together:
I know I am loved, I am worthy, I am enough
You are loved, you are worthy, you are enough
   Khalil spoke:
Wandering on golden Giza sands, under the Sirius star
I do believe déjà vu will awaken us, to who we truly are
Today our ancestors rejoice, as bells of divinity chime
I do pledge love and commitment, until the end of time
   Celeste spoke:
I'll dance festively on Nile shores, leaving my footprint
I do believe my prayers were heard, you're heaven sent
Surfing your vibration, I am rejuvenated by the motion
I do promise unconditional love, loyalty and devotion
   Khalil spoke:
Submerged in your passion, the beast within me tame
I love to hear your hypnotic voice, whisper my name
Existing turned to living, with a love known by few
I love your sweet lips, smile and laughter that renew
   Celeste spoke:
There's a look in your eyes, assuring me you care
I love when you run, your fingers through my hair
Blessings for my ashes, a lush green garden has grown
I love your strength, and gentle heart I've never known
   Together:
I know I am loved, I am worthy, I am enough
You are loved, you are worthy, you are enough

Khalil spoke:
Moving through life, vowing alone I would stay
I spoke to The Creator, about a solitary pathway
You emerged out of fantasies, I dared not dream
I speak now of possibilities, with you on my team
Celeste spoke:
My broken heart once unleashed, waterfalls of tears
I spoke candidly to loved ones, about my deepest fears
Before family and friends, we stand here best dressed
I speak to this blue ocean, about now being blessed
Khalil spoke:
My queen, my light in the darkness, we shall survive
I see us striving for our family, until we can thrive
My velvety African violet, flourishing in fertile ground
I see your blooms unfolded, turning our lives around
Celeste spoke:
You've cleared tears in my eyes, blinded by pain
I see brilliant rainbows, appearing after the rain
Your love engulfed me, I'm transformed inside
I see my warrior king, standing by my side
Together:
I know I am loved, I am worthy, I am enough
You are loved, you are worthy, you are enough
I know working together, we'll reach our goals
The Universe long-ago, intertwined our souls
I know our hearts beat as one, eternal and pure
Love is all that matters, you've proved that for sure

"Khalil Sloane, do you take Celeste Alexander to be your lawfully wedded wife?"

"I do," he replied, smiling at Celeste.

"Celeste Alexander, do you take Khalil Sloane to be your lawfully wedded husband?"

"I do," she answered, fighting back tears.

"The ring is an ancient symbol of the unbroken circle of love. Unconditional love has no beginning and no end. No giver and no receiver for each is the giver and each is the receiver. May these rings always remind you of the vows you both have taken." The minister then blessed their marriage and asked for the rings.

Khalil turned around, signaling Robert to step forward with the gold wedding bands, which Celeste and Khalil exchanged.

"By the power vested in me, I now pronounce you husband and wife. You may kiss the bride."

The newlyweds engaged in a long passionate kiss. Robert, embarrassed by their public display of affection, giggled and fidgeted before Talib and Eli held their nephew's hands. The new Mr. and Mrs. Sloane turned to face the roaring crowd and raised their clinch hands in the air, before jumping the traditional African wedding broom. Celeste went to stand next to Kennedy and Bianca. Dr. Sullivan handed an envelope to Mr. Alexander, which he then gave to Khalil.

Khalil knelt down in front of Robert. "Robert, thank you for allowing me to marry your mother and become a part of your life. Thank you for trusting me with your mother. I truly wish you were my natural son, not just my step-son. I was wondering if you would allow me to adopt you so that I can be your real dad. It is totally up to you, and I won't be mad if you don't wanna do it. And you don't have to decide today."

Robert looked over at his grandfather before bolting into Khalil's arms. Celeste and Bianca burst into tears, while Kennedy comforted them.

"I've got the papers right here," Khalil said, hugging Robert tightly. Robert buried his head in Khalil's chest, allowing no one to see him crying. Khalil picked him up and stood in front of the minister, who announced that Khalil is officially Robert's father. Khalil used his handkerchief to quickly wiped away Robert's tears before putting him down. Celeste, Robert and Khalil holding hands, faced cheering family and friends and posed for their first family photos.

The wedding party descended onto the beach, with the ladies carrying their heels. Celeste adorned her feet with pearl barefoot sandals. "Those are sexy," Khalil said, while he and his brothers helped Celeste climb to the top of the lifeguard tower. The bridesmaids, flower girls and ring bearer were strategically positioned around Celeste. Khalil stood in front, between his brothers, posing for beach wedding photos.

"Let's take pictures at the shoreline," Celeste suggested, heading for the ocean. Celeste threw her mother's corsage of red roses, which was wrapped around the handle of her bridal bouquet, into the water.

"This is where we scattered her mother's ashes," Mr. Alexander told Khalil and his brothers. "Celeste has been connecting with her mother here, ever since she was a baby."

"Must have been difficult raising a daughter without her mother," Khalil sighed.

"Hi, Grandma!" Robert screamed, running towards the ocean.

"I miss you, Butterfly," Mr. Alexander said, joining them.

"Hi, Mama," Bianca said. "I finally got Celeste married off!"

"Mama, this is my friend Kennedy. Her twins have a crush on your grandson." Kennedy stood there, awkwardly.

Khalil slowly approached apprehensively, taking Celeste's outstretched hand. "Mama, this is my husband, Khalil. I wore your pearls today for our wedding ceremony. It was beautiful. I wish you were here. I love you." Khalil stood behind Celeste, with his arms wrapped around her, gazing over the ocean.

The wedding party returned to the reception where their guests were enjoying champagne and hors d'oeuvres on the patio. Mrs. Sullivan announced that dinner was being served in the reception hall and herded the guest inside. An elegant California surf and turf meal was served. Toasts were made by Elijah, Bianca, Mrs. Sullivan, Dr. Sullivan, and finally Mr. Alexander.

Khalil and Celeste stood up together, holding hands. "We'd like to thank all of you for helping us make this special day memorable. Thank you, Mr. Alexander, for welcoming me into your family, trusting me with your amazing daughter and grandson, and *my* special gift, Raiders season tickets!"

"Daddy, thank you for my dream wedding! Robert, thanks for giving me unconditional love. Dr. and Mrs. Sullivan, thank you for loving and caring for me as your daughter. I am so fortunate to have three wonderful parents."

"We'd also like to thank Mr. Alexander and my brothers for helping us purchase our new home," Khalil added. "Dr. and Mrs. Sullivan, thanks for our honeymoon in Jamaica.

I'm looking forward to spending ten days on a tropical island with my *wife!*"

"Mr. and Mrs. Sloane, thank you for raising the man of my dreams. And thank you for welcoming Robert and me into your lovely family."

"Mom and Dad, thank you for holding me to high morals and standards, and showing me the importance of love and family in this hostile world."

"And last but not least, thanks to our wedding party, Bianca, Kennedy, Elijah, Talib, Robert, India and China," Celeste smiled, raising her champagne glass in a toast.

The wedding reception continued with dancing, bridal bouquet toss, and garter toss. Khalil and Celeste were enjoying themselves dancing in the middle of the ballroom floor when Bianca joined them, leading some white man by the hand. "Khalil, I'd like to introduce you to my husband. Khalil, Wade. Wade, Khalil."

"Finally we meet," Khalil said, shaking Wade's hand.

"About time. We're family now," Wade acknowledged.

"I hear your family is expanding. Congratulations."

"Thanks," Wade replied, rubbing Bianca's belly. "Congratulations to you on marrying a wonderful human being, and adopting an amazing child. Robert is our nephew, but more importantly, we are also his Godparents."

"I didn't know that. Thanks for being there for Robert and Celeste. I've got them now."

"Are you continuing your involvement in the civil rights movement?" Wade asked.

"I'll complete my political obligations through the 2018 midterms."

"Are you eventually going to get involved politically here?"

"Possibly, but my main focus will be real estate development."

"I'm an architect working on some projects here in Southern California. Let's meet when you get back from your honeymoon to discuss the market here."

"Sounds like a plan."

Bianca grabbed Wade's hand, leading him away.

"Why didn't you tell me, her husband is white?" Khalil inquired.

"What difference does it make?"

"Was it a secret?"

"No."

"I'm sure you know I assumed he was Black."

"Why?"

"Because you never said otherwise. People usually mention something out of the ordinary. And Bianca's involvement in the movement has grown."

"You don't need to be in a relationship with someone Black, or for that matter be Black yourself, to support civil rights. And even Black women have the right to love whom they please."

"Did she ever date Black guys?"

"Her first love, back in high school. He cheated on her."

"She ever give another brother a chance?"

"Nope. Only dated white guys after that heartbreak."

"I'm glad you didn't have the same reaction to *fuck boys*."

Bianca, leading Wade by the hand, approached Kennedy on the dance floor. "Kennedy, this is my husband, Wade! Wade, this is Kennedy!"

"Hi, Uncle Wade!" Robert shouted, dancing with the twins.

"Hey, Robert," Wade replied, waving.

Kennedy, visibly shaken, shook his hand. "Wade, this is Eli, Khalil's brother, and my twins, India and China."

"You pretty flower girls did a great job!"

"Nice to meet you," Elijah said, extending his hand. "Congratulations on your two new family members."

"Thanks. We all love them."

Bianca and Wade continued moving through the guests on the dance floor. Kennedy and Elijah left Robert and the twins dancing, and headed directly to Celeste. "What the hell?! Wade is white?" Kennedy exclaimed.

"When was I supposed to announce that Wade is white?" Celeste inquired.

"Anytime would have been good!" Kennedy responded.

"It was never relevant to any of our conversations. Why did anyone need to know that?" Celeste asked, looking at both Khalil and Kennedy. "Does that make her any less Black? Does being mixed or the descendant of slave owners make us any less Black?"

"Hard to trust a sista or brotha's commitment to the African American community who is married to anyone who isn't Black," Khalil said. "Clearly, they've given up on Black love."

"You don't trust Bianca?" Celeste asked.

"I trust her and her husband if you do."

"We are losing too many of our Black queens to white men," Eli responded.

"We are losing too many of our Black kings to white women," Kennedy added.

"Fortunately, that's not a concern for you. *Woke* Black men are attracted to beautiful, intelligent, *woke* Black women like yourself," Eli flattered her.

Kennedy blushed and gave a quick smile.

"Let's get Bianca, some champagne and sparkling cider so we can go down to the beach for our toast," Celeste said to Kennedy.

"You can't go nowhere!" Khalil teased, pulling Celeste close to him. "You my wife!"

"Mr. Sloane, I hate to break the news to you, but *checkmate*! You are stuck with me and Robert. We bought a house. You're locked in! We go together!" Celeste replied, pushing away from him. "Mom can watch the twins. Can Robert stay with you a few minutes?"

"Of course. He's my son now. We'll be out on the deck watching you."

"The twins and I can hang out with Khalil and Robert until you get back," Eli suggested to Kennedy. "Maybe you and I can take a walk on the beach at sunset."

"I'd love to," Kennedy smiled, looking into his eyes.

"We'll be right back," Celeste said, kissing her husband on the cheek.

Bianca and Kennedy, each carrying a glass of sparkling cider and an empty champagne glass, followed Celeste who was carrying a gold-trimmed Waterford crystal fluted champagne glass and bottle of champagne. They stopped at the waters edge barefoot, where Celeste filled their empty champagne glasses. "We did it!" Celeste cheered, raising her glass.

"To the new Mrs. Sloane!" Bianca replied, toasting Celeste.

"Congrats on a moving ceremony!" Kennedy added, sipping her champagne.

"I can't believe Kennedy is drinking alcohol! I wish I could drink champagne!"

"I'll drink for you," Celeste offered, taking Bianca's glass and downing it.

"Thanks for your help!" Bianca laughed. "You're getting *turnt up* today!"

"She's just getting ready for tonight. Khalil can't wait to get out of here!"

"Tonight you'll enter your new home for the first time," Bianca said, sipping her sparkling cider.

"Tonight she'll consummate this marriage in the home Khalil prepared for her."

"You nervous?" Bianca asked, taking her dark brown braids out of the bow-tie bun.

"She better be. Khalil looks at her with bad intentions!"

"No!" Celeste chuckled. "Well, maybe a little bit!"

Bianca and Kennedy burst into laughter.

"When do you leave for your honeymoon?" Kennedy asked.

"Monday. Our first two nights will be in our new home! Tomorrow I'll pack."

"Right!" Kennedy doubted. "You'll be wiped out tomorrow!"

"I've already packed most of what you'll need. You won't have much to do," Bianca said. "I also burned sage throughout the house."

"Thanks! Maybe I can relax before we go."

"Where is Robert gonna be?" Kennedy asked.

"At home with his Grandpa. They've got plans. Daddy's taking him to Catalina, by helicopter next weekend."

"They're both sad Robert's moving. Your father is going to spend every moment he can enjoying his grandson," Bianca added.

"They'll still spend time together several times a week," Celeste reassured.

"Mom, Dad, Quentin and Wade are going to be fighting for time with Robert," Bianca warned. "Nothing's changing for Robert and me!"

"I can't believe I'm married," Celeste sighed. "I needed Khalil's love. Every cell in my body is dancing."

"You two are so cute!" Bianca grinned.

"Speaking of cute, what's up with *Elijah*?" Celeste teased Kennedy.

"I don't know, but I'm gonna find out!" Kennedy giggled. "He's so sexy!"

"He's a nerd!" Bianca informed Kennedy.

"What does he do?"

"He's an NAACP Attorney," Celeste answered.

"Where does he live?"

"New York. You can find out whatever else you need to know on your *sunset stroll*!"

"What does Talib do?" Kennedy inquired.

"He's a rapper."

"Looks more like your type!" Bianca teased.

"No, she prefers older men."

"Y'all don't know my type! I don't even know my type. I'm gonna try something new."

"Life's a chess game," Celeste replied. "Your choices create your reality. There are infinite possibilities and multiple universes, depending on the choices you make."

"Your goals, what you choose to focus on and talk about, your friends and associates, and the places you spend most of your time determine the quality of your life. You become what you see!" Bianca declared.

"Low-class people gossip about people. Middle-class people discuss life issues. And upper-class people contemplate the universe."

"Education provides opportunities to earn money and gain freedom," Kennedy said, sipping her champagne. "I'm taking that route."

"You can squeeze in a long-distance affair!" Bianca laughed.

"I'm more concerned with my growth right now. But I might be able to have some fun with Eli, occasionally!" Kennedy giggled, looking a little tipsy.

"For the first time as an adult, I feel like I matter," Bianca reflected. "Wade and our baby are all that I need. I'm thankful I can work from home and at my own pace."

"There have been some heartbreaks, disappointments and shattered dreams, but we survived and kept striving. The compromises we chose ultimately led us to thriving lives."

"We've found inner peace and purpose," Bianca smiled.

"We have all we need to lead fulfilling lives!" Celeste cheered, toasting with her best friends.

"We're creating heaven in this chaotic world!" Kennedy declared. "Girl Power!"

Celeste looked back at the men in her life, watching her from the deck. Robert was standing between Mr. Alexander and Khalil, holding both of their hands. She smiled, blew them a kiss, and sighed, "I'm so blessed to share my life journey with those kings."

Made in the USA
Monee, IL
02 February 2021